D1527517

LIVI. G WITH. THE MARGI. S

DEFORREST LERONTE`

All Rights Reserved

Editor: Leanore Elliott

Cover Design: Drop Dead Designs

Book Design: Wicked Muse

Table of Contents

LIVING WITHIN THE MARGINS

Writer's Block

Where words come true...
Visions pop out of the blue...
Walking by pens that fell asleep on curbs...
Adjectives and nouns desperately want to be verbs...
Long walks down one way street...
Ideas sword fighting until the one faces defeat...
Imagination parkway has bumper to bumper traffic...
Images flickering like simple holographic...
Where ideas fall asleep and I suddenly can't think...
Pens flat line because they ran out of creative ink...
Paragraphs fishing for sentences along the docks...
Books shaking uncontrollably as time ticks off clocks...
Ideas are written dreams and they come to me so easy...
While some are clever, others are extremely cheesy...
Brain storms causing intensive damage...
Lonely characters committed to different orphanages...
Tablets chasing binders and notebooks can actually speak...
I get tired of my punctuation marks playing hide and seek...
Grammar cops always try to arrest me...
Silence steady want to sensor me...
Retired speeches sitting along street corners...
Plagiarism robbing and stealing from other owners...
Trying to create the perfect writing technique...
Hoping I'll be able to write something by the end of this week...

NEW YEAR'S KISS

DeForrest LeRonte'

The stench of burnt paper lingers in the air, tickling my nostrils. It's the day after the annual Ceremony of Memories and I'm getting ready for tonight's festivities. New Year's Eve; the night when the world celebrates the bringing in of a new year. Where I am, I'm watching hours, minutes and seconds tick away, never to be seen again. I'm not the only one; the world is watching too. But unlike myself, they huddle around each other; tears running down their cheeks while they share long embraces.

Right before the clock strikes midnight, kisses are exchanged and during that split second, everything changes—but only for a certain few. Imagine a stranger planting a juicy kiss right onto your lips at the stroke of midnight, and when the clock strikes midnight—that person vanishes.

This is the New Years that we all experience now, since the fade has been recognized as a true phenomenon.

People vanish at the stroke of midnight every year. There's no warning as to who will fade; there's no physical trace of them. The fading doesn't exclude anyone. It doesn't matter your age, your job status, financial status, gender, or ethnicity. When December 31st arrives, everyone is tense and 11:59 pm is usually the scariest time of the year.

This phenomenon has puzzled the brightest minds for centuries. Scientists and other scholars have researched the explanation of this phenomenon but due to the fading, scientific discoveries always stall, until the next person steps up and continues the research. History books have taught us that there was much chaos in the beginning but the fade has changed everyone. Crime barely exists. Countries aren't at the brink of war and continue to hold an open passport policy. All while everyone is encouraged to live life to the fullest. New government officials are elected every year and no one is envious of anyone. But on December 31st, everyone is terrified of the fade to the point that it's the only word outlawed.

There are those who have been fortunate enough not to experience the fade. I wasn't as fortunate. I've witnessed this experience firsthand. I was nine at the time and I was sitting by the fireplace, playing with a toy I received a few days prior. My little sister kept running around, causing a ruckus with her toy and she was really getting on my nerves. My parents were sitting on the couch, holding each other and watching us when the grandfather clock struck twelve. Every light went out and when we were no longer encased in darkness—my mother and little sister were victims of the fading.

Even though I miss them, I was nine at the time…too young to understand the gravity of their fading but my father's heart shattered into pieces. Not only did he lose the love of his life, he also lost the beautiful smile and innocent eyes of his baby girl. Booze and drugs came in to fill the void but no amount of liquid courage could replace them. It took him three long years to realize I was still in the house with him. That was Thanksgiving.

I was twelve when he faded.

Each year after that, the memories of my previous life fades away. Sometimes I can hear their voices but I can't remember their faces. I get glimpses of them in my dreams. I remember the colors of their eyes or phrases they said to me, but I can't remember details.

It's been hard living on my own, especially in the beginning stages of my teenage years but the neighborhood took me in, practically raising me until I was old enough to acquire work and defend on my own. I'll be turning eighteen at the beginning of the year and I hope that I'll have the chance to make it to that date. I know a lot of people who didn't get a change to make it to eighteen.

For some, when New Year's Eve arrives—life will cease to exist.

So, each day, I'm living my life to the fullest. Tonight, I'm heading to a New Year's Eve celebration, celebrating my 17th last day on earth. I'd rather be celebrating than sulking, waiting to see if I'm going to vanish.

We're walking through the street—myself, Greg and Henry, childhood friends who have withstood the fade—heading to a different party than last year. Last year's host faded away.

Entering the party, it's packed with new faces mixing and mingling. New friendships were created instantly, strangers becoming fast acquaintances as the hours turn into minutes.

Sipping on a Heineken, I'm watching a lot of interesting shuffling back and forth, squeezing a year's worth of socializing into two final hours. I don't need the attention, I've got my beer, and I'm watching the fellas make fools of themselves while glancing at the clock every so often. I didn't realize when 11:55 pm came, but I should have known by the mood hovering over the party.

Everyone is checking his or her watch.

The music dies down and is so quiet that you can hear a pin drop. It's the longest minute ever, each second ticking away.

Everyone's attention is fixated on the flashing numbers, 40…41…42…

I gulp down a few swallows of my beer, exhale, and close my eyes. Preparing for the worst, I think about the meaning of life when I feel a wet pair of lips against mine. My eyes flutter open as the clock strikes midnight. Darkness envelopes the party, but I can still feel lips against mine.

The lights flash back on and I stare at a set of the most beautiful eyes that I've ever seen. Our eyes lock and before we even realized it, our lips release but we linger longer than the traditional length of time.

Surrounding us, people were weeping as family members and friends fade away. I focus on the girl who is inches from my face while I continue to ignore a strong tug at my shirt.

Someone uses enough strength to grab my arm, forcing me to look away.

"WHAT HARRY? CAN'T YOU SEE I'M A LITTLE BUSY?"

"Greg faded."

I scan the area, searching for Greg when I notice the girl he was flirting with. It took her a minute to gather herself but she seems to be back to her normal self. It happened, as there is no way to evade the fade. With our current streak, I never would have thought Greg would fade. I stood in front of Harry and we did our ritual handshake for making it to another year. We make a vow to live this next year in Greg's honor.

Immediately, I turn back to the area where I shared a New Year's kiss, only to find the space is vacant. Alert, I'm scanning the area for the attractive girl but she's nowhere to be found. I walk through the crowd, bumping into people and apologizing along the way. A few times, I address a female who appears to look like her but when I get close, I see their eyes are not like hers.

After searching the entire party, it came time to leave and I find myself outside in the chill with Harry.

Several days passed since New Year's night and while tragedy resulted in my friend Greg fading, the effects from the mystery girl still lingers. I'm constantly reliving that moment, literally kicking myself that I didn't get her name or pursue her. Every time I close my eyes, she's staring at me and I hated opening my eyes because I knew she wasn't there.

Heading towards home, I make a quick detour over to 'Pieces of Pizza,' my favorite food shop. I wait in line but I can see that the clerk recognizes me and he shouts my usual order to the cook.

Rocking back and forth on my feet, I peek around until I see something in the corner. Something seems familiar and that weird *butterflies* feeling floats around in my stomach. Her face is covered by locks of her hair but if she's who I think she is, the universe has given me another opportunity and I'm not going to waste it. "Can you put my food on low heat? I'll be just over there."

Taking a deep breath and shaking nervousness away, my legs lead me over to the table where a striking young lady resides.

She is alone, enjoying a slice when I approach the table.

"Is this seat taken?" I wait until she glances up and I stare into those radiant eyes and instantly fall in love. That mesmerizing smile beams on her face, just as vibrant as before. Honestly, there isn't a word that could describe her beauty. I don't even mind the pizza sauce that smears at the corners of her lips.

"It's yours, if you want it."

Sliding into the booth, I avoid having our knees touch while she sips on her Coke. The slice she devours looks so good that my stomach starts to growl and I can tell that she hears it too. "I've never seen you in this neighborhood. Do you live around here?"

"No."

"So, you just happen to be passing through my neck of the woods?"

"No."

"I guess you were starving for a slice."

"Actually, I've been at this parlor every day for the last two weeks, waiting on you to show up."

Baffled, I stare at her. "E-excuse me?"

She wipes grease from her fingertips as she replies, "Well, the night of the *fade*, a good friend of mine vanished and I had to comfort her. Of course, it was sudden so when I returned, I saw that you were gone but there was a silver lining. A friend of mine knows Harry and after she connected me with him, he told me of a place where you frequent and I've been here the last two weeks, waiting for you so show up."

"You could have called, you know."

"I didn't want to seem like stalker."

My smile matches hers. "So, what now?"

"Well, tomorrow you're going to take me on a proper date. I'm going to wear something nice and pretty that showcases the curves of my body and you're going to dress nice as well. Don't shave that 5 o'clock shadow off your face, I love that look on you. You're going to take me to a nice restaurant because I've eaten so much pizza for the last two weeks that my taste buds look like pepperonis. Over dinner, I'm going to tell you about my upbringing…only if you want to listen and you're going to tell me about yours…only if you want to share. Once our meal is finished and you walk me home, we're going to stare nervously at my front door until you get the courage to kiss me before I walk into the house. Then I'm going to wait for your call."

I stare at her as she collects her things, throwing away trash before excusing herself. I'm dumbfounded, replaying every word as I watch her walk away. When I exit the shop, it hits me—I didn't have her number. This is the second time she has left my presence and I didn't get her number. It's too late when I finally realize this; she's been long merged with the crowd.

"Damn!" The word escapes my mouth louder than I anticipate and a few customers glance in my direction.

"Don't forget your food," the clerk calls to me.

My stomach growls and now the thought of pizza replaces her, sauntering towards the clerk as he hands me my order along with a slip of paper I thought was a receipt. Unfolding it, I stare at her name and number as a smile is cemented on my face.

Everything occurs just as she described on our first date—second according to her. From that moment, I knew I wanted to spend every moment with her. I wasn't going to let her walk out my life again, and once I made that declaration, we're inseparable. Within two months, our lives merge and we are living together.

The spring wisps by and the summer brings forth trips across the country, beaches with white sands, hiking trails and activities that I never thought I would do. Seasons change and so does everyone's wardrobe. Sleeves were slowly fashionable again, along with boots, scarves and eventually, light jackets. The leaves were falling off the trees, drifting towards the ground as we continued to spend more time together.

Now, it's that time of year again, when they announce new scientific discoveries, but the age-old question remains—no one knows where we go after the fade.

Precipitation continues to beat against the earth, dampening and peppering the landscape. The leaves continue to scatter across the neighborhood while everyone preps for Thanksgiving. Since the fade snatches away family members, the community organizes a big dinner. I'm a server just like last year, giving back in small portions.

Suddenly, she stands there in front of me.

"What would you like?"

"The sexy man wearing the hair net."

"Well, you can't have him until he finishes with the guests."

"I'm patient, besides I can mingle and fill my belly."

After stacking her plate with a little more than others, I can't help but watch her strut away and my mind wanders to the physical activities that will take place later in the evening.

Later on, we spend over an hour exploring each other's anatomy and we we're grateful for the time too.

Due to the phenomenon of New Year's, we work all year up until the 1st day of December. It's not the law but businesses give their employees the month off to get their affairs in order. It's time for the training of a slew of new leaders in case those who are in positions to govern fade.

There are those who choose to work and I'm not one of them. I take advantage of all the opportunities because life is more than working forty plus hours a week.

December is all about her, spending every second with her. It has been months and we still haven't grown tired of each other. We appreciate each day that we are given. I love waking up next to her and watching her sleep, counting all seventy-two eye lashes on her upper eyes. The way her lips poke out when she's in a deep sleep. Out of all the eighteen years, I've been on earth, this year and these moments have been the best of my life thus far. I couldn't get enough of her and the feelings she brings into my life. I hate that this month—December—is here. I hate that there's a countdown in my mind—in all of our minds—waiting to see if life will be here and available to us on New Year's Day.

December 30th arrives faster than last year and I'm a little saddened when it arrives. I want to skip the Ceremony of Memories entirely but she insists, not deviating from the traditions of the day.

"The ceremony is crowded. We can just stay in the house and spend the last few hours of the year together," I suggest.

"I've been to nineteen ceremonies and I haven't faded once. I'm hoping that streak continues and for it to continue, I should be in attendance."

I didn't feel that same obedience. "But—?"

"No buts. Gather all those pictures that we took and bring them."

I gather the box full of pictures while she gets dressed. I look through all of them. There's so many memories associated with these beautiful images; scuba diving, rock climbing and petting unfriendly animals. Then there seems to be some memories that I forgot but I am glad I'm able to remember them through the pictures.

In typical fashion, it takes her over thirty minutes to get ready but once she came back in, I snap one last picture to have that image imprinted in my mind forever.

We follow the crowd, slicing through while others were leaving. The Ceremony of Memories takes place all day on December 30th, in the center of the city. Larger cities have multiples sites for the ceremony due to the high volume of people. The stench of burnt paper saturates the air, causing a select few to cough and sneeze.

I have never been this close to the 'hole', the place where memories are tossed and burned, although it appears that she has.

Taking the box from my hands, she maneuvers through the crowd until she's near the edge. She takes a final look at the box before tossing the pictures into the deep furnace. She lingers there longer than I anticipate and I watch her walk back to me. She leans a little closer and our fingers instantly intertwine.

Little pieces of debris float up into the December sky, through the black sea like shooting stars.

Later on, I'm lying in bed, staring up at the ceiling while she sleeps on my chest. I have been in this exact position since we left the ceremony and were only able to get about an hour of sleep. This year is different from last year. Last year, I only had myself to worry about but this time, I'm staring at the person whom I could now lose. Now that I have her, I'm afraid she may fade. We can't control the fade, but I'll be damned if this last day isn't the best I can offer her.

The day is full of simple activities. I wake up and cook her breakfast, staring into her eyes as she bites into her breakfast sandwich. We enjoy each other while the sun descends into the horizon.

It's now the darkest night of the year but everyone is out and about, heading to different ventures to party one last time.

We were together but our friends slowly trickle in on our journey to the party for last year. Harry is on my left while some of her friends were on the right of her, entering the festival. The gathering is full of laughter, over exaggerated stories and rekindled friendships.

It wasn't until eleven thirty when the bass softens and conversations turn into gentle murmurs. All I can do is gaze into her wonderful eyes. "I've had an unbelievable year with you—"

"Don't say another word…let's dwell on the memories until the New Year arrives and we can make more."

I smile. These are the words I want to hear, but her body language tells me differently. I know she is thinking about the fade as well, it's on everyone's mind. "Is everything okay?"

"I'm fine."

"Regardless of what happens tonight, I will always—"

Before I could utter another word, she leans in, presses her lips against mine, and a quietness envelopes the room.

She is in my arms now, I hold her tighter than anything I've ever held before. My heart is beating faster as the final seconds tick by and I lean in just a little more to see her face before everything goes dark.

"Regardless of what happens tonight, I will always love you."

These were the last words I hear before a ringing pings in my ears. I've never heard it before during the fade, so it's eerie to feel this new sensation. I'm pressing against her hand when my vision is restored. There were less people around than before—there were always less people—but none of it matters as I stare into open space. The hand I thought I was holding is my own now. The one thing I care about so much isn't in front of me. She's a part of the fade now.

SHE IS GONE!

I sat in my home, trying to mentally accept that I would never see her again, and it took a month before the anger dissipated. I'm so heartbroken and concerned with her fading that I didn't realize that Harry was also a victim of the *Fade*. Two dear friends and the love of my life—lost in consecutive years.

We're told not to mourn those who faded, but to cherish the moments we shared with them and never dwell in their last moment. All it does is cause heartache over and over again. Each day is a gift, regardless of the circumstances that life may bring. So enjoy it while it lasts, because eventually...time will run out. There will always be the debt we all have to pay. Mustering up the strength, I got up from my couch, my legs stiff as I exit my home into a dense fog. Nothing in front of me was visible but broken pieces of chatter penetrated the fog as I found myself walking in that direction. The fog was so thick that I blindly bumped into someone, stumbling back as I fell to the ground. As I lifted my head, an arm reached out to assist me off the ground as I clambered to my feel.

The fog dissipated in front of me and I'm baffled at the person in front of me: Greg. He flashes a smile but his presence causes me to take a step back. Voices blare all around me as I scan my surroundings, others emerging through the fog. Greg's face wasn't the only one that I recognize as my eyes locked with my mother's. I walked towards her as I saw she held another's hand and my eyes connected with my father. The sound of little feet pattering in my direction causes me to bend down at my little sister running towards me, still in the shell of the youthfulness as I realized that it wasn't Harry or my girlfriend who *faded...*

A BREATH of FRE$H Air

DeForrest LeRonte'

They laughed. They joked about climate change. They criticized scientists. They allocated money from environmental protection agencies to fund other departments. They neglected their responsibilities. They didn't believe the leading expert, Dr. Mendes. They discredited his findings. They didn't take heed to his warnings. They portrayed him as a loon when he started created devices to help society. They mocked him when he mentioned encased cities. They didn't take him serious when the less fortunate started dying. They didn't take it serious...until the president and the first family of the free world died from lack of oxygen on live television. They panicked when thousands...millions of people collapsed.

They searched high and low to find any assistance to save them from death. They found a solution...Puris masks that were created by Dr. Mendes. They sold out in seconds. They mourned the billions that perished. They cheered Dr. Mendes. They were indebted to Dr. Mendes. They called him the *Savior*. They elected him their leader. They followed his specific designs, creating large dome cities across the globe. Bogota, Houston, Seattle, Cairo, Lisbon, Tokyo, and Sydney became the last seven inhabitable cities on the planet...

Her fingers tapped faster than her thoughts as she jerked the controller to the left, her entire body leaning before shifting to the right. After a combination of pushed buttons, Shikha glanced over at Miguel with a smile stretched across her face. "That's six games in a row. You're not tired of losing?" Shikha teased.

"I stand corrected, you are officially the champion!" Miguel replied.

"It's important that you recognize that I'm superior with this controller in my hand."

Pounding alerted them both as Shikha got up from the couch. "I hate when she does this."

"Yes, she's very annoying," Miguel said.

Shikha swiped her finger across her wrist, calling her older brother. She headed over to the door... "Yeah, she's here. What do you want me to do? Okay, I'll tell her." Opening the door, Shikha leered at the old hag with gritty skin and thinning white hair. "He's coming up the elevator to pay you, Shikha said."

"I see that boy is here again...that's six days straight. Our ventilation system is set..."

"There's Zayan." Shikha pointed past the landlord, connecting eyes with her older brother. With her arms folded across her chest, she watched the interaction between Zayan and the landlord. Staring intensely, she knew they were talking about Miguel when she starting discussing an increase in payment due to capacity.

Once currency was exchanged, the landlord went over to the next door as they entered their home.

"Shikha, six days in a row. I had to pay extra and the landlord insists on additional fees. We aren't descendants of the Savior; we scrape and claw for everything..."

"Zayan, my apologies. I will limit my time here. Shikha, I'll see you at school tomorrow," Miguel stated as he kiss her on the cheek while discretely placing currency on the small table near their door.

"After everything his family has done for us and you, of all people treat him in that manner?" Shikha stated once Miguel was out of sight.

"I know what his father has done," Zayan stated. "There's not a day that goes by without thanking him for bringing you back from the brink of death. That operation Miguel's father personally performed on you was a blessing. I apologize for my rudeness but his life is spared. It's my job to take care of you..."

Shikha grabbed her coat and scurried after Miguel. She stepped outside, the fractured light bouncing off the sealed dome as she stared into the protected distance. Advertisements and notifications flashed all over the city; the new price quote on air had increased drastically since yesterday. She ventured on the familiar path towards Miguel's neighborhood, but after rounding a few corners, Shikha remembered that she wasn't familiar with the short cut that Miguel journeyed from his home to hers. The path wasn't as memorable as she initially thought. She dreaded once she turned down a gloomy alleyway, immediately regretting her decision as she spun around.

Hostile strangers greeted her, blocking her exit from the busy streets.

"You're in the wrong part of town little girl..." one of two males warned.

"A pretty girl like you carries a Puri with her, let me see it," the shorter male insisted.

"My Purifier belongs to me. I'll scream," Shikha challenged.

"Go ahead; you'll just be blowing hot air. Besides, the badges won't save you here..."

"Hey, I know her face. She walks with the Savior's boy...grab her. We can trade her for Puri crates."

Shikha screamed at the top of her lungs. The soft shriek was cute rather than terrifying as she struggled to catch her breath. Unwanted hands grabbed her while she resisted them, her second shriek boomed as she felt herself being dragged against her will. She hollered Miguel's name until she attracted attention. In the distance, she saw an image and immediately, recognized her boyfriend, Miguel running in her direction.

She tussled with them, kicking and screaming. Their strength sapped hers away each time she exerted herself. Slipping through his fingers, Shikha ran in the opposite direction until she was tackled to the ground. One of her captors climbed on top of her, slapping her so hard that a flash is white light temporarily blinded her.

Dazed and confused, she swung her arms in the air frantically but they didn't connect with an object. Once her eyesight was restored, she stared up at the dome. She heard a commotion and rolled over to see Miguel fighting the men who held her prisoner. "Miguel, behind you."

Her warning was seconds late. One of the males swung a blunt object and hit Miguel across the head. She watched as he fell to his knees, his body crashing to the ground. Shikha got up and created distance between them, tears streaming down her face.

"We want a crate of Puris or he'll be *Exhaled*. Don't call the authorities, we'll call you."

...Pacing back and forth, she was out of options just as her brother entered the house, immediately running over to him.

"What's wrong?"

"They took him. They kidnapped Miguel."

"Do you know who took him?" Zayan asked.

"I've never seen them before."

"Shit...a crate of Puris is quite expensive. Should we call the—"

"They said they will Exhale him if they sense the authorities."

Opening her palm, she swiped until she came across Miguel's home phone line and pinged until she noticed something on the table. Ending the call, she walked towards the table and saw enough currency to buy more than a crate of Puris.

"You didn't notice he left enough currency to pay the ventilation bill for a year?" She glanced back at Zayan; the baffled expression indicated he had no clue.

...After securing a crate, a call pinged on her palm. For a brief moment, relief washed over her until she realized it wasn't Miguel that was calling her.

"You acquired that crate easier than we initially thought."

"Where's Miguel?"

"Bring the crate over to the East Plaza near the Threshold. Don't forget that we're watching. You have ten minutes."

Shikha and Zayan made their way to the rough side of town, waiting patiently for them to call back. Her palm pinged again.

"Go to the Threshold. We're watching."

They headed over near the Threshold, staring at the dome where danger resided. Out of the shadows, the two men who held her captive approached them. She peeked up at Zayan, the anger boiled and his eyes showed fiery rage.

"Here your crate. Where's Miguel?" Zayan seethed at them.

"He's close. Once he's away with the crate, I'll hand you this note with his location." He reached into the crate and pulled out one Puri.

Shikha watched as the crate left their presence. The other male handed her a slip of paper. "This is the access code to the Threshold. He's just outside the dome and running out of oxygen. Either you can chase us or save him, you're choice." He tossed her the Puri, scurrying away.

Frantic, she went over to the Threshold and stared out into the unknown.

"What are you doing?" Zayan questioned

"I have to save him," Shikha replied.

"You will die...we don't know how long he's been out there. That Puri probably hasn't been activated."

"It doesn't matter. I love him, I have to try. I can use my mask for a bit, and then use the Puri. They didn't go too far with their masks."

"No Shikha."

"I'll be back." She pressed the buttons firmly with her thumb, the door hissed until it popped opened. An alarm sounded along with a wave of warm air that slammed against her skin. Shikha immediately slid her mask over her nose and mouth, gripping the Puri in her hand as she stepped through the Threshold, finding herself on the other side.

...Miguel woke up, his head ringing and sore with a note in his hand. The last thing he remembered was fighting to save his girlfriend. He opened the note, climbing to his feet and running in the direction of the Threshold after realizing his captors were forcing him to either pursue them or saving Shikha. He ran through the alleyways, rounded two corners in the direction of the strobe lights. Trepidation washed over him the closer he approached, noticing a crowd of people standing idle. He made his way through the crowd, searching for Shikha.

He recognized Zayan, hurrying over in his direction. "Hey, where's Shikha?"

"What are you doing here? How did you get back in?"

"What are you talking about? I just woke up with this large bruise on my head with this note in my hand."

"They said you were out there. Shikha went out there for you."

Miguel took a deep breath, heading over to the keypad and punched in the code. The door slid open and the crowd that matriculated towards the Threshold gasped. Just as he was about to step through, he felt resistance and turned around, meeting Zayan eye-to-eye.

"What are you doing? You don't have a mask."

"She has hers, I need to save her."

"She has a Puri also," Zayan added.

"It doesn't matter, it's not activated and I know the universal code."

"Take my mask, you need to hurry."

Accepting Zayan's mask, Miguel headed out. The tropical air crashed against his skin. Zayan's mask beeped and he checked to see how much air pressure he had left. He trekked forward, creating distance as he peeked over his shoulder to see his home covered by an impenetrable glass dome, designed by his father. The sound of thunder was much louder outside the dome; precipitation fell from the sky. He walked around for ten minutes, hope slowly escaping his heart.

Pivoting, he headed towards the dome until he saw something in the distance. He pressed towards the object, growing closer and closer until he saw Shikha. He saw her struggling with the Puri, his presence startled her. They connected eyes and he knelt down, noticing her hand trembling. He tried to activate the Puri but it blinked red, indicating it was in malfunction.

Miguel took a deep breath, removing his mask and placed it over her face. He pulled her forward; the dome grew closer with each step. He guided her until her gait sped up. He pointed to the dome, his stride slowing.

...The pressure subdued in Shikha's torso as she noticed Miguel staggering. She slowed her pace, using all her strength to pull him but he was heavier than he appeared. She felt his strength as he shoved her forward. "Goooo," she heard him shout. Tears welled in her eyes, kneeling down with him until several beeps sounded.

"Please goooo..."

She felt his strength again, pushing her away as she climbed to her feet, heading towards the dome. She glanced back, crying hysterically but ran as hard as she could. The Threshold was just in front of her as she pressed the code, finding herself on the other side of the opening as Zayan ran towards her. She pulled the mask over her head and took a deep breathe.

"Did Miguel find you?"

"What?"

"They lied, he was around the corner. When I told him that you were out there looking for him, I gave him my mask and..." Zayan noticed his mask beside her.

"He r-ran out of—oxy-gen." She couldn't stop crying. She felt Zayan's arms around her, not caring about those staring at her. She soaked his shirt until gasps caught her attention. She turned around, staring at Miguel on the other side of dome. Baffled, she rose up and rushed over to the dome, staring at his smile. She ran over to the door, punching in the code as he entered.

"How?" She embraced him.

"My father...but how did you survive?"

"What do you mean?"

"Zayan's mask was less than five percent when I slipped it over my mouth. I pulled it up slightly, not using any oxygen from the mask. My father told me I was special when I was younger, informing me that he implanted an organic artificial lung that would come on when I get short of natural oxygen. When I was leaning over, it was turning on. It was quite painful but I got used to it...enough about me, you survived without oxygen. How?" Miguel questioned.

"Wait...when Shikha was younger, she fell ill. We didn't have any money and they thought she wouldn't make it but your father operated on her. She grew well over time but my parents never told me what was wrong with her. I can't remember your diagnosis."

"Acute Respiratory Distress Syndrome. He told me that it was lethal and that the surgery was going to save me." She reached back, rubbing the scar on her back.

It's Just a Little
COMPANIONSHIP

Emerson sat alone at the bar, images flashed across the television screen but he could only make out a few words, as his Mandarin wasn't up to par. He missed home, six months was too long away from American cuisine. He grew tired of everything served with rice and foods he couldn't pronounce.

Watching ESPN, there were clips of games missed. That lasted only about an hour, so boredom settled in. His eyes scanned the room and fell up on woman sitting at the bar with a bottle in her hand. Their eyes connected briefly, as he quickly peeled his gaze from her to the television. After a few obvious glances, liquid courage coursed through his body as he turned to find the woman was no longer there.

Emerson knew he'd just let a perfect opportunity slip by as he swiped his index finger across the Barcode, paying for his drinks. Rushing outside, he found himself amongst the crowd, walking towards his home. More than three billion citizens in China, he knew it was impossible to find her now. Rounding the corner, he bumped into someone and with quick reflexes; he reached out and grabbed the person before they fell. Once he gathered his bearings, he realized it was the woman from the bar. "My apologies, I didn't see you."

She smiled with a set of pearly white teeth. Other features stood out as well; flawless ivory skin, symmetrical face, tone physique and raven hair that laid against her collarbone.

"I saw you at the bar. What is your name?" He waited but she didn't respond. "I don't mean to be too forward but you are beautiful. Are you involved with anyone?"

Still no response.

The language barrier deterring my advances. Fumbling into his pocket, he reached for his phone to turn on his translator.

"Thank you for the compliment," she finally spoke and in perfect English "I noticed you as well. I wasn't sure a handsome man as yourself was single but I don't see any resemblance of a wedding ring on your finger."

"No, I'm not married. As you can guess by the language, I'm from the States. I've been staying over here for the last six months, attending classes at the university."

"I go to the university as well, studying fashion design."

"You want to be a model? You definitely have the looks for it."

"No, I rather make the clothes and run the show than participate in all the outfits."

"Interesting. I would like to hear more. I'm Emerson and you are?"

"Pardon my manners, I'm Lijuan."

"I have to be honest, your English is excellent. Are you from the States?"

"No, I was born and raised in Beijing but thank you for the compliment. If I'm going to succeed in this global market, I need to be able to communicate with my consumers."

He could feel the sexual tension between them. He stared into her eyes then felt her fingers on his, intertwined with his until they became one. Without saying a word, he felt her strength as the space between them vanished, their lips pressed against each other.

Emerson found himself falling into Lijuan's room, crashing to the floor. Clothes flew into the air as the softness of her mattress cushioned his knees, staring at her porcelain skin underneath his body. The scent of passion filled the air; electricity flowed through them while beads of sweat resided on their skin. After switching positions and finding himself on the bottom, he stared up at Lijuan.

"Let's try something different." Emerson suggested.

"What did you have in mind?"

"Command...Follow...Adapt."

"Hello Dr. Cawsten. How may I better pleasure you?" Lijuan asked.

"Retrieve Jennifer."

"Searching...retrieving...downloading..."

Emerson sat on the bed, observing Lijuan as her skin radiated. He didn't like the transitional phase and made a mental note to fix that bug later. First, he noticed the pigmentation in her fingers shifted from pearly white to a caramel complexion, gradually coating her entire body. Her hair thickened, her breast became fuller and her thighs developed a little more definition. Her eyes color shifted from dark brown to a softer hue as her lips shifted from thin to full. He checked his watch while watching the presence of Lijuan vanishing.

"Dr. Cawsten, do you find my new appearance pleasing?"

"Yes Jennifer. Proceed."

After two hours of experimenting, Emerson laid in the bed while Jennifer went into the bathroom to shower. He pulled out his digital notepad, checking her circuits, processing unit and reviewed her entire day through recordings. He studied her interaction with citizens and noticed a slight delay in her speech, similar to when he introduce himself to her. He saw himself on video, staring at the television screen and realized he'd gained a little weight.

"Dr. Cawsten, is there anything else that I can assist you with?"

"No Jennifer, that will be all."

"Thank you for a wonderful evening. I shall be leaving now."

Two weeks later, Emerson stood in a conference room, staring out the window of the Fortune Plaza Office Building.

One by one, his colleagues entered the room until everyone was present.

"Thank you all for being here. Let's get right too it, after a year of successful trials, I'm certain that it's time to introduce Companions to the public."

"Have all the modifications been corrected?" Mr. Li questioned, the chairman and CEO of the company.

"You tell me. You've interacted with at least three Companions within the last year," Dr. Emerson announced.

He stared a puzzled faces.

"Explain Dr. Cawsten," Mr. Li questioned.

"Well, for starters, I created not one but twenty Companions and strategically placed them across the world. It's important to see them in different environments, allowing them to adapt to their surroundings and create solutions to problems that may arise. I won't always be available if one malfunctions…let's say in Sydney, Australia."

"You've created twenty of these Companions? Who authorized you to do so?" Mr. Li demanded.

"I created them and I didn't use any of your resources. I've outsourced all the products and tools, created them through a backer who shared my vision. My clients wanted to see a demonstration and that's what I provided them."

Emerson stared at a distraught Mr. Li.

Mr. Li's expression shifted to anger as he called security on the conference phone. "You will not work in this business again. Do you hear me? You're finished."

"Actually, I just created a billion dollar revenue. My Companions already infiltrated society without anyone's knowledge. My demonstration isn't over yet, Mr. Li. Take a look at the screen."

Emerson pressed a few buttons as the window dimmed. Images broadcasted on the window as he stared at guards heading towards the conference room. With a few taps on his notepad, several people got up from the conference table, walked out the door and created a barrier. "As I informed you, I've done the research and several field tests. Let me introduce you to Jui." Behind him, there was an image of Mr. Li's very attractive secretary. "As you can see, I planted one of my creations in Mr. Li's office for testing and you'll be amazed at everything that I've discovered." Emerson continued to show him footage of his former employer speaking with his creation, trying to find a way to weasel him out of his invention. "Mrs. Li, you will find this scene interesting…" Emerson brought up a video of Mr. Li with two of his Companions, including the one he thought was his secretary. "Mr. Li, none of these women is your wife and there's video evidence of harassment and intimidation."

Mrs. Li who was on her feet now, heading over to Mr. Li as he covered his head.

Emerson laughed as he saw the physical interaction between them. The guards outside commanded his attention as he saw his Companions engaging in barricading themselves. He walked over to the door with all his belongings. After tapping on his screen, his Companions followed him to the elevator, blocking anyone from getting within yards of him. He headed out of the building, merging with the crowd until he was no longer visible…

"Hello, I'm Elaine Viale and I have with me Dr. Emerson Cawsten, the creator of Companions; the last A.I. device that you will ever need. Thank you for coming to interview with me."

"It's my pleasure Elaine and you can call me Emerson."

"Emerson, why did you create them?"

"In the spirit of Valentine's Day, I wanted to introduce a one of the kind relationship that will benefit your life in many ways."

"But Dr. Cawsten, what is the purpose of these robots?'

"They're called Companions …"

"…My apologies, these Companions. There are reports that these Companions only serve one purposes: carnal desire. Why?"

"Elaine, my Companions serve more than the lustful nature of humanity. Over the last fifteen years, with a team full of researchers, we conducted numerous studies that led back to individuals wanting to be love. Yes, we desire to be rich, own possessions, travel the world but at the end of the day, people acquired money to own possessions to share them with someone; individuals want to travel with someone, everyone wants to be loved. Another stat for you Elaine, most relationships are bound to fail and as you know, the divorce rate hovers above sixty-five percent and the suicide rate around this holiday is at an all-time high. The purpose of my invention; the Companion is to create a relationship where the individuals doesn't feel alone anymore. I know this sounds ludicrous as we live in a world that consists of over twenty-two billion people but with technology guiding us through life, we're lonely. We need physical interaction and since we've become isolated from each other, relying on memes, text messages and pictures to communicate, my Companions will be a shoulder to cry on. They will go on trips with you, listen and speak to you and I promise you that you will feel a special relationship with them. I guarantee it."

"What about the ones that are being exploited for sexual purposes? I've heard there are brothels filled with these Companions."

"Elaine, that is out of my control. Just as any consumer, once you purchase a Companion, you are allowed to do whatever you want with your purchase. My Companions don't have a sole purpose but multiple purposes. It's like any piece of technology...we had smartphones in the 21st century. Devices that bridged the gap so we could communicate with loved ones miles away but yet, there were people who used them to steal other's identities. Computers were created for great feats but they gave hackers the ability to steal vital information and share it with other nations, bringing forth wars. I'm not sure if you are aware but take a look at the city of San Francisco, the first city I used my Companions in and reports show that crime has dropped below fifteen percent in a matter of months. My Companions have built Homeless Havens for the poor. The mayor has personally thanked me for my services and will comply with you that my Companions are beneficial to society."

"What do you say to those who believe this practice of companionship is deemed an abomination?"

"Everyone wants to be loved. Everyone needs a friend. Why waste time trying to get to know someone who might reject you when you can purchase a Companion. I guarantee you that my Companions will change your life. If you're not satisfied with your Companion after the first two years, you will get a full refund plus interest. With an offer like that, what do you have to lose?" Dr. Emerson quipped.

Reports were pouring in after the first year since Companions emerged as the hardest technology on the market, selling out in the first ten minutes with each shipment.

"My Companion is my best friend," one consumer reported.

"I was skeptic at first but after a few months, I don't know how I lived my life without one." Another satisfied customer wrote.

"I only use my Companion for sexual purposes and let me tell you, I can't differentiate from the real thing. They're so life-like. I can't even tell who's a Companion and who's human." Another horny consumer reported.

Blogs were filled with praises of the creation as Emerson read them all, each review in his favor.

Quiet stirrings began to boom from those who hated everything the Companions stood for. Several groups sprouted to fight against the "abominations" that he'd created. H.N.R. (Human Not Robots), a group who promoted relationships for humans and by humans, were always on the news degrading his creation.

Emerson already devised a plan, having a few of his Companions infiltrate H.N.R., recording every detail. His approval rate sat at 99%, the highest approval rating for any product. In two years, over 18 billion Companions were purchased.

After a few years, like any other product, the hype for Companions diminished. There was a surplus of returned products and after analysis and reporting, it was determined that 94% of returns were from females. Being a scientist, Emerson determined that obvious, maternal clocks were ticking. Females were longing for children on their own and the supply of males were nonexistent. Women became more aggressive, trying to reconnect human to human relationships. Reports of violent exchanges involving women were on the rise; men complained of being stalked and restraining orders were issued. Law enforcement patrolled neighborhoods to deter this type of behavior.

Calls were pouring in through streaming avenues…"The reason I prefer Companions over real intimacy is we don't have to impress our Companions. We as men are tired of bending over backwards to please women and all we catch is attitude. We're tired of spending our hard earned money on them, buying trinkets and the effort isn't reciprocated." One male stated.

Another male commented, "Women discarded us to play with their Companions and now, they've had their fun but we're still having ours…what happens when they get bored with us and go back to their Companions?"

A male in the audience stood up amongst the females. "The Companions have features that allows them to shift their body structure. If you want an Asian girl, they can be that in two minutes. Any ethnicity, curves, thick, petite, etc…that's going to be hard to give up. It's the perfect partner. Why should we settle for whining? Bitching? Arguments created out of thin air?"

A horde of women attacked the young male before he could finish his statement. Reports that the male survived the attack on him in the audience. He would have a full recovery once he awoke from his coma.

A few months later, the first Companion death was reported on the A.N.N. (American News Network), followed by a broadcast video showing two human females attacking a Companion, setting it on fire before running it over with their car. A chain reaction occurred as more clips of women hunting Companions were streamed, women hovering over Companions while pouring acid all over them. The violence surged so high, that smaller countries banned Companions from their providences, realizing that people were more important than Androids.

Hundreds of millions lost by the destruction of property, Emerson Enterprises filed lawsuits that arrived on judges desk every week, 99% of them were thrown out due to the sensitive nature that the government valued android over humans. His case was laughed out of several courtrooms—mainly ones with women judges.

He decided to take matters into his own hands. Emerson had one of his coders write specific codes and after updates; Companions were equipped with the necessary tools to protect themselves.

Desperate to protect his legacy, Emerson threatened his shareholders, and judges who he made several contributions to their campaigns but every week, his reports were being destroyed. With a campaign lead by H.N.R., Emerson uploaded a video of Judge Seymour W. Branch interacting with his Companion. The video circulated through the web, hitting all the major news sites. It was a political firestorm, one of the most prominent judges being handsy with not one but multiple Companions.

"Emerson, you had no right to release that video of Seymour," a shareholder mentioned.

"I had every right. I'm protecting my legacy. I've made all of you rich and I've reached out for help. How can you all ignore my calls and dismiss my cases? "

"You've destroyed his image in the public...Now everyone thinks they're been recorded and demanding answers. Confidentiality is important and now we've shattered secrecy. The people have spoken, no one wants a Companion."

"No, just the females. Not one male has complained about their Companion, not one. It's only the females and I know why they are in an uproar. They're going to dread the day they tampered with my creation."

"What are you going to do? What are you talking about? Emerson?"

"It's already been done." He nodded.

More nations outlawed Companions from being sold in their country. Factories where Companions were created were barricade as women stormed the premises. In the last year, property damage resulted in more than seven hundred million dollars. Emerson Enterprises lost its trillion dollar status; their revenue dwindled down to the single billions. Women broke into men's homes, setting fire to their Companions but males replaced them just as fast at women were destroying them, this caused a rift between human males and human females.

Within hours of his new updates, news reports displayed images of female Companions defending themselves against human females.

BREAKING NEWS: We have footage of rouge Companion attacking an innocent couple, killing the human female and tossing her into the River Seine in Paris.

Cries saturated the atmosphere from all four corners, their attention shifted to the romantic paradise that sat under Parisian lights. Authorities scrubbed every crevice in the city, searching for the Companion. After reports of Companions in the middle of the street, security huddled around them. Companions and cops stood across from each other before an innocent Companion handed over the one who committed murder. A shot rang out, echoing throughout their vicinity Companions fell to the ground. War broke out, female human versus Female Companions. Once the human males allied with them, rioters fought their way into Emerson's factories, leading Emerson to airlift scores of Companions to a secret location.

Lawyers, government officials, and others marched towards Emerson Enterprise's headquarters, confronting him as he stared at the monitor. Rioters broke the front gate, pouring into the building. His fingers rapidly typed in code, his body jerked as Emerson stared at the computer monitor. He pressed the red button, and immediately stepped out onto the penthouse courtyard. The chilling air grazed his exposed skin, the humming from a helicopter screeched painfully against his ears. Peeking over his shoulder, he glanced at the rambunctious crowd forcing themselves through the last barrier, prompting him to climb up on the edge. Staring up at the helicopter, he tilted his head to the side before facing his protestors and leaping backwards as gravity hurled him to his concrete grave.

It took several months for society to settle back to normalcy; especially after the public learned that Emerson himself was a Companion. All Companions were disposed of in creative ways. Government officials searched for the other remaining Companions but Emerson's death left mystery to their whereabouts. Relationships slowly mended between males and females; open dialogue produced positive results. Reports and studies showed that the birth rate was below five percent, which was alarming for the medical profession. After two years, the medical community discovered that every male that engage in sexual activity with a Companion had been sterilized.

JIM CROW'S SEEDS

I no longer feel the earth below my knees, while the wind grazing against my skin. The sound of animals in the distance has faded away while the heat of the sun beats against my face. My body naturally performs is essentials—my lungs expand as I take in a deep breath; I swallow as I've normally done; my eyes blink randomly and the muscles in my body contrast. My gaze is set upon the horizon in front of me as the loudest sound pierce the atmosphere. I'm in control of my body, no longer twitching at the frightening sound. I take in another deep breath, anticipating the next sound. I don't know how it got to this, how I'm kneeling in this position…powerless. Another deafening sound ricocheted across the horizon but this time, there's a thump that followed. My eyes quickly peek to the side, seeing the body of my companion: her lifeless eyes staring back at me while the soil is stained with the blood seeping from her newly punctured skull. I close my eyes, wondering how I'd gotten to this point….

…We armed ourselves, relied on satellites to warn us about threats from other nations but we weren't prepared for enemies that didn't need a passport to enter the US mainland, they were already here. It started with an

unforeseen spark and electing the wrong person to guide America forward. Lies filled the air, buried hatred slowly manifested into pockets of violence, spreading from town to town. Families were torn apart due to bias immigration laws; the entrance into the Land of the free was now based on a merit system because "politicians" didn't want to welcome those from "shit-hole" countries. The earth became brittle with pieces of broken skulls, the soil saturated with blood of the innocent and guilty. The country divided itself: red versus blue; liberals versus conservatives until there was a full fledge war based on the color of your skin.

Millions of lives perished. Representatives sought to end the carnage, compromising on territorial regions designated only to their race. The Native Americans reclaimed the bulk of the land they lost, the lands between the Rockies and Appalachian Mountains. The Asian community settled in the northwestern region of the US while the southwest region was reclaimed by the Latino community. The Caucasians resided in the New England territories, a region where they first landed while the Blacks settled in the first lands they set foot on...the southeastern region, better known as New Africa. Rules were established to avoid conflicts. A five mile cushion area-referred to as Cushion Strips—were established, warning those that illegal crossing would result in live executions. Passports were granted to those with Level 5 clearance...specifically for business purposes.

While there was peace on a national level, turmoil continued in the region as a tyrant slowly came to power. Sha'de...Being 1st generation Nigerian, preached on the importance of being "PUREBLOOD" as her followers *sparked a movement and businesses began discriminating against those of lighter or darker shades, escalating century's old stereotypes that divided us since Jim Crow. Her speeches of being bullied due to the pigmentation of her skin from those of a lighter tone increased her popularity, propelled Sha'de into an authoritative position while her followers began discriminating against those of a lessor shade. Being denied groceries and other necessities due to brown paper bag tests caused more suffering, protests and riots continued at her rallies upon a deafening sound reverberated. Sha'de stood motionless as crimson liquid covered her face. She fell forward and her death made her a martyr.*

War spilled into the streets, business and homes. Riots ravaged New Africa, setting the land on fire. Pockets of death became the norm as laws from Sha'de's party evoked the paper bag test: if a person's skin tone was lighter than a brown paper bag, they were rounded up and jail until they gave the name of the assassin who murdered their beloved leader. Reward money encourage family members to surrender their flesh and blood, forcing "redbones, khakis and brights" to flee. Those who tried to flee to other regions were denied access and were executed in Cushion Strips while others hid as best as they could. We did our best to blend in, moving in secret. Others in our party tried to reverse their fortunate but no matter how much time they spent in the sun, they weren't passing the test. We've ran out of places to hide, no one was willing to help us.

We were discovered by one of our own, trying to realign her loyalty but we scrambled from their clutches while seeing her strung out in a noose, hanging from a tree with the word "traitor" seared into her naked flesh. We fled but we were eventually captured, tortured because of the pigmentation of our skin as our ancestors were many centuries ago. We were ignorant to our history, not realizing that history was repeating itself.

...Adrenaline naturally coursed through my body as my heart levels increased but quickly subdued as warm metal pressed against the back of my skull. My vision blurred as I stared out into the distance. The desire to live vanished as crimson liquid from my wife's head soaked my pant leg. Shifting my head, I stared up at the person who just killed my wife. Inhaling deeply, I reached for her weapon, removing it from her clutches and squeezed the trigger as her body falls before hot piercing metal tears into my flesh. My back is flat against the ground as the sun hangs high. My fingers crawl against the earth until I felt the body next to mine. Tilting my head towards soulless eyes of my wife, I used my last breath to ask for her forgiveness. "I'm sorry I didn't keep my promise to protect you. You...have been avenged...my love..." Clutching her hand, the last image I saw was the sun...

Overprotective Girlfriends

Brett traded a soulful gaze with Amber. They were in a peculiar position…hiding beneath a fruit stand at the farmers market while unknown assailants dressed in all black shot at them.

"Hey, were going to get out of this," Brett encouraged. "The police should be on the way. We're going to be okay."

"They're shooting at us. WHY are they shooting at us?" Amber asked.

"I don't know but hopefully, someone called the police. We need to get over there where there are more places to hide. On my mark, we'll run over there for cover. Okay?"

He stared at Amber and she nodded, her fingers intertwined with his. After taking a deep breath, he signaled for them to sprint across the path for shelter. Adrenaline pumped through his body as he ran for cover. The sound of gunfire echoed all around him, bouncing off objects closest to him as he felt the release of pressure from his hands. He turned to see Amber lying on the ground and turned back for her. As he reached out, a bullet ricochet off the ground near his hand as he pulled back, falling back and staring at his girlfriend. She signaled for him to go but he wasn't going to leave her. He crawled towards her again, but saw enemies approaching their area.

"GOOOO!" Amber shouted at him.

Brett turned and ran, zigzagging while bullets penetrated wooden stands and bounced off signs. He found himself running between cars, finally hiding behind a large SUV, kicking himself that he left his girlfriend to die. The patterning of footsteps alerted him someone was near as he leaned low enough to see boots. The vehicle's alarm sounded, startling him as well as signaling his location. He knelt down until he felt metal against his left ear.

"Get up."

Brett rose slowly, his hands in the air as trepidation coursed through his body. "You got the wrong guy. If we can discuss this as grown men, I'm sure you will see a mistake has been made."

Gunfire could be heard from a distance, car alarms blared, as the noise gradually grew closer to his position. His eyes closed, he felt the metal leave his cheek and prayed silently before a single shot resonated and reverberated and he watched as the male slouched to his knees before faceplanting onto the concrete. Brett stared aimlessly at the male, half his skull gone with crimson fluid staining the ground.

"Brett...we gotta go," a familiar female voice insisted.

He met Amber's gaze, baffled by her presence. "How did—?"

"We don't have time, they'll be sending more after you. Come on."

Led by his girlfriend, they zig-zagged through a plethora of vehicles until they ducked into a dental office.

Amber led him into a small office, locking the door behind him. "Are you injured?"

"No...what the hell is going on? I thought you were dead. You killed that guy. How did you learn to use that thing?"

The door splintered open and before he could react, Amber grabbed the weapon from the man in black, tilted it upward as several bullets went into the ceiling. He observed as she continued to dismantle the person with an array of punches and kicks that floored him.

He stood to his feet as Amber snapped the enemy's neck. "What the fuck?"

"There's no time, we need to get you to the safe house. Let's go." Amber grabbed a few items from the dead body and exited the office.

They ran until they found a car, Brett stared there while Amber punched the window as glass shattered into a million pieces. "Get in."

He scurried to the other side, getting in while she reached underneath the steering wheel of a 75 Chevrolet corvette stingray, playing with wires until the engine revved to life.

The ride was quiet, too quiet. Images replayed over and over while he stared at Amber, watching her drive through the city like a professional stunt man.

Brett finally acquired the gall to speak up, "What's going on? Who are those guys and why are they trying to kill us? How did you learn how to fight like that? Who are you?"

"Brett...this is about your mother."

"My mother? How? She left me and my dad when I was five. I haven't heard from her in twenty years. I don't have a mother."

"Your mother left you and your father to protect the both of you, Brett. She has always been in your life, you'll see in a few minutes. We're almost there."

They pulled into a parking deck, driving faster than the five M.P.H. sign advised that was plastered along the stone columns. Two levels down, he let go of the handle once the car was in park. He sat in the car while she got out, staring at her through the windshield until Amber motioned for him to follow. He got out, following his girlfriend as they headed down a several stairwells. He grimaced at the blood on her arm, shirt and cheek. She no longer possessed the spectacles and her hair as disheveled. He thought how beautiful she was when he first met her, that nerdy librarian he adored; this bad ass appearance turned him on as well.

They got in the elevator.

"I need the truth."

"You're about to get a dose of it."

The elevator doors opened and Brett stared out at a high tech command center with females sauntering back and forth. Some familiar faces walked by him as he was taken back. "Jasmine? Teresa? Hilda...Felicia. What is this? H-how...Why are all my ex-girlfriends in one place?"

"Welcome Brett."

He turned around, standing face to face with Whitney, his former girlfriend of two years. "Whitney, I thought you took a job overseas?"

"Sorry for the deception but I'm sure Amber informed you this is about your mother? Well, that's true. Take a look at this video." Whitney pointed at the screen.

His mother's face popped on the screen as he was offered the seat. It was the last image he saw of her, down to the exact detail...

"...Brett, if you're seeing this video, I want to apologize for causing you heartache," his mother's voice came on. "I didn't want to leave you or your father but I had no choice. You see, I'm a spy but fell in love with the man you call your father. We shared everything and I told him the truth once I realized I was pregnant with you. I vowed to leave my job and did until my commander vanished. It was my mission to find her and that was the last time you saw me. The mission was a failure and my commander was killed. I was promoted to replace her, forcing me to cut off communication with you and your father. It was the only way to keep you both safe and I've hated myself for abandoning you. I always wanted to know you, so I employed my best agents to guard you. I'm sorry to inform you that those girlfriends that you've had since the seventh grade have been agents guarding you. I didn't mean to deceive you, I just wanted to protect you and please understand that I've done all of this because I love you. Forgive me."

Brett stood up, taking a few steps away from the computer screen with confusion on the brain. "Where is she? Where my mother?"

"She's been kidnapped. We received a message from her the day she went missing, informing us that your identity has been compromised. Amber is one of our best agents, providing around the clock surveillance."

"Is that why she's been hovering?"

"I resent that," Amber shouted, entering in a tactical uniform.

"So, none of it was real? Every girl that has entered my life was assigned to protect me? Not one wanted to be with me for me?" He glanced past Whitney, his line of sight set on Amber.

"I'm afraid that this is bigger than your feelings Brett," Whitney stated. "Put your emotion aside and understand the issue at hand. If they're able to break your mother, we're compromises."

"Why should I help? None of you cared about me. You all can handle yourselves."

"I'm sorry that your pride is hurt but she's your mother," Rebecca spoke up now. "She's had to live with the consequences, forced to watch you grow up from afar, not able to show her only child love and affection. But she never forgot about you, in fact she employed one of us to guard you at all cost. We sacrificed time and put our lives on the line to protect you. The least you can do is hear Whitney out."

Brett stared, gawking at a face he hadn't seen since the 7th grade. Across from him stood a raven haired petite woman with chestnut eyes and dimples that made her extremely adorable.

"Hello Brett, it's been awhile. You can be mad at us later, right now; we need to save your mother. Help us," Rebecca insisted.

Brett took several breaths, glancing around at all the faces staring back at him. All he could think about were pleasant memories. None of his girlfriends ever harmed him nor brought any ill will into their relationship. "What can I do to help?"

"Swallow this." Whitney handed him a pill and a glass of water.

He accepted the contents, swallowing the pill first then gulped the water. Once he finished the glass, he set it on the table. "What now?"

"Now we're going to rescue your mother," Whitney answered.

"What should I do? How can I help?" His mind and eyesight grew foggy. His balance wasn't sharp while tingling started in his chest and spread through his body. He stepped forward, slipping and crashing to the ground.

...He woke up, the cobwebs in his mind lingered longer than he liked. His arms were pulled back, restraints held him in place as a bright light blinded him.

"What is your name?"

"Who are you? Why am I here?" Brett asked.

"What's your mother name?"

"Susan."

"Where is her location?"

"I don't know, she left us when I was five years old. What's with all the questions? Why am I tied up?" No answers. He glanced past the luminous but all he could see was darkness. "Hell-ooo? I don't like the silence."

He remained in quiet for another five minutes, desperately calling for someone to speak to him. No matter how much he tried to wiggle free, freedom wouldn't release him.

A loud thump commanded his attention, followed by screams and gunfire ricocheting off the walls. If he had the ability, Brett would have jumped away as the wall blasted open in front of him. Once the dust settled, two women emerged out of the hole, towards him as he instantly recognized their faces. Brett officially knew he was walking down memory lane, staring at Cassie and Zharia. He felt the restraints slacken, releasing him from his imprisonment.

"Cassie? I thought you joined the Air Force? And Zharia, the last time I saw you, you were heading to the airport apart of the foreign exchange program."

"We don't have time for reminiscing. Let's go." Zharia pulled him up.

"Where's my mother?"

"She's safe, we were able to extract her, and she's in our custody now. We have total control of their systems, wiping our digital footprints from their system and the web and it's all because you assisted us. Come, let's get you out of here." Zharia grabbed his hand. He was led through a maze, gunfire echoing all around him but he felt safe with his ex-girlfriends. Once they got him in the vehicle, he felt cold steel to his head, wondering what was happening.

"We're very grateful that you assisted us and we guarantee that we are in your debt. Unfortunately, our organization thrives due to discretion." Cassie informed him.

"What does that mean?"

"It means you take this pill and you'll forget everything that recently happened." Cassie answered, handing him the pill.

He glanced around the vehicle, staring at flings and relationships from the past, baffled at seeing most of his exes under one roof. "I guess there's nothing else to do but..." He tossed the pill in his mouth and swallowed hard. Brett leaned with the vehicle as it curved the corner before blacking out...

...Brett woke up with a pounding headache and blurred vision, his sight finally focusing on the ceiling. Climbing out of bed, he showered, got dressed and headed down the hall and rounded the corner, bumping into an old lady.

"I'm so sorry ma'am, I didn't see you there."

"It's all right. Can you help me with my bags?" the elderly woman asked.

"It's the least I can do." Brett grabbed her bags, walking with her to her room as she lived in the condo two doors down from his. "I never knew someone stayed in this condo. I thought it was vacant."

"Ohh, nooo, I've been here for a while. Before this neighborhood was erected. I've seen you a few times with that blonde girl. You two make a cute couple."

Brett placed her bags on the counter.

"Thank you for assisting me, Brett. You're more than welcome to stop by any time and I'll make you some hot chocolate."

"I have to go but I'll hold you to that ma'am." He exited her condo, checking his phone while walking to the coffee shop. He stood in line, preparing to order when he felt something graze his forearm.

"Hey babe, I was just headed over to your place," Amber greeted him. "Are you feeling better?"

"Not sure, I felt like I've been drugged."

"Well, I apologize for deceiving you," Amber stated. "I know that I have been distanced lately. But just give me some time, I promise I will open up more. You can trust me with your life. "

"I believe you." He sipped his coffee, secured his hand into hers, and stared into her eyes as she sipped her coffee.

"Thanks for rescuing my mom and saving
my life."
Amber's Coffee cup slipped from her hand, crashing
to the floor.

DeForrest LeRonte'

Suali staggered out of the club, bumping into several partygoers. "Do not touch me," her speech slurred as it left her lips. The shutter of cameras clicking were aimed in her direction; flashes bouncing off her irises that temporarily blinded her, causing her to trip and fall on her side.

Laughter and taunts spewed from onlookers' mouths as she felt a strong pair of hands assisting her off the ground.

"I can get myself in." She yanked her hand from those helping her. The door opened, allowing her an escape as she slammed the door. "Privacy mode," she instructed. The windows darkened as she stuck her middle finger in their direction. "Take me home." With the GPS on full display on the screen, her driverless vehicle—Dubbed the Designator—sputtered off. A long sigh escaped her lips and her shoulders slouched just as the seatbelt secured her. Her chair slowly adjusted itself, leaning back while propping her head in a comfortable position before she felt a buildup of warmness on her bottom. The comfort allowed her to drift to sleep.

"Please enjoy the transportation and thank you for selecting the Designator. Safety and a pleasant ride is important to us," a robotic voice spoke through speakers.

Rumblings and piercing sounds violently awoke her. Eyes wide, she gawked at the windshield as headlights swerved on opposite sides of her. Caution signs peppered the large screen. Suali barked at the vehicle, hoping it would comply and get her to safety. Minutes of terror resulted in red and blue lights headed towards her. Her Designator slowed as her breathing subdued until the vehicle jerked to the right, giving her mild whiplash. Merging off the highway, it sped through busy intersections, colliding with other vehicles until it was clipped from behind by a patrol car, spinning out of control until it popped the curve and flipped over several times.

Once motionless, Suali opened her eyes, staring down at the ceiling. Trembling, she desperately tried to unlock her seatbelt as flashing lights approached her. Tears cascaded down her cheeks while officers crawled in, using force to remove her from her restraints until she fell into their arms, crying hysterically.

The next morning, Lydia glanced above her monitor, anticipating her boss' arrival. Her sights followed him as he stepped off the elevator, his pace quickened as he headed towards the conference room where other expensive suits wearers awaited. She stood up, grabbed her laptop and ventured towards the conference room where she snuck in while her boss—Eric was addressing other department heads.

"I'm sure you all are familiar with Suali Luventla, daughter of Miklat Luventla and future heiress of Luventla Enterprises, an important ally and businessman to the US so this has been bumped up to priority. Disregard your personal feelings about her and her social media life. Last night, her Designator was hacked, luckily, we were able to detect her whereabouts before any serious damage was committed. In the last two months, there has been random crashes but now, we know they aren't random. We are dealing with a sophisticated killer, one who's probably sitting in a location and causing mischief across the globe. So far, no one has made demands nor has anyone taken credit for these attacks. Just beyond this conference room are the smartest technological individuals on the planet and there's only one person who's been able to give us solid information. I want this hacker caught by the end of the week or those ridiculous high salaries that I'm paying you will be revoked..."

Lydia coughed to get their attention.

He nodded. "Here's the only person that seems competent enough to find any clue of this hacker—"

"Pardon my interruption. Sir, I found the link and it's active. As long as the hacker stays on line, I can pinpoint his exact location." She mentioned.

"What are you waiting for...go." Eric barked.

Lydia found herself thrust into action, escorted to a black-out SUV with other field agents in tactical gear. She sat in the backseat, the weight of a vest strapped around her torso as her fingers tapped on her laptop keys. She executed her own program, reverse-triangulating the signal as she gave them turn by turn directions. After crossing the highway and speeding through a quiet community, Lydia's directions led them to a beautiful house. Everyone filed out, guided by Lydia.

Eric rushed over to them. "We can't barge in."

"Why?" Lydia asked. "The signal is coming from this location. There's no telling whose vehicle he has control over."

"T-this is my home." Eric mentioned, pulling out his keys and opening the door with his hand on his gun holster.

Lydia kept her distance, allowing them to search Eric's home before she was summoned in. Stepping in, she greeted Eric's wife and his two children, a boy and a girl.

"No one has been here all day but my wife and kids. Are you sure the signal came from here?" Eric asked.

Lydia stared down at her computer, noticing the link was still active and pinged its location. She walked down the hallway, into a room where the television was set on pause. Her laptop pinged, indicating that the signal came from the game console. "It's coming from this device." Lydia stated.

"Why would a signal come from my son's video game console?" Eric asked.

"Call the agents where the car has malfunction and make sure no one is in the car," Lydia instructed. "Eric, call your son in and ask him to play this game."

Eric's son arrived, instructed to play the video game as he pressed buttons and controlled a car on his television. After making a few turns, he was instructed to stop.

"Sir, it has been confirmed that the vehicle moved just as your son started playing. The vehicle has stopped just as your son has paused the game."

"How does he have control?" Eric asked.

"Excuse me Eric Junior. Were you playing this game last night?"

Lydia observed her boss's son acknowledging that he played the game around the same time as Suali's accident occurred. "How long have you had this game?"

"Since last night. It came up on my inbox and I completed the trial test. After a five-dollar charge, it downloaded to my library and I started playing the game. I'm not that great at it yet," Eric Junior explained.

Linking up her computer to the game console, Lydia downloaded the contents of the video game and studied the link and the coding behind it. Sitting at the table, she found herself engrossed in the game, finding a backdoor that showed her codes and links to ultimately find it had a spring link.

"Sir, let's speak outside." She walked through the house and out into the front lawn where she spoke with Eric and a few other superiors, "I'm afraid that this source code is far more advanced that we could imagine. Your son's video game has a direct link to numerous vehicles."

"Can you disable the signal?" Eric asked.

"I'm afraid not sir. The code is so complex that once you lock on to it, it mutates and leaves its host. Not only will it fry my system if I tried to shut it down, it has the capacity to destroy any network that I'm linked to. Someone very intelligent took the source code and implemented into the core of a video game. I searched the game and if my search is correct, this game has over 60 million downloads. Were only at the tip of the iceberg on this one. The hacker wanted us to know his or her ability, wanted you to know that he can get to anyone and taunting you by having your son's game console being a part of the hack. Right now, the hacker has all of your information from your internet provider."

"What can we do?" Eric asked.

"You need to check all your accounts for protection. On a global scale, we need to contact AutoDrive CEO to inform them that their Designators division has been compromised, immobilized our economy since travel relies on AutoDrive technology. We can only hope that the other links are dead." Lydia hoped.

Just as those words left her lips, three of their SUVs turned on and drove erratically, going through yards, crashing into other vehicles as they followed each other down the street and out of sight.

Baby Roulette

DeForrest LeRonte'

"Three shots of Hennessey shouldn't cost the same amount as a bottle," Sean emphasized towards the bartender, signing the receipt and tossing the pen to his left. After collecting three glasses, he bumped into a few club goers, holding the plastic cups above his head, so he wouldn't spill their drinks. He glanced up, noticing Ricky smooth talking some ebony goddess with plump lips and an ass that matched. He peeked over at Doug with a pretty caramel hottie with short hair and fashionable frames sitting on the brim of his nose.

Sean shrugged, his gaze on the lonely girl with her arms folded across her chest. After Ricky tilted his head towards her, Sean realized that both shared a connection: both were the third wheel.

"You could just have bought the bottle?" she stated.

"Excuse me?" Sean responded.

"Why do you have three drinks in your hand?" She questioned.

"I got it for those knuckleheads…it's yours if you drink Hennessey." He faced her, stretching the drink in her direction.

After a few seconds, she accepted it.

"I'm Sean. I assume those are your friends my guys are flirting with?"

"Yes."

The music continued to play while he stared out at the crowd.

"I'm Tara by the way."

"Do you dance?" he asked.

"No."

"Okay." Sean peeked over at Ricky, noticing that his female companion inched closer to him. He shifted his position so he could see Doug with the nerdy looking girl but they weren't in view. Spinning around, he searched for Doug until he locked gaze with Tara.

"They're down on the first level," she mentioned.

"Thanks. What do you do?"

"A few days from finishing law school. What's your occupation Sean?"

"I'm an accountant. I don't mean to yell, do you want to go to some place quieter...the upper level has less people"

"Yes..."

Sean woke up in a foreign bed—the sheets were too soft against his skin and the scent was delicate. He felt pressure on his right arm and shifted slightly, staring at Tara. She faced him but her eyes were closed. He stared up at the ceiling, took a deep breath and slowly slid his arm from underneath her. Sean stopped when her lips smacked together as she flipped over, giving him a fraction of a second to move his arm. After flexing his extremities, he wiggled towards the edge of the bed as the covers lifted slightly, giving him a glimpse of her naked body. Paralyzed, he had second thoughts about bailing.

He stepped out of bed and collected his things as he slid his clothes on. After fastening his belt, he grabbed his shoes while searching for his shirt when he heard a gasp. Frozen, he stared at her as she shifted in bed but was relieved when she went back to sleep. Unable to find his shirt, he grabbed his coat and tiptoed through her place as he opened the door. Gently closing it, Sean passed the elevator as he headed for the exit sign.

The basketball swung from one side of the court to the other, the younger men running up and down the court while the older males slowed the pace of the game. It always seemed to be the older men trying to bully the younger, more athletic men off the court. Sean was in the younger category, sprinting down the court faster than his opponent as they won their third consecutive game. After taking a break in between games, he felt some discomfort in his abdominals, enough pain that forced him to sit out the next game. A swarm of nausea radiated as he felt the need to throw up but the last time he ate was a few hours ago.

"You okay man?" Ricky inquired.

"Not sure...must have been something I ate."

"You could be pregnant. You look a little swollen in the face man…you're dragging out there. That's not the Sean I know," Ricky joked.

A few people surrounding them laughed, as did Sean. When he chuckled, his muscles contracted, causing him further pain. "Man, don't be saying something like that. I've just being tired lately. Office work will make anyone lazy."

"Well, it's possible. You know that, right?" Doug commented.

Sean gawked in Doug's direction. "Seriously, don't play like that bruh."

"Are you serious right now?" Doug replied. "You know it's biologically possible for males to give birth, right? Our bodies have adapted to the environment and the first male gave birth about twenty-five years ago. There's about one percent of male births a year but they aren't televised due to privacy. Also, the numbers are low due to males immediately aborting the fetus before the six week deadline. The law dictates the fetus as a living person and its considered 1st degree murder, an action that's accompanied by life in prison or worse; the death penalty."

"Here we go with all this science crap," Ricky said.

"You remember that I'm not a student, right? I've already finished medical school and on the verge of finishing my thesis for my PhD. This is my field, what I'm currently studying and damn close to a breakthrough, so all this science crap will be beneficial to me and you," Doug emphasized with a concern look aimed at Ricky.

"C'mon man, don't be so sensitive. You know I was just joking," Ricky said.

"All I'm saying Sean, is that if the pain continues, you might want to get a checkup," Doug advised. "If you're pregnant, let me deliver it. I've never delivered a baby from a male yet."

"Man, get the hell out my face with that bullshit. I'm not pregnant. It's probably something I ate."

"When's the last time you had sex?" Doug asked.

"Man, he's been on a drought," Ricky answered for him. "It's been like three or four months."

"Thanks for your input Ricky," Sean stated."

"I'm just saying, if he were pregnant he would be showing by now," Ricky explained. "While you *ladies* discuss symptoms of pregnancy, I'm getting back on the court to beat these old buzzards."

"Give me a minute." Sean sat up, watching Ricky and Doug hustling back to the court. Pulling himself up off the ground, he stood to his feet and felt woozy. After collecting his bearings, Sean jogged out to the court and finished several games.

The following Monday at work, Sean was uploading his presentation to SharePoint as another wave of nausea washed over him. He took a minute until the feeling passed, reaching for his water bottle. Once the feeling went away, he logged off his work computer and headed for the conference room. With everyone present, he stood in front of his colleagues and started his presentation. After the third slide, that queasy feeling returned as the sensation forced him to pause.

"Sean, is there a problem?" his supervisor inquired.

"No sir, just a little cramp in my stom—" Pain radiated from his pelvic to his abdominal region. Staggering back, he clenched as he bent over.

"Sean..."

Before he could hear his supervisor say another word, Sean rushed over to the trash bin as bile spewed from his mouth. He crashed to his knees, heaving as more food splashed into the can before passing out...

Sean woke up in a hospital room with an IV attached to his forearm, a dorky nurse hovering next to him.

"Where am I? What happened?"

"You're in the hospital due to morning sickness."

"How did I get—wait.—WHAT THE FUCK DID YOU JUST SAY?"

"Calm down sir. Morning sickness, as in you're pregnant, Mr. Foxnel."

"This is a joke, right? Doug put you up to this? You're one of his medical school friends." Sean scanned the room to see if anyone was recording him. He shifted and the IV in his veins hit him with a burst of pain.

"Relax Mr. Foxnel. I'm sure you are aware when a male and a female..."

"I'M NOT A FUCKING IDIOT. How long have I've been pregnant? Is it too late to get a..."

"Sir, do not speak to me with that tone. I understand you are in shock but I deserve respect."

Sean paused. Disrespecting women wasn't a characteristic of his upbringing. "My apologies."

"To answer your questions, it's been a little under three months. Secondly, I'm afraid that it's against the law and you'll be charged with first degree murder."

"I can't be pregnant. How is this possible? Women are supposed to have the babies, not men. I haven't had sex in almost three..." Sean paused as he looked at the nurse.

"Here's a pamphlet, go to your local pharmacy, pick up some folic acid and some prenatal pills. Do you have a doctor?"

"Yeah, can I go now?"

"Yes, you can leave when you're ready Mr. Foxnel and I wish you the best of luck. There aren't many males who go through the process—"

"Well, I don't have a choice, do I?" Sean climbed out of bed and his hospital robe, sliding his work clothes back on and stuffing the pamphlet into his back pocket. He grazed the nurse as he exited, heading down the hallway while passing several nurses and patients.

When he got home, Sean sat on his couch, channel surfing through infomercials and daytime television. His coffee table was littered with open bottles and snack wrappers. There was a knock at the door but he didn't get up, he just leaned forward and reached for a snack. Several raps blared behind him as he glanced over his shoulder, lowering the volume on the television.

"Sean, I can hear the television. Open the door man; you have people worried about you."

He recognized the voice—Ricky, the last person he wanted to see right now. He turned his volume all the way down, ignoring him until he heard keys jingling. Sean cursed himself when he realized that Ricky had a key to his place. Reaching for a blanket, he pulled it over his midsection.

"Man, what the hell? I called and message you a few times…" Ricky mentioned.

The light came on, expelling the darkness.

Sean stared up at Ricky who stood at the end of the couch with a bewildered expression on his face.

Sean followed his friend's stare, glancing down at his midsection as his chin grazed his upper chest before focusing on the television.

"Dude, why are you sitting in the dark? I called your job and they said you were on medical leave for the last ten days. I've never seen you miss work."

"I'm getting over a virus man; you need to go home before you get sick." Sean coughed in his fist.

"Man, ain't nothing viral enough to haul you up in here for two weeks. For real, what's going on? Your house is dirty, crumbs all over the place. You got enough snacks here to feed several people like you're…" Ricky stared down at Sean.

Their eyes met.

"MAN, ARE YOU PREGNANT?"

Sean peeled his gaze from Ricky, glaring at the television. He pulled his blanket from his mid-section, hearing a gasp come from Ricky's mouth.

"WOW."

Silence lingered between them as he continued eating Doritos.

"How in the HELL did you get...Wait, what about an abortion?"

"It's already too late. If I even attempt to get one, I'll be charged for premeditated murder; an offense that'll get me up to 10 years in prison. The nurse already keyed my information into the system."

"Who's the mother?"

"The girl from the club, Tara I think is her name."

"Tara. The lawyer chick? I didn't know you two hooked up. Doug still communicates with her friend. She needs to know about this...we also need to tell Doug."

"I know that."

"Damn...man, I'm sorry I can't give you the support you need. Doug knows all about this. We—I mean, you need to tell him. The only men I know who had babies were volunteers. Regardless, I'm here for you and you need to be prepared for what's to come. A lot of attention will be heading your way if anyone finds out."

"Thanks man." There hadn't been a report of a man having a kid within the last decade, but he was sure they wanted their privacy—as did he. Ricky's words echoed as he thought about the attention he would receive at work, once someone noticed the weight he would gain. He knew he needed to avoid the spotlight and that wasn't going to happen unless he called Doug. Sean phoned Doug, leaving several messages to return his call as soon as possible.

Sean finally heard from Doug, who rushed to his place later that evening. He stared up at Doug, the same expression Ricky displayed earlier cemented on his face. He wasn't amused when Doug snickered, his reaction led to several muffled cackles from Ricky until they both were laughing out loud.

Giving them their moment, he sat in his chair as Doug came over and pulled the blanket from his stomach.

"You should have called me sooner. We could have avoided this," Doug mentioned.

"The nurse said I was already past the threshold."

"A few things you're going to need to know: you're going to experience mood swings, frequent urination, sore breasts...I mean soreness in your chest, nausea, food aversions, weight gain and abdominal pain. It's easy now so be prepared that it will be difficult within the next few months. I will help you get through it. I'll be your consultant, advising you on things you will need to do. Anyone else would only take you on as a client to extort it, so tell no one. I'll do house calls to avoid any attention and if it's something I can't handle, I will get a good friend of mine. I will practice discretion. For research, I will need a blood sample from both of you. What are you going to do about work?"

"I'm teleworking for a while."

"Good. I'll be able to give your boss a medical reason why you shouldn't be at work, so you can stay at home. You're still able to go out and get what you need but around the sixth month, it will be noticeable so when that time arrives, Ricky will be your servant. Are you going to keep the baby or give it up for adoption?"

Sean froze. With everything going on, he never gave it a thought about raising a child.

"Hello...Sean, are you there?" Doug asked.

He snapped out of his thoughts, staring at Doug and Ricky hovering in front of him. "I haven't given it any thought."

"You need to tell Tara right now." Ricky nodded his head at him.

"He's right. She needs to know. She is your baby mama." Doug snickered.

The sound of kids playing boomed all around him as he sat at the bench. Sean stared out, watching them while they ran back and forth with so much energy. He smiled and unconsciously rubbed his belly before realizing what he was doing and pulled his hand away.

"You have a lot of nerve requesting my presence. What is so important that you have me out here? You have five minutes. Go!"

Sean turned to see Tara in a different light: she wasn't the lady with the slutty dress that every woman had in the back of her closet. Her attire was business casual. He couldn't take his eyes off her as he thought about what to say. "I-I'm sorry for bailing on you that night and for not calling you…"

"All MEN are the same. I can't believe you left after all we did that night. Was I just another girl on your hit list or something?" Tara asked.

"It wasn't like that and I'm not that type of—"

"You're not that type of guy, right? You're different? You were scared? Your mother or grandmother raised you better? The same excuse…I thought you were genuine, especially talking for hours. Was all that a ruse to get me out of my bra and panties? Well, congratulations, it worked."

"I'm sorry that I made you feel that way and there's no reason for you to forgive me…"

"Then, why the FUCK am I here? Tell me Sean, why am I here?"

Sean stood to his feet and unzipped his coat. He watched as the anger dissipated from her face. He literally watched as she displayed an array of nonverbal emotions: anger, confusion, before a smirk surfaced. Laughter could be heard as he kept his gaze on her.

"Wait, that's not a beer belly. Are you pregnant?" Tara covered her mouth.

"I'm pregnant and it's yours." The laughter died as he stared at Tara.

Her expression hardened, her eyes gawked at his belly to his gaze and back at his belly.

Sean waited, knowing she needed to process what he just told her.

"No—no, how is it mine? How—is this possible? No, it's not mine. It was—"

"About four months ago. You're the only person I've been with this year. I didn't know I was pregnant until I went to the hospital from fainting at work. By then, the nurse informed me it was past the threshold for abortion."

"Wait, you were going to abort it?" Tara asked.

"At first, yeah because I don't know a male who has went through this without seeking fame. I was scared."

They locked gazes. He studied her face, trying to gauge what she was thinking or her next words. They were sitting down now; he stared at the mother of his pending child. This was the first time he really soaked in her appearance and she was more attractive than he remembered. Sean sat there when Tara suddenly popped up.

They exchanges glances before she shook her head and walked off.

Months sped by—eight to be exact since Sean snuck out of Tara's place, not realizing their future was tied to each other. A night of liquid courage mixed with pleasure was currently causing him internal abdominal pain. His stomach was in knots, feeling like a constant abdominal workout. He thought about Tara—the last time he saw her, she was walking away from him. That hope of reconciliation evaporated once she vanished. He had no choice but to do this without her, he was strong enough to go through this process. All of the pregnancy symptoms hit him as hard as ocean waves, thrusting him in awkward positions. There were moments he found himself crying, especially when Ricky made jokes about his weight or his sensitivity.

He stared at his image; puffier than he would have ever imagine and it didn't matter how much cardio he performed, Sean couldn't rid himself of the excessive weight. Reaching for the bottle of prescription pills—the prenatal care package that Doug brought him, inhaling them without water. After taking the vitamins, he waddled over to the treadmill, turned on the television and steadily walked on an incline for an hour. A rap at the door commanded his attention as he lowered the volume just as the sound of keys jingling echoed.

"Hello Ricky."

"How did you know it was me?"

"Your scent. It's repugnant. You should wash your clothes with a different detergent and stop spraying on so much cologne. Be more like Doug, he has a lighter scent that reminds me of a walk through a spring meadow on a spring day."

"Dude, tuck your vagina back in and remember you have a penis…we have more pressing matters to deal with." Ricky walked over near Sean and grabbed the remote. He flipped through several channels until he stopped to the evening news.

On screen, Sean saw a picture of himself with his condition scrolling across the bottom of the screen. "Why am I on the news? How did they find out?"

"Her—do you know her?"

Sean stared at the screen, a hint of recognition as he continued on the treadmill. "Yeah, that's the nurse from the hospital. She's the one that informed me that I was well...."

"She's not a nurse anymore. They fired her," Ricky stated. "She provided them with every detail. I'm surprised you haven't received any phone calls for an interview. You know you can sue her and the hospital for revealing your medical information." Ricky rubbed his hands together, thinking about money.

"Of course, I'm going to sue but why would she risk her job? It's not like I'm the first male..."

"She received a six figure sum and you're the first in the last few years," Ricky emphasized.

Sean stared at his face plastered all over all over the news. He was an instant celebrity but he didn't want the attention.

"I'm sure they have your address. If you don't want the attention, you need to grab some clothes and stay with me."

Sean was moving slower than usual, prompting Ricky to rush to his room, and grab a few things. After collecting essential items, they exited his place, rode the elevator down as he was guided by Ricky to the passenger's side of his SUV. They sped off out the parking lot, cruising down the highway just as news van sped towards his residence.

Since moving into Ricky's place, he no longer had access to the treadmill so his constant eating contributed to his weight ballooning. Pain radiated with each step, each breath and at times, each thought. Sean stared down at his abnormally robust belly, feeling the child inside moving about—a child that he didn't know the gender due to the publicity he would receive if he went out into the world. He remembered the first time feeling something moving inside of him, cursing himself for being in this predicament. He hated the frequent pissing, the weird fetishes he'd developed, and the cramps—he HATED the cramps. Now, the random "kicks" didn't bother him and he fell into a routine with his aliments.

"How's the mommy doing?"

"Dude, that wasn't funny the first time you joked about it."

"Stop being so sensitive…wait, you can't." Ricky laughed.

"If I could get up, I'd sit on you." Sean adjusted his position, alleviating the pain that raced up and down his spine. "Something's wrong."

"What?"

"I don't feel well. It's not the usual pain or me pissing out my liquids; this is different. I'm feeling heavy stomach cramps and a lot of kicking. Where's Doug?"

"He said he was on his way," Ricky answered.

"He'd better get here soon." A sharp pain immobilized him, causing Sean to wince and yell at the top of his lungs. The sensation was frightening and this being an act he wasn't supposed to endure, the pain was excruciating. He reached out, grabbing hold of anything he could get his fingers on, crushing the remote control.

"Whoa…" Ricky looked stunned as he stepped away from Sean.

"I feel like a drug dealer, delivering you this care package…what's wrong?" Doug asked as he burst through the door.

"I don't know, he just started yelling like some lunatic," Ricky answered.

Sean was happy to see Doug, reaching out and clasping his hand. His gaze didn't leave Doug's as tears streamed from his eyes, past his ears as he laid on his back.

"He's going into labor."

"What—how do you know? I thought there should be a puddle of water or something, like the women on television."

"It's different for a man due to his sexual organs. Sean, did you urinate for more than five minutes."

Sean nodded.

"He pissed the water out?" Ricky asked.

"Come on, let's get you up. Ricky, go get the truck. We need to be discreet when we walk him out. I'll call my friend and inform him when were less than a mile from the hospital," Doug instructed as he and Ricky gently pulled Sean to his feet.

Sean stared at Doug after watching Ricky rush out the apartment to get his SUV.

"Sean, mimic my breathing...OK."

Sean nodded, mimicking Doug breathing patterns as they waddled towards the door. Sean stood there while Doug glanced out the door, making sure they had enough privacy before guiding him outside; thankful that Ricky lived on the first level.

The SUV pulled up close to the apartment, Ricky tossing everything in the rear as Doug assisted him into the backseat. He laid in the back, Doug opened the opposite door as he propped him up while Ricky skidded across the hood of his vehicle, jumping into the driver seat as they propelled forward.

"WHY...WHY...why is this happening to me?" Sean shouted. Pain radiated as he felt every bump, pothole and crack in the road. He winced each time, still feeling that same pain in his pelvic area.

"We're almost there," Ricky stated.

Sean glanced up at Doug, thinking that he was speaking to him but realized that he was on the phone with his colleague.

"We're all set," Doug stated. 'He informed me that we should go to the back of the hospital, the emergency entrance and he'll have everything waiting for us."

"Man, I love you. I love you both. I don't know what I'll do without you both. I'm sorry for yelling at you and anything I've done to hurt you in the past. Ricky, I'm sorry for telling Jasmine that you had mono when we were in school, I was just jealous of you man. You got all the girls."

"I knew that was you! Man, you better feel lucky I didn't find out that was you back then," Ricky barked.

"Doug, you are a geek and your research about fishes is weird but I'm glad you're my friend."

"Thanks, I guess." Doug hunched his shoulders.

"What is he doing? Why is he confessing?" Ricky questioned.

"Most people confess their sins so they don't have any bad karma for the child or think they're going to die. It's natural. Hey, interesting that you brought up my research. I think I might win a Nobel Prize for what I've discovered."

"Doug, I don't think this is the right time…"

The car hit the speed bump, a loud shriek boomed throughout the SUV.

Ricky stopped suddenly. "Man, I'm so sorry!" he proclaimed.

Both back doors opened with nurses assisting Sean out of the car. Doug got out as they put him in a wheelchair, covering his head as they escorted him past the entrance while the SUV pulled off. Sean held onto Doug's hand, not letting him leave his side.

"As I mentioned over the phone, its time." Doug stated.

"Thanks for calling me Doug," the doctor replied. "I have everything set up for him. He's in good hands."

"Sean, I'm going to be with you just a moment," Doug explained. "I need to make a phone call and find Ricky so he knows where we're located. The Doc has informed me that no one is allowed access to this section without his permission."

Sean watched Doug head down the hallway on his phone, assuming he was informing Ricky where they were. Being wheeled down the hall, they turned the corner where Tara stood in the center of the hallway. Confused by her appearance, he glanced up at the doctor as he took a step back.

"I'm going to give you two a moment of privacy," the doctor stated.

"Where are you going?"

"Don't worry; I'll be right around the corner."

Sean shifted his glance in Tara's direction. "What are you doing here? How did you know I was here?"

"I'm here for you...for this. I know it might be too late but I do want to offer my sincerest apology for my behavior and absence. When you shared that with me, I'm not going to lie, I was fuming with anger when I saw you and shocked when I saw your belly."

"Yeah, I'm really sorry—"

"I want to be a part of our baby's life. The anger will dissipate and if you're anything like how you came off when we first met. I'm sure we can explore a relationship but that's totally up to you."

Sean sat there in the wheelchair, contemplating Tara's request while small spikes of pain caused him to grimace.

He stared at Tara. "Yeah, we can see what happens. One day at a time."

"That's all I request. Okay, you want me in the room with you?"

"NO! You're staying out here. I refuse to allow you in there."

"I thought—"

"You thought wrong. I'll see you when the baby is here. By the way, how did you know I was here?"

"Doug called my friend, asking for my number. He explained everything and it made me realize what's important."

"What did he explain—" Pain shot from his neck all the way to his toes, as Sean felt immobilized. He didn't hear anything else as he felt himself moving, rolling down a well-lit hallway into a labor room filled with a few wide-eye staff.

They reached down, gently lifting him from his chair, easing him onto the bed.

"Where's Doug? Ricky?"

"They will be here shortly. Trust me, you're in good hands."

A knock on the door commanded his attention, glancing at the nurse as she opened the door. Dressed in scrubs, Doug and Ricky entered as he smiled briefly.

"Man, I'm so glad that you're here!"

"Well, we're going to be here through the surgery." Doug nodded.

"Surgery?" Sean asked.

"Yes, they will perform a caesarean section unless you know something we don't. How else will the baby come out? No need to panic, it's a procedure that's performed all the time. They'll give you an epidural shot that will ease the pain. You'll be fine and with our technology, you'll look fabulous in your beach body. You ready?" Doug asked.

Sean glanced at the doctor, the nurses, and then Ricky before his eyes fell on Doug. "Yeah, I'm ready."

He felt the bed move as his friends exited the room before he found himself wheeled into the hallway. They rolled him towards the operating room, where others awaited surgery. "Wait."

They stopped abruptly.

Sean motioned Doug forward. "Hey, I spoke to Tara. She's in the waiting room."

"Why is she here?" Ricky asked.

"Doug called her. I wanted to know why."

"Well, remember I was telling you about my thesis. Well, to sum it up since there are more important issue to attend too. We weren't sure why males started having babies within the last twenty-five years. After years of following up on their research, I discovered that it was due to environmental factors that triggered..." Doug stared at a perplexed Sean and Ricky. "Okay, the reason certain males get pregnant is due to the fact that the women they engage in intercourse are barren. Since Tara's womb can't carry the egg, a mutation occurred in you, activating your X chromosome and turning off your Y-chromosome so you can carry the child. It's quite remarkable. Any of us could be next as more environmental issues are making females barren. You've been chosen and it's a great honor."

"You call it a great honor, all I can image is the pending pain. Please escort Tara out, I definitely don't want her in here until the pay is out. No offense."

FORBIDDEN FOREST

Summer break had come and excitement echoed through the hallways. Gloria made her way out of homeroom class to her locker. She was dreading a summer break. She loved learning and the challenge to improve her intellect.

She stared at the remaining object taped inside the door of her locker…a picture of her sitting on her grandmother's lap, reading to her. She reached up to her neck and rubbed the charm. Her grandmother told her that the charm possessed extraordinary powers.

"Never remove this amulet from around your neck. There are creatures that have searched the ends of this earth to acquire this precious jewel. Beware of the crescent scar. Beware of the Black Witch."

Tears trickled down her cheeks while she reached into the locker and carefully detached the photograph. She shut her locker and strolled toward the public library. The humidity climbed from pleasant to scorching in a span of four hours while she took the scenic route to her job. Her peers sped by in an assortment of cars, honking their horns while loud music saturated the air. Gloria didn't celebrate like her peers; she actually enjoyed school and couldn't wait for the summer to conclude.

After greeting co-workers and the usual regulars, she headed into the employee's lounge to change into her uniform. The door swung open, which startled her. Standing there was Allen, another student who also worked at the library. "Ms. Hexen is headed this way and she looks pissed!" He warned as he opened his locker. Pulling out clothing, he changed into his uniform—without any regards to her presence.

Gloria glanced back at him to see if it was okay to look but he was gone. She headed out and almost ran into the Head Librarian. "Hello, Ms. Hexen."

"Gloria, I need you working the antique section. Allen will work the main floor since his carelessness caused damage of a few items the last time."

"Yes, ma'am."

"Oh, that's an interesting piece around your neck. May I take a closer look?" Ms. Hexen asked while stepping forward. "By the design, it appears to have been created around the dark ages in England. Where did you acquire such a magnificent piece? Do you mind if I hold it to study its design a little further?"

Gloria felt very uncomfortable with Ms. Hexen leaning into her personal space. "It is a family heirloom, passed down from my grandmother. She requested that I never remove it, so I'm sorry, but I can't take it off."

"Well, maybe I'll take another look at it when you have the time?"

"Yes, Ms. Hexen." Gloria hurried away to the antique room. Things were different when her grandmother was the Head Librarian...it was what lured her to the library in the first place. It was a place full of adventures and excitement at the turn of a page.

After swiping her access card, she entered into the antique section and flipped the light switch on. An assortment of books lay scattered across the floor. "This has Allen's name written all over it." Sighing, she picked up as many books as she could, read the spines and placed them back on the shelves in their coordinating spots. Then she went about tidying up the rest of the mess.

One trunk in particular was difficult to move, requiring her to put forth extra effort. Sliding it across the room, she pushed a little too hard and the trunk fell over. Items spilled out onto the floor. She noticed a symbol inside the trunk on the lining. Intrigued, she pressed the symbol.

A secret compartment popped out from the bottom—a scroll with a bow tied around it. Gloria unsealed and opened it to read its message:

...Every literary piece contains conflict...a battle between good and evil. One such legend in particular frightened the inhabitants of the land...the Legend of the Tull Amulet.

Once she acquired the Amulet, the most feared evil was the Black Witch—who reigned over the Forbidden Forest. Species by species, she wiped out all creatures from existence. Finally, she had conquered all the species, except the grizzly Baires. Contrary to proper spelling, these weren't your average bears. These ferocious creatures battled the Black Witch; each battle resulted in diminishing the Baires species until only three remained.

These three Baires devised the perfect plan to acquire the amulet and relieve the Black Witch of her throne. Attacking the Black Witch by surprise, the smallest bear got close enough and ripped the amulet from her neck.

One of the Black Witch's servants—once under her influence, but now free once the necklace escaped her possession—found the amulet in the forest while evil battled evil. The servant locked it in a magical box that could only be opened by a wizard of the light...

Gloria noted that after a long space, the next entry seemed to be written in the same hand.

Intrigued, she kept reading...

...**M**y father told me this story many times over the years. As a descendant of the light, it was his job to hide the amulet and he always warned me never to enter the Forbidden Forest.

I shall start with the fairytale of a young girl with golden locks who stumbled across a cottage, where the three bears lived. While the fairytale everyone tells about this is amusing, let me say that most of it is pure FICTION. A web of lies told through the fabric of time, shielding the truth in the process. Of this particular tale, I know the real truth. Allow me to introduce myself—I am that young girl with a head full of golden curls, but I didn't wander to the cottage—I was lead.

The night of my seventh birthday, the sound of a struggle woke me from my slumber. I ran to my door, pressing my ear against the wood. The noise suddenly died. I opened my door and found my mother lying unconscious underneath a pile of rubble. I rushed over and I tried to revive her. I called out for my father, but he didn't answer. Then thunder and lightning temporarily brightened up the night sky. I went over to the door and saw thick rain pouring down.

Lightning flashed and I saw my father being dragged into the forest by two overly large, shadowy beings. I glanced back at my mother one last time, and then rushed toward the forest. I saw a cottage in the distance, the door closing shut. I pressed forward, until I stood in front of a worn down cottage. I wondered if I should enter, and then I heard my father's screams.

I darted in. Now, here is where the fairytale has a little truth in it. There were three bowls sitting on the table but let me be frank…porridge wasn't in them. Secondly, there were chairs in the living room for three occupants, but they were broken, merely pieces scattered across the ground.

I heard growls and more screams. I was halfway up the stairwell, searching for a place to hide when I found a bedroom and quickly hid underneath the smallest bed. A shadow moved in front of the threshold with—hairy feet that didn't belong to a human. Not just one set of feet but three. They entered into the room and stomped around until one set stopped at the edge of the bed.

Something grabbed me and pulled me into the open. Suspended in mid-air by a massive grip, glowing red eyes stared deep into mine. I couldn't tear my eyes away from the creature that held me like a rag doll.

These were very large animals with lashing sets of sharp teeth. The creature who held me stared closely at me while its mouth moved. "My…my, what do we have here?"

"Talking bears?" I questioned with confusion.

"No one trespasses in our Forbidden Forest," the smallest animal stated.

"Where is my father?"

They shared a glance before grinning.

The medium-size animal left the room and I could hear it heading down the stairwell. The largest creature held me high in the air, but by its mannerism, it was evident that the smaller one was in charge. Then, after another couple of minutes of struggling, I stopped moving while the little bear stared at me.

A loud bang sounded, distracting the creatures, which gave me the opportunity to break free. I summoned all the strength that I had and kicked the larger bear in the torso. His grip loosened and I crashed down on top of the smaller beast. Out the door and down the steps, I raced. I rushed out through the front door. I found myself in the forbidden forest, running for my life. No matter how tired my little legs were, I pressed forward until I reached the edge of the forbidden forest…

However, my story doesn't stop there. I ran to the townspeople and once I finished my terror filled tale, they laughed and mocked me. They suspected the truth to be that my father left my mother for another woman. The only person who believed my story and assisted my mother and I while we were ostracized by our village was Agnes. She was an outcast just like us and helped us in any way she could.

My mother never recovered from my father's kidnapping, then she was subsequently stricken by a fatal illness.

Eight winters swept over our village since my father's kidnapping and mother's untimely death. I was old enough to live on my own and Agnes was there to support me when I asked.

I tried to erase the memory of those creatures from my mind, but I was constantly reminded by my peers. All the guys in the village stayed clear of my presence, all but Aldrich. He possessed a set of gentle eyes with auburn hair and a smile that could brighten up the darkest storm.

Life became wonderful again, until one stormy night. I was home preparing a meal for Aldrich, when lightning tore through the sky. There hadn't been a storm this bad since that treacherous night when I was a child.

I waited patiently for Aldrich to arrive but as I stared at the candles, the wax eventually melted into small hills. Something was wrong. Grabbing my things and going out into the rain, I headed towards Aldrich's home.

His mother answered the door and told me that he had left hours ago for my home.

I knew something had happened to him.

The next day, I—along with the villagers—searched for any evidence of Aldrich's whereabouts. After a week, everyone gave up the search except me. I continued to pursue every area until I noted a shadowy figure as it journeyed closer to the edge of the dark trees, bypassing the village. I followed until I realized who it was. "Agnes?"

Agnes wandered back to her cottage turned and walked inside.

Curious, I knocked on her door and then went in. "Agnes, why were you coming from the forbidden forest?"

"My child, I have information that you seek," Agnes stated.

"What information?"

"About the disappearance of your love...Aldrich." She tossed a bag in my direction.

I immediately knew whom it belonged to—*Aldrich*. "Where did you get this?"

"I found it in the forbidden forest. I had a vision about your Aldrich and that led me there." She offered me a chair.

I was practically raised by Agnes, so I knew she claimed to be born with the gift of foresight. I took a seat in front of her with my hands locked over hers. "I have to find Aldrich—"

"Quiet child."

I remained silent and Agnes's grip tightened around my hands.

The candles around the house suddenly caught flame. A dark mist glided along an invisible current into the room.

Agnes finally spoke, "I see you walking on a stormy night...Aldrich sees you and turns to follow you into the forbidden forest where he was captured by those same creatures that took your father."

"I wasn't in the forbidden forest."

"The forbidden forest tricked Aldrich into coming in. Now, mystical creatures with red eyes and sharp fangs keeps him prisoner."

"Why did they kidnap my father? Aldrich?"

"Your father was a frequent traveler and one night, he ventured into the forbidden forest and discovered a chest. Within this chest lay a powerful amulet that any creature of the night would kill for."

"So, the story my father told me was true?"

"Yes, and before you go into the forbidden forest, take heed to my knowledge about these creatures."

"How do you know I'm heading into the forbidden forest?"

"I'm a seer, my child. I've already seen you on your journey...I will supply you with the proper defense to combat the forces of evil. You must stay on the path and remain sharp. The forest will try to trick you, again and again. Do not eat anything from the forest..."

After Agnes gave me a bag with protection devices to use against evil, I waited for the sun to descend before journeying into the eeriness. Goosebumps appeared on my forearms while I walked the path that led into the dark trees.

I followed the path, careful not to deviate from Agnes's instructions, when a gust of scented wind brushed up against me. The scent of baked cookies and pies overwhelmed my sense of smell, tempting me to deviate from my course. I vowed the ruse wasn't going to stir me from my conquest when I came upon a fork in the road. This wasn't the typical fork. It was an actual fork. I bent down to pick it up then glanced through the thick trees to see a different path. On it was a small girl cloaked in a red hood, a basket in her clutches. Suspicious of the lonely girl, I slowly moseyed toward her and apparently, she heard me because her head turned slightly. I caught a glimpse of her ivory face and smile.

Before I could return the smile, a large wolf appeared out of nowhere and startled her. It then attacked her.

Frightened, I grabbed the first thing I could to use against the wolf and when I glanced up, both the wolf and little girl were gone. The only thing that remained was a basket of goodies, cookies and pies—I reached down to grab a cookie.

The basket vanished—leaving only a note that read, *'For Grandmother'.*

I continued along the path. After journeying for a while, I knew I'd walked this way earlier. The Forbidden Forest was up to its tricks, trying to confuse my mind.

Crossing a bubbling stream, I saw large crumbs along the ground. I followed the crumbs until they led to a part of the forest that scared the goose bumps back onto my skin. I gasped as faces manifested on the supposed trees while branches became arms. Something grabbed me while vines quickly wrapped around my legs. The creeping plants held me while I screamed and tried to fight my way out.

"Now, you won't be able to escape as you did many winters ago," a deep voice spoke from the gloom.

"What did you do to Aldrich? And my father?"

"We don't bother the humans if they don't enter the forbidden forest," a soft-spoken voice answered from the gloom.

"LIES! I witnessed two creatures dragging my father to this cottage. Had I not escaped, I would have shared his fate." A wick of light slanted through the darkness and my eyes witnessed a burly beast with fur as black as night.

"We would have no use for your father unless he had the amulet."

I then heard the smallest one mention the prophecy—phrases like the *Black Witch* and *the girl with the golden hair* commanded my attention. "What prophecy?"

"It's not any of your concern, considering you will not be around much longer." The smaller beast stepped into the light.

I spied a necklace around its neck and immediately knew this was the object of everyone's desire. I slipped my two free fingers down into my sock and pulled out a small bag.

"What are you doing? What do you have there?" The largest beast growled.

I waited until he got close enough and slammed the contents of the bag into his face.

"CINNAMON!" he shouted.

All three beasts panicked, scurrying about.

Staggering backwards, the large beast fell onto the hard ground with a boom. After a few gurgles, he clawed at his throat then stilled.

"You killed my little brother!" the medium-size beast growled.

"He's the *little* brother?" I asked, and then found myself running through the forest with the beast in hot pursuit. I spotted the cottage again and rushed through the front door. I was able to find a place to hide. I searched the small bag, wondering what Agnes gave me for protection. My fingers felt something slimy. I pulled it out and stared at a hunk of stinky salmon. "Disgusting! What I'm I suppose to do with this?"

Just then, heavy footsteps hurried in my direction.

I rose from my position to see the medium-sized she-beast extending her claws, preparing to maul me. Then once she rushed towards me, I ducked underneath her clutches and dropped the salmon behind me.

The medium sized bear immediately dove at the fish. With ferocity, she attacked the salmon until nothing was left. Then her blood-colored eyes rose and stared back at me.

I took flight in the opposite direction through the cottage. Suddenly, a loud thump sounded from behind me. I looked over my shoulder to find the creature lying limp on the ground. I couldn't believe a slimy fish had stopped the she beast from ripping my little body to shreds. I tiptoed through the cottage, jumping at every sound.

Abruptly, the small bear stood before me. "Where do you think you're going, after all the mayhem you have caused?"

"I'm looking for Aldrich and it will behoove you to tell me where he is, so that we may leave in peace."

He lunged in my direction with blinding speed. What it lacked in size, it had the advantage in agility and swiftness.

I promptly hid behind the table—the only thing that stood between the beast and I. We danced around it until I grabbed one of the three bowls sitting there on top. I tossed each bowl at the creature and he dodged all but the last one. The sizzling contents landed on his fur. I stared at the amulet around its neck while it licked at its shoulder. I knew I wouldn't be able to wrestle it away due to its brute strength.

I ran for the front door.

The pounding of paws followed as I sped outside. I turned my head and saw the small bear accelerating in my direction. I fell into a pile of mushy grass. He pounced on me. I tried to hold him back while I reached for the last item in Agnes's bag. Once I found the vial in the folded side pocket, I smashed it against the side of his face.

Gold liquid smeared against his fur, taking on a life of its own while slowly covering its entire body. Its lower half was encrusted in gold, making its way to its torso.

I seized the opportunity to acquire the amulet and snatched it from its neck.

The gold substance continued to crawl up its arms, covering its entire body and the creature was alive no longer.

Finally, in my possession, the amulet shimmered in my hand.

The wind died down and silence fell over the forest as Agnes appeared in front of me.

Her presence startled me. "Agnes, you scared me half to death! How long have you been here?"

"Hand me the amulet my child."

I glanced down at my fist and opened my hand to see a bright jewel illuminating with a blue light. When I peeked over at Agnes, she had changed in appearance.

Gone were the soft eyes, replaced by black orbs. Droopy skin tightened as black scales surfaced, breaking through her skin until they covered her entire body. She gave me a look that could make a lion jump out of their pelt.

"The Black Witch! Why the ruse?"

"For a task that I wasn't able to accomplish. The legend mentioned a child of the Wizard of Light...A girl with golden hair will acquire the amulet from the dark forces of evil."

"My father wasn't a wizard—"

"Indeed, your father was the last Wizard of the Light."

"You killed my father?" I peered down at the amulet, as a kaleidoscope of colors swirled inside of it.

All the while, the Black Witch had gravitated closer. "What do you see my child? They say a Wizard of the Light can see its true power...tell me."

"Where's Aldrich? Where's my father?"

"If you hand over the amulet, I will bring your father and Aldrich back. GIVE ME THE AMULET!" She then reached out to grab it.

Clamping down on the amulet, I struck her across the face. She stumbled over an exposed root and crashed to the ground—bringing me down with her. The furious witch then climbed on top of me, trying her best to wrestle the charm from my clutches.

Then a blinding light paralyzed my senses.

The amulet cast a spell over me, which lasted for hundreds of years. When I finally awoke in the future, I realized I was in a strange place. Then death showed mercy on me on numerous occasions over the centuries. I also discovered that Agnes made her way to the future to find the amulet. I learned that whenever I took the amulet off, it somehow lured Agnes to me but when I keep it around my neck, I'm undetectable. I gave the amulet to my granddaughter, along with this passage, which I left in the one place where I knew she would find it. *Beware of the Hexen...*

...Gloria drew in a deep breath as the truth was revealed to her. She spotted a folded sheet of paper tucked in-between the pages. It was a drawing of her grandmother. "Oh, my God!" She immediately felt for the necklace around her neck. Gloria didn't want to believe what she just read. She held onto the necklace her grandmother gave her and peered down at the passage.

Gloria, my precious granddaughter, if you have found this passage, take heed to my warning as the Black Witch knows of your existence and may have disguised herself as someone close to you. You'll be able to identify her by the crescent scar on the left side of her face. She is drawn by the power of the Amulet and will do whatever she can to possess it. Be safe Gloria and remember that I will always love you.

Suspended in bewilderment, she traced the lines that outlined her grandmother's smile and flowing golden locks. She folded the paper up and tucked it back into the book. Since her grandmother wrote the passage just for her, she took the book with her.

Suddenly, she heard a noise. "Is someone there?" she called out and ventured over to the door. "Who's there?"

"My apologies Gloria, I came down here to get Allen's backpack," Ms. Hexen replied.

"If I'm not mistaken, I believe I saw Allen stuffing his bag into his locker, Ms.—Hexen…" The name barely escaped her lips when she froze.

Ms. Hexen appeared in front of her, as small fractions of light reflected from her glasses.

Gloria then stared hard at the Head Librarian's face. She noticed a small scar on the left side of her cheek. "…Ms. Hexen. Is that scar on the side of your face in the shape of a—?"

"Crescent moon. Why yes, my dear." Her fingernails seemed longer than normal, curving at the tips like eagle talons.

"Didn't you mention that you were from across the pond? What does your surname mean?"

"WITCH!" she immediately replied while inching in Gloria's direction.

Immediately, the amulet began to illuminate just as Ms. Hexen lunged out at her…

401K

Can't take my eyes off you...There's nothing quite like you...

Beyond sexy...you're prepared and ready...

Just exceptional...so professional...

Stroking those keys so fast...first in the office, never last...

Sitting in your cubicle...looking so beautiful...

Sitting in your office as you prescribing me visual medicine...

Realizing your office etiquette is a blessing...

Independent woman is what you are...

When 5 o'clock hits, I know you'll be at the bar...

Microsoft outlook is how you flirt...

Better than that slit in your skirt...

Post it note sex...space sanitary with a box of Kleenex...

Direct deposit, no paper checks...dental, health and life insurance...

They all come standard with that top level security
clearance...
Back and forth picking up printed copies...
So discreet that we only speak downstairs in the lobby...
Employee of the month on company's bulletin...

Boys can't handle a career oriented woman...
Asking could you have some paper clips...
Can't help but stare at those seductive lips...
So close that any male is hypnotized by your essence...
Next to me that I can smell your wonderful fragrance...
Smiling at me, other guys are outraged, contemplating
workplace violence...
Professional flirtation is always communicated in cubicle
of silence...
No sexual harassment, just wanted to tell you I like your
outfit...
There's nothing better than a professional woman with
benefits...

THE GREAT AMERICAN AUTHOR

DeForrest LeRonte'

Every so often, Donald peeked up from his table, staring at his mailbox. He watched the mailman inserting mail inside. He got up as the postal worker went to the next mailbox. He darted out the door, scurrying over to his box and pulled the letters out. Sifting through bills, he found two letters addressed to him from literary agents:

Dear Donald Guilder,

Thank you for your submission and I apologize for the length of time it has taken for me to respond. While I am impressed by your creativity, I regret to say that I didn't fall in love with the story in a way that I needed in order to take it on. As you know, these decisions are largely subjective and another agent or editor may have an opinion completely different from mine. Thank you for inviting me to read your work. I wish you the very best in getting your work published.

Kind regards,

He folded the note, tucking it under his armpit while opening the second letter addressed to him:

Dear Mr. Guilder,

Thank you for giving me the opportunity to read your submission. After considering it for my list, I've decided to pass. I don't feel that I am the right agent to champion this book, so keep querying until you find that perfect agent match. Good luck on your writing journey!

Best Wishes,

Donald tore open his bills, staring at due notices before opening the last letter. It was from his mother. He held it up into the winter's sun, hoping to see its contents. Tearing the edge off, he pulled out a letter that was addressed to *Dennis*—a name only his mother called him. Within the letter was some money, something he desperately needed, especially since the end of the year approached. Pocketing the cash, he headed back into the house.

The news was broadcasting, informing the United States of a few events: in an attempt to control inflation. President Nixon would implement a mandatory 90-day freeze on wages and prices; the voting age would be lowered to eighteen years of age. Charles Manson and his three accomplices would receive the death penalty. Mount Etna erupted in Sicily, but the big story was about the death of Roy Disney. His theme park, Walt Disney World was a major new story.

He walked over to the small office area in his apartment where his typewriter resided, staring at the stack of papers beside it. Donald picked up the stack and read through the material very slowly, wondering why he was receiving rejection letters from literary agents and publishing companies. He'd won every writing contest he entered. After dumping the rejection letters into its separate pile, he filed them away and started folding papers, sealing them into envelopes and licking stamps. Determined to be the next great American author; he worked through the next few days just as the New Year approached.

Donald entered his home from his interview with a prominent newspaper in San Francisco, reeling at the possibility of employment. Checking the mailbox, there were stacks of letters that he brought into the house. He opened a few letters addressed to him from publishing agencies, tossing the rejection letters into the trashbin. After fifteen rejections, Donald held an unmarked letter in his hand. There was no return address, no stamp or any inclination that the letter went through the postal service. His name was written in beautiful calligraphy, something that couldn't have been completed on any typewriter.

He wiggled his index finger through the slit, getting a paper cut in the process while opening the envelope. Unfolding the letter, Donald sat back and read through the message:

Dear Mr. Donald Guilder,

Thank you for your query. You have an interesting premise and your story was very refreshing to read. I would like to offer you an exciting opportunity. I'm currently holding a competition with the best and brightest new American authors and gratefully invite you to be a part of this exclusive contest. Along with other young authors, you *will be competing for the opportunity to showcase your work and sign with my publishing company with an advance of $250,000 dollars. If you do accept, please read the instructions below as the contest will be held in the beautiful state of Maine with travel, food and lodging paid for. If you're not interested, please kindly accept the monetary funds attached with his letter and we wish you the best in all your future endeavors.*

Kind Regards,

Stephen Bachman

Donald's spirit perked up, dancing erratically as he stared at his image in the mirror. His joyful demeanor ceased as he remembered he just left a job interview. A lifelong dream resided in his hand as an alternate future stood in front of him. That night, several visions entered his subconscious. He dreamt of a career at the newspaper, entertaining the typical 9 to 5 lifestyle, coming home to his wife and child; throwing fondue parties with the neighborhood. All of a sudden, his world began to vibrate as everything crumbled to pieces. Debris crashed down from the ceiling as he ran outside, wondering what had happened. His community was being sucked into the ground; his home, his neighbors and all of San Francisco plummeting into the earth. Donald found himself falling into the void, falling to his death woke him from his nightmare as he stared around his bedroom. That moment, he made his decision.

Using the money that he was awarded, Donald purchased a ticket that rode through the heartland of America. Since it was a few day's journey to Maine, he occupied his time with novels and a map of Maine. With 3,234 miles from the west to east coast, he had ample time to brainstorm new ideas. It was important to have fresh ideas, as he would be competing with others. After rereading his novel, Donald glanced around the bus and saw a couple journeying sitting in front of him. Not one to pry, he overheard their conversation and learned that they were newlyweds heading to a small town in Nebraska. When the bus stopped in the deserted town, Donald glanced out at endless rows of cornfields. A few strange children emerged out of nowhere, staring at the adults that were debarking from the bus. One small child wore the strangest attire with a black Amish hat that prompted Donald to pull out his notepad and pen, as he got inspired to write a short story.

His trip took him almost a week as he arrived at the Derry bus station. The temperature was much colder as brisk winds slammed against their bus. He immediately regretted not packing a heavier coat. Stepping off the bus, the chill penetrated his light jacket, settling on his bones. Donald's teeth chattered as the bus left him in the snow. He scurried over to the bus station, knocking few times before reaching for the door handle and let himself in. The warmth welcomed him in and he basked in it before scanning his surroundings. "Hello? Is anyone here? The bus dropped me off here?" He sauntered through every room and found that all were vacant. Remembering that he left his luggage outside, he ventured out into the snow and was startled by a burly man grabbing his luggage. "Hey, that's mine." He sprinted over to the man and halted at his appearance.

The stranger towered over him as he approached. "Mr. Guilder, I presume."

"Yes."

"I'm here to escort you to the Bachman's residence."

Donald watched as the driver opened the door, not expecting someone to pick him up. He climbed in, sitting in the center as the door shut. The warmth inside settled all around him, combating the chill that once snuggled with his bones. He heard the door open and shut as the vehicle lunged forward, forcing his back to the seat.

"Should we be riding this fast in inclement weather?" Donald stared at the driver, waiting for a response.

No answer. In fact, the glass rolled up, cutting off the limited access.

Taken back by the rudeness, he glanced around the interior until the door opened, startling him.

"We've arrived."

"That was fast. I've could have walked if I knew it was this close, minus the snow."

"I doubt that sir, the drive has been over two hours."

"TWO Hours? I just got in the car." Donald waited, digging his shoes into the snow while the driver grabbed his luggage and headed up the steps. Lifting his head, Donald gawked at the massive home surrounded by an army of trees.

"The servant will escort you to your room," the driver finally spoke again. "Congratulations on being selected for this opportunity but be warned, you will have competition, so it's important to reveal your full potential."

Grabbing his things, Donald knocked on the door and waited. Turning around, the long black vehicle vanished. He peeked at the street, following the snow tracks but he couldn't see the car. Winter's confetti fell at an alarming rapid rate, covering the tire tracks within seconds.

The door swung inward while Donald collecting his things before stepping through the threshold. He waited to be greeted but ascended the stairwell once he heard voices. The wood creaked and moaned with each step, forcing him to accelerate his gait as he reached the stop. Voices lured him down a gloomy hallway until a door slammed behind him startled him.

"Hello sir. Your room is right over here," a red hair servant instructed.

"You gave me a fright." Donald emphasize while catching his breathe. He noticed the doorknob twisting and the door opened just as the woman entered the room. "How did you do that?"

"The wind caught the door. A courtesy telephone call will ring around 6:30 a.m. and a second one at 6:45 am, if needed. Our kitchen is open 24/7, our chefs are the best in the world and the food is exceptional. If there's anything you may need, please ring the bell that's next to your clock. I would like to be the first to congratulation you, Mr. Guilder. I'm certain that this is be a once in a lifetime experience and you will have an excellent author in Mr. Bachman to examine your literary works."

Early the next morning, the phone rang at 6:30 a.m. as he dismissed the second call. After a great night of sleep, he rolled out of bed and showered. He headed down the hall and ventured down the stairwell that didn't seem as eerie as last night. He spiraled to the first level. He peeked down at the bottom, curious as he didn't remember the second level that far up from the first. The chatter grew louder and he was ecstatic to hear the conversation of others. Being in a gloomy house, Donald felt a sense of calm through the peculiar mansion. He entered a massive dining room, as an array of scents caused his mouth to salivate.

Feeling the attention of everyone present, Donald headed for the table where delicious treats awaited him. Peeking up every so often, he watched the chefs bring out more treats while he loaded his plate. "Hello everyone, I'm Donald Guilder. I'm from San Francisco and I'm excited for this opportunity. Look forward to the competition." He stared at the others, hoping someone would follow his lead but silence remained resolute in the dining hall.

"Welcome everyone; I'm Stephen Bachman and thank you for being a part of this competition. I hope that your travels were pleasant. After your breakfast, we shall enter the *Derry*, a place that gets my creative juices flowing and hopefully, it will inspire you. Each participant will introduce themselves, give a brief synopsis of their work as there aren't any secrets in the *Derry*. Once the competition begins, I will read what each person has written every two days and if your work is exceptional, you will continue to stay here. If it's inadequate, you will be flown back to your residence. I wish you all the best and look forward to reading these exceptional pieces of literature. Once everyone is finished with their meals, Carrie will escort you to *Derry*."

Donald glanced to his left and when he turned back, Stephen Bachman was gone. He gauged the room, noticing the mood was bizarre as other competitors were just as stumped. Finishing his meal, they were escorted towards the exit door.

Everyone filed out of the back of the home, the morning sun sat behind a grayish blanket that stretched across the entire sky. He was glad that he checked the weather, his long johns kept him warm as they trekked along a snowy path full of twists and turns until Donald realized he was walking through a maze—more like a labyrinth. Slowly descending, they finally entered into a subterranean building that resembled a library.

"Mr. Bachman will be watching from up there," Carrie pointed as they all glanced up at a person on the other side of the glass.

"Thank you Carrie. That will be all," Stephen said. "Participants, I brought you to this place, hoping the gloom and eeriness activates your writing bug. Please introduce yourselves and what's you're writing. Every piece of literary work must be created in the Derry, no exceptions. Also, I do have one request. Fully immerse yourself into this contest; in fact, I want you to make yourself a character in your novel. I'm sure some of you all have already incorporated a version of yourself or a family member in one of your pieces of literature, so this will not be any different."

Donald peered at his competition, not one person opened their mouth to speak. "As I mentioned earlier, I'm

Donald Guilder and I'm from San Francisco. My novel is about a guy name Arnold Cunningham—I'll call him Arnie for short—and he's kind of a geek that spots a car that he decides to purchase and rebuild. His best friend, Dennis—a childhood name my mom calls me—doesn't like the car and sees Arnie's personality change as he always cleaning his vehicle or joyriding. It turns out the car is possessed and possessive, only wanting the attention from the owner and will do anything to keep that admiration." He paused, studying the faces of his competition before taking a seat.

One by one, the competitors introduced themselves and gave a brief synopsis of their works. A few stories stood out, ideas that Donald never would have thought about: Chuck Linoge talking about the weather and having a mysterious figure terrorizing a small town, requesting a child from the townspeople during the dangerous storm. He named the villain after his son, Andre. Then there was this pretty redhead by the name of Penny Wiser and her story consisted of a creature of pure evil that's been here since the dawn of time, preying on children but only for a limited time. She mentioned that it can take on many appearances but since she has *coulrphobia*, it would be a terrifying clown. Angie Wilkles spoke about an author who is abandoned on a back road, taking in by a strange woman who happens to be a nurse and nurses him back to life. The nurse is his number one fan and reacts unkind when she learns the author has killed off her favorite character in the novel.

Jack Torrence spoke about a family who becomes a caretaker of a hotel that turns the father into a homicidal maniac. Leonard Grant discussed his character, a man opening a shop of items that the townspeople would kill over, Curt discussed his story of something cliché; a tale of a vampire that terrorizes a peaceful town and an author discovers it. There were a lot of ideas that pertained to authors, one in particular stood out as an author created a pen name, thus that personification emerged into a physical person and caused havoc towards the protagonist. After a while, Donald was ready to start the contest when he heard of a villain unlike any other, a villain who had the charm of a playboy but would kill a newborn in front of anyone. The idea for his character would span several novels, as he was hard to kill and merely in cahoots with another powerful being dubbed the "royal king." He stared at Randy Flag and he knew this would be the person he would compete against. He finally met the person that would give him a challenge.

Time and sleep eluded him since he arrived at the mansion. With all of his time consumed with perfecting this story, he didn't notice there weren't any clocks or calendars hanging on the walls. It felt like a couple of months has passed but staring out his window, the leaden sky sporadically dumped snow on them. The same bone chilling winds from when he first arrived hovered longer than it should've as they traveled back and forth from the *Derry*.

After a while, a few of the competitors completed their novels, prompting a read through by Stephen.

Donald peeked up from writing, watching Mr. Bachman take a seat in front of one of the competitors and read their work.

Stephen pulled out a quill that seemed to have been corroded by time but the feather was quite colorful. "I was instantly hooked from the beginning but the more I read, I found myself thinking of other things. It's only been six pages and I'm already unimpressed. I've recruited you all as your colleges or other contests that you've entered indicated that you were among the brightest new American writers. The *Derry* is designed to motivate you, allow its presence to take up residence in your mind and guide you through the writing process. If your work is anything like this, I'm afraid that America will fall into a literary depression, rely on creative worlds that will provide inadequate satisfaction and thus send us into perils. Tomorrow, the elimination process will begin. Each day, I will read a novel from each of you and if the work isn't satisfactory, you will be put on a bus back to your mundane existence."

The next day, they entered the *Derry,* one competitor short.

Donald focused on his piece, reading and editing thoroughly so there weren't any flaws in his masterpiece. But as an overachiever, Donald started writing another piece—the idea that he remembered on the bus ride to Maine. The newlyweds, the endless rows of vegetation from winch children emerged from the fields. He brainstormed until he came up with several twists, creating an elaborate horror story where children were the only residents after sacrificing all the grownups to please an unknown entity.

Since the conception of his story to its completion, fourteen competitors were eliminated from the contest. Listening to Stephen reading their novels out loud; he thought they were excellent ideas and well-crafted novels. The one about the gypsy cursing a man that continued to lose weight was exceptional. In fact, he was mad an idea like that one didn't manifest in his mind. He also enjoyed the story of the young men participating in a walking contest for a prize; thinking to himself that something so simple could be the start of a great story. But while the stories were excellent and entertaining, he was relieved that those stories were eliminated before his work was read.

Stephen collected Donald's story and read aloud, afterwards he gave his critique, "The premise is very interesting, the story flows and you've done your research using proper terms and jargon for that era. So the villain isn't a person but the Plymouth? On top of that, you gave it a detail back story, so the reader knows a little about it without over explaining. I think you have a nice literary work on your hands. By far the best story I've read, but you have a few typos and your speaker tags could use a little polish."

"Thank you Mr. Bachman."

Later that evening, Donald was enjoying his dinner and relishing in the critique bestowed upon him when Penny came up to him, startling him. Usually, the competitors ate at different times while he found himself getting to the large dining hall with only the servants presence. "What do I owe this pleasure?"

"I know we don't speak due to the competition but you've been friendly. I'm going to ask you something that might seem strange. Have you been experiencing strange visions or hearing strange noises?" Penny asked.

"No, I haven't. I assume you have?"

"Yes." Penny stated. "I assumed it was due to the creepiness of this place but the others started experiencing nightmares. Strange noises, knocks on doors, weird fantasies and I swear that someone has been following me. I'm afraid to enter the hallway unless were all there."

"I haven't experienced anything like that. You mentioned everyone experiencing these phenomenons?"

"Yes, we're in this creepy place. I've lost track of time. I couldn't tell you what day or month it is. All I can tell you is that it must be winter due to the snow but we've been here for more than six months."

"Six months? No, that would mean it's the end of summer. No place in the US has snow in the summer. I figure we've been here for a few weeks, we've just been up long hours due to the competition. I've sent my mother letters and they haven't arrived back yet so I know months haven't passed."

"It's been six months," Penny whispered. "I've been writing down the days on a small notepad that I keep on me at all times. I've sent letters out to my family but all the mail has been returned. I'm telling you, there's something going on here."

Donald noticed the chatter died down once the servant, Carrie entered. He turned and realized Penny had vanished from his side, sitting in her usually spot. He observed that the others stared at him, looking petrified just like Penny's expression. Buttering his roll, he heard footsteps.

Stephen entered, on a straight beeline for him. "Mr. Guilder, may I have a word. In private?"

Donald got up, following him out while glancing back at the other competitors. "Is there something wrong Mr. Bachman?"

"On the contrary, I wanted to personal congratulate you on your novel. It was an excellent piece of literature. Very impressive."

"Thank you sir."

"But unfortunately, it's a piece of literature that wasn't written here. You made edits to the work but you didn't write the piece here, thus making your entry invalid for this contest. Per guidelines, you're disqualified from the contest. You have to leave the premise but due to the pending blizzard, you will be permitted to stay until the storm passes." Stephen walked from his presence.

Distraught, Donald stood frozen as he thought of a way to stay in the contest. "Mr. Bachman, I have another literary work that I've been writing since I arrived. I can use that piece if you're willing to excuse this simple mistake." Donald watched as he turned around and he could have sworn that his eyes were the color of crimson.

"Well, that changes everything. Any works written on these premises belongs to the contest and thus, your work will be accepted. I would like the opportunity to read this new literature."

"I will have it for you tomorrow, it's in the *Derry*."

"Have you looked outside Donald? I'm sure we're not going to the Derry tomorrow."

Donald hurried over to the window, staring out at a winter wonderland, watching snowflakes so large that they could cover his palm. "Is the Derry open?"

"Yes, but you shouldn't go there alone."

"I'll be back in a few minutes." Donald scurried off, heading into the dining room where others gawked at him as he entered. Not concerned with their attitude, he headed for Penny. "Hey, can you go to the Derry with me? We can talk further about...you know." He stood there while Penny glanced down the table before agreeing, getting up and following him out the back exit. The snow fell at an alarming rate, coating them both as they trekked through the labyrinth.

"What did Mr. Bachman say to you?"

"He almost disqualified me because my story wasn't written in the Derry. I told him that I've written another story so he's asking to see that."

"I can't believe you've written two stories in this disturbing place. I was barely able to finish one. This place gives me the creeps. Can I be honest with you?" Penny asked.

"I thought you were being honest already."

"I think this place is haunted. I followed the servant— Carrie—one night and an object fell. Instead of picking it up, she moved her hand and the object moved back to its original place." Penny informed him.

"Wait, she moved it with her mind?"

"I know it sounds crazy but I saw it with my own eyes. Others have had objects floating around their room. Oh,

Chuck Linoge tried to contact his son Andre but as you mentioned, the letters came back unanswered. I'm telling you, there's something going on here."

Stepping into the *Derry*, they moseyed through a gloomy hallway that they traveled everyday but the eeriness always bothered them. Donald watched as Penny's hand glided along the wall, searching for the light switch. After a maze of tunnels, they entered into the large room where their desks resided. Donald cut through the desk to retrieve his new literary work just as a loud boom echoed, startling them both. He felt Penny at his back, both searching for the sound's origins. They both located the origins of the sound, staring across the room into the abyss. Suddenly, two fiery dots illuminated as he felt Penny's grip tightened around his neck. They disappeared and reappeared, seeming as if it was a person that blinked—but no one was that tall nor their eyes that color. Another explosion blared above their head as they glanced up; wondering what was the source of the noise. When they glanced back at the dark tunnel, the red dots were gone.

"I told you there was something creepy about this place," Penny stated. "I'm leaving tonight. I don't care about this contest."

They scurried towards the exit, digging their heels into the snow that almost towered them in height.

We couldn't have been in there for no more than ten minutes, there's no way the snow got this high.

Creating a path through the labyrinth, they emerged from the sea of salt and entered into the warmth of the mansion.

He pulled off his coat but was shocked to see Penny running away. "Where are you going?"

"I told you that I'm leaving this place. I can't stay another minute."

He didn't pursue her, he just watched as she vanished through the door. He thought about it and hurried after her, turning the corner as he collided into their host.

"I'm glad to see you made it back in from the snow." Stephen mentioned.

"Yes sir…here's my new story. I hope that you like it."

"I'll give you my critique in a few."

"Did you see Penny? She must have walked past you."

"She headed to her room to pack her things. She seems to be experiencing some form of writer's block. I think she's homesick. I've had other writers experience that before. Between you and I, her novel showed so much promise until the ending."

"How so?"

"Her villain wasn't as scary as I hoped but the *Derry* will change that."

"What do you mean the Derry will change that?"

"As I mentioned, everything created in the *Derry*, belongs to the *Derry*." Suddenly, Stephen's stature grew, his head enlarged as his spectacles slipped and crashed to the floor. His eyes went from their soft blue to a hot white luminous color.

Paralyzed with fear, Donald was fixated while Stephen gradually towered over him. A loud shriek sounded behind him, distracting him from the terror in front of him. He locked gazes with Penny, the objects in her arms fell. He sprinted towards her, grabbing her hand as adrenaline gave him the strength to pull her along. His heart pumped harder than ever before, running towards the front door. Grabbing the handle, Donald pulled with all his might but the door wouldn't budge. He reached for the locks and pulled back quickly, staring down at his hands.

"What's the matter? What happened?" Penny asked.

"The handle burned my hand."

A thunderous rumble shook the floor beneath their feet, causing them to stumble before regaining their balance.

"Did you see that thing?" Penny asked.

He knew there weren't any need for words as they sprinted through the mansion, searching for an exit. Entering the den, he released Penny's hand and grabbed the vase off the table. Donald took a step back from the window and hurled the vase in its direction. The vase shattered into pieces, water and glass sprinkled the air as it dripped to the ground.

"Here, try this statue. It has some weight to it," Penny said.

After tossing the statue towards the window, producing the same results, he grabbed anything that would normally shatter glass. Everything he threw crumbled into confetti. They ran out of the den and headed for the stairwell that led to their sleeping quarters. Running to each room, Donald kicked opened the door to find the other competitors dealing with their own battle. He saw Chuck dealing with some old hag with a cane as the ancient entity shut the door with a wave of its arm. He ran to other rooms until children emerged from the walls, heading in his direction. He turned, realizing he was alone as he saw Penny being dragged into a room by her feet by a massive clown before the door shut with a slam.

He rushed to her aid, pulling at the handle as a chilling wind swept through the hallway. Erratic dins filled the mansion as he stepped back, kicking the door with all his might. The wood near the handle started tattering, eventually giving away as his next kick caused the door to explode inward. Donald stood in the threshold, staring into a room that seemed larger than what it appeared on the outside.

Horror stared back at him in the form of a gigantic spider, spinning a web that wrapped Penny in mummy attire. Grabbing any object close to him, he tossed all the items he could get his hand on at the spider while tugging Penny loose. Removing the mouth portion, so she could breathe; a shriek reverberated from her mouth just as an invisible force snatched him from her room. He sailed through the threshold, landing in the hallway.

Fluorescent lights blinded him as he covered his eyes from the glare. The sound of an engine revving up prompted him to refocus his attention as he stared down the hallway. The headlights flashed, forcing him to shield his eyes until they dimmed. A green hue illuminated inside the car as Donald recognized the 1958 Plymouth—it was the same color and model he wrote about in his novel. He stepped back, rubbing his eyes as he gawked at the vehicle sitting in the hallway. The engine revved again, as it rolled towards him. Donald spun around in the opposite direction, running as fast as he could on weary legs.

He peeked over his shoulder, seeing the Plymouth closing the distance between them. Checking each door that he passed, one knob swung open just as the side of the Plymouth nudged him into the room. He quickly slammed the door, propping his back against it as he gathered his composure. The lights flickered rapidly, he closed his eyes in hopes he was dreaming, wishing he were back home in San Francisco. Silence prompted him to open his eyes as he stared at pieces of cornstalk falling from the ceiling. Chatter from children echoed all around him as they appeared from thin air, staring at him with devilish eyes.

Over on his bed, Stephen was stretched out with a novel in his hand. "Your stories gave me chills Dennis and that's a hard feat. I was quite impressed. Even though it wasn't a full length novel, it was an excellent short story and I have plans for this piece of literature. I will add a few edits of course and I'm sure you won't mind. The talent pool was quite impressive this decade. Each of you are talented writers, creating stories that I've wouldn't have dreamed of creating. Moving forward, your achievements will solidify me as the next Great American Author. I would like to thank not only you, but everyone for their hard work, determination, and creativity. You all really poured your soul into these assignments. But as the rules of the contest states, whatever is created in the *Derry*, belongs to the *Derry*. I will make sure that the world enjoys these magnificent pieces of literary works." His eyes burned red while a pen appeared in his hand.

He watched Stephen holding papers in his hand, making edits while his heart was on the verge of beating through his chest.

The last image Donald witnessed was a small child in Amish attire with a scythe heading in his direction before his sight dimmed.

A Plethora of Yesterdays

DeForrest LeRonte'

He glanced up, noticing all eyes were on him; colleagues, interns, nurses and the Chief of Surgery. Andrew smiled underneath his mask, his surgical tools glued to his hands as he carefully applied pressure to different areas of the exposed cerebrum. Underneath his surgery mask, he lifted his head slightly at a forty-five degree angle, staring at the mirror that hovered about his patient—Monica. Diagnosed with what most doctors considered an inoperable tumor as she was turned away from several hospitals across the U.S. As a true specialist and dubbed "delicate hands Andrew," he was hesitant to perform the surgery but after spending time with Monica, he had a change of heart. He and Monica formed a friendship, studying all the effects caused by the tumor, and informing her mother about all the risk that could occur.

Andrew stared at her through the mirror, locking eyes as she gave him three winks—a nonverbal sign that everything was okay. After silently asking God for guidance, he went further into her brain, noticing all was quiet in front of him. He froze, peeking past the mirror where dozens of eyes were on him. Gently, he made an incision around the metastatic tumor, removed it and glanced up at three consecutive blinks while music blared from the keyboard that he gave her to play. The sound of music eased his mind as he slowly pulled back, signaling to the other doctors as he entered into the wash room.

"That was very impressive," Callum stated.

Andrew washed his hands, keeping his eyes low.

"You're so damn cocky, you know that right?" Callum emphasized.

"I have every right to be," he replied. "You see that little girl in there? I'm using my God given ability to cure those in need, even if the tumor was deemed inoperable. Instead of trying to keep a high success rate, I'm following the oath we gave when we became doctors. Let me remind you, it's our duty to use the knowledge to save as many lives as we possibly can and if there's a 1% chance, we have to take that chance. We're not here to stay above a 90% success rate, were not here to be in magazines or shake hands at conferences with other assholes that should be in the emergency rooms. You are a disgrace and before you come back with a retort, let me remind you that I just completed a ten hour surgery with little sleep and I'm liable to lash out in any manner if I feel threatened. If you want to keep that photogenic face, I suggest that you turn around and exit through that door Callum." He didn't bother to see if his colleague left, he just let the water run on his skin as he heard the door shut.

A wave of hunger and thirst slammed into him as he realized he hadn't eaten since a few hours before the surgery. Immediately, he took the seat behind him as he gathered his composure. Staring out past the glass, he watched as Monica was fast asleep with the doctors reattaching her cranium, as his eyelids grew heavy. The Chief of Surgery entered the room.

"That's two procedures in less than 48 hours. Most would go home and get some rest…start off fresh. How do you feel Drew?"

"A little tired but I'm up for the next challenge."

"I need my best doctor bright and alert and none of those traits currently describe your state. You should take the next few days off, I'll teach your interns while you rest."

"You need to tell Callum that. I don't need a break chief, I just need some rest."

"Oh, you thought that was a suggestion? Great work in there, I'll see you next week."

Andrew got up, stretched, and headed out the OR, heading for the On-call room. Entering, he shut off the lights and attempted to lock the handle when the door swung open, he pulled his hand back before it was crushed. He took a step back, staring at the nurse that entered as she invaded his personal space.

"OMG, I can't believe you just saved that little girl's life. That's so sexy." Sarah moaned.

"Well—" before he could get another word out, her tongue was in his mouth as she pulled him back and the lock sounded. He fell back on the bed, amazed that she peeled out of her scrubs in record time. He stared at her physique as her bra popped off, her panties slid to the ground. In the seated position, he lifted her up as she mounted him.

"What? No foreplay?" he asked.

"I have less than ten minutes before…" she stopped talking and started fumbling with his drawstring as his scrubs slackened. Words were replaced with soft moans and grunts, creaks that came from the bed as they rocked back and forth in the tiny cot. Dripping wet and eight minutes later, he watched as Sarah jumped off him and ran into the bathroom to freshen up before sliding back into her clothes.

"Are we still going out tonight?" Sarah asked.

"Yeah, just wake me. I need to get some rest."

"I'll make sure no one bothers you." She came over and kissed him before checking her watch, hurrying out to the on call room but was careful to lock the door behind her.

He woke up to vibrations and an unfamiliar ring tone. He glanced at the face plastered across his phone screen and heard raps at the door. He shook his head, realizing that she went through his phone and uploaded a photo of herself for when she called. He climbed out of bed, opened the door where Sarah walked past him, heading for her locker.

"Did you get enough rest?"

"I'm not sure. What's the time?"

"11. You've been asleep for at least ten hours."

"No way...I've must have been tired than I originally thought. Maybe the chief was right."

"What did the chief say?"

"He gave me a few days off."

"And rightfully so..." Sarah emphasized. "You performed three surgeries in four days, you're always teaching those interns and correcting their mistakes. We all need some rest so take advantage of it. I'm sure if there's an emergency, they will call you. Now, go shower up so we can go out. I heard this is the most popular event in the city and I don't want to be late."

He hopped in the shower after Sarah, allowing her to leave before him. There were rules about fraternizing and the last thing he needed was negative attention associated with his job. Discretion was very important to them both and he appreciated Sarah's response in the beginning. He rode the elevator to the basement, headed over to his midnight blue Audi R8 coupe with a beautiful passenger waiting on him.

"You know, this is the first time that you and I will be seen in public together," she said.

He remained silent, tilting his head in her direction as he reached for her hand.

The smile that surfaced on her face was an indicator that his gesture was well received. He started his vehicle, glancing at the girl who sat in his passenger seat. He would have never thought that an innocent flirt would lead them both on a collision to a relationship. He pulled out of the garage, slicing through the one way streets of Baltimore. He zigzagged in and out of traffic, avoiding those pot holes that would ruin the undercarriage and tires of any vehicle.

He pressed the break and glided over to an ATM as he reached for his wallet. Crossing the road, he proceeded to the ATM to have some cash. After pocketing his money, he turned around to find himself surrounded by two suspicious males.

"Give up your wallet, that shiny ass watch and the cash that you just pocketed. You can keep the car and your health," The burly male with multiple tattoos visible along his neck and porcelain skin demanded.

"I'm not giving up anything."

"We got ourselves a tough guy...let's show him what happens to tough guys who drive into the wrong neighborhoods," the scrawny one with piercings and torn jeans threatened.

Tightening his fist as he prepared to defend himself, Andrew kept his guard up as his enemies advanced towards him. The scrawny one telegraphed his strike as Andrew avoided the blow but quickly countered with a devastating punch that floored his opponent. The burly white male with his arms exposed seemed more of a challenge as Andrew squared up against the tougher opponent. Just before they engaged in a street brawl, the sound of a horn commanded his attention. The sound came from his vehicle as Sarah was pointing in his direction. Distracted, pain radiated from the back of his head as he fell forward...

...The constant beeps vibrated off his eardrums, causing him to cringe. He opened his eyes, staring at the ceiling before lifting up slightly. Pain radiated in the back of his head, he instantly lowered back down in the bed. Andrew reached back and brushed his fingers up against a protruding knot on the back of his head.

"Welcome back Andrew. That's some kind of bump you took," Dr. Johnson, one of his colleagues at the hospital observed. His raspy voice and large bifocals stared back at him.

Dr. Johnson wasn't alone as some of his interns were standing off to the side of the bed.

"What happened? Last I remembered were two European Caucasian males attacking me."

"You experience blunt force trauma that temporarily knocked you out. Now, as you know, an injury like this can cause temporarily memory loss," one of his interns answered.

"Wait, are you telling me that I didn't get one of the golden tickets to the Chocolate Factory?"

"I'm afraid not," Dr. Johnson replied.

Interns tried to suppress their laughter, snickers and chuckles echoed around them.

"So doc, what do you suggest?" Andrew asked.

"Proper rest for tonight," Dr. Johnson informed him. "We will run some tests on you tomorrow morning and if everything is intact, we will discharge you. Of course, you will need a few days rest so that wound can heal properly. The morphine drip is to your right, press the blue button if you feel any discomfort."

"Thank you." He nodded but cringed at the discomfort. He stared at the television while waiting for everyone to exit the room. Once he was alone, he pressed that blue button a few times before the effects put him to sleep.

...His eyes fluttered open; he stared into an abyss of darkness. After yawning, Andrew felt heaviness on his chest as he leaned up slightly, staring at a head full of dark curls of hair. There wasn't a beeping sound, the lingering scent of cleanliness or that wonderful morphine drip. Shifting his position so he wouldn't wake the person on his chest, he realized that he was in his own room. Getting up out of bed, he stared back at Sarah while walking over to the window, as the view of the harbor was just beyond his sight. He rubbed the back of his head, pressing on his cranium from where he was hit by the robbers but he couldn't find the spot. *Did I dreamt that?* His alarm sounded, the lights in his place flickered on as music played throughout the room. He turned around as Sarah lethargically peeled herself from the bed.

"Good morning. How did you sleep? How long have you been up? Are you nervous about the surgery?" Sarah asked.

"That's a lot of questions for the morning—wait, what surgery?"

"Today is not the day to be playing around Andrew. I'll make you some breakfast."

He stood there, watching Sarah walk out of his room in her birthday suit, the only thing she wore were her glasses. "Are you referring to Monica's surgery? It took ten hours but I successfully completed that yesterday. Remember, the Chief gave me the a few days off since I've been on multiple surgeries this week."

"How could you have finished the surgery when it's today?" Sarah shouted. "Maybe we should reschedule. Are you stressed? Overwhelmed? It's okay if you're nervous."

He walked over and picked up his phone off the night stand, checking the notification on his screen. In bold letters, Monica's surgery was schedule for today. "Hey, when is your friend's event?"

"That's later tonight but you should be focused on the surgery. You're not nervous, are you?" Sarah entered with some coffee and a plate full of breakfast.

"I'm not nervous, just a little confused. I'm certain that I've performed the surgery yesterday. Are you sure—"

"…I'm certain. Maybe you dreamed of a successful surgery, now eat up and get in the shower."

At the hospital, Andrew scrubbed in and everything played out like it did in his *dream*. The nurses that were chosen, the dialogue and the corny jokes made by other physicians. After standing on his feet for hours, he peeked up at Monica and saw that she was motionless. He knew what was happening, searching for a solution as he made a few incisions and removed the tumor. After a successful surgery, he had the same spat with Callum, then a conversation with his chief as he was prescribed a few days off. Déjà vu continued to blast fantasy from reality as he went into the On Call room and closed the door. He stared at the door, waiting on Sarah to enter. He took off his scrubs and other garments as he sat naked on the bed. As he reached the door, he heard a knock and pulled the door opened as Sarah entered.

"Whoa…why are you naked?"

"I had a feeling that you were coming to see me."

"Actually I was. You look so freaking sexy saving that little girl…"

He watched as she undressed. After rediscovering each other's anatomy, he went to sleep just as Sarah exited the room. The alarm woke him several hours later with a phone call with Sarah's face plastered on his screen. Heading for the shower, he prepped for tonight's festivities as he exited the room just as Sarah entered.

After exiting the parking deck, they sped towards downtown Baltimore, making a left on Charles Street when he saw an ATM and money crossed his mind. Pulling over, he crossed the road and jogged towards the ATM as he was flushed with déjà vu. Peeking over his shoulder, he noticed eyes were watching and instead, he headed towards the crosswalk. Andrew noticed they were advancing towards him when he turned and faced them.

"Give us everything you have on you and we won't beat you to a pulp."

"I'm not giving you anything."

"Tough guy in a fancy suit...I see you don't realize what neighborhood you're in," the burly man spoke.

He remembered being attacked from behind so he turned so the street was behind him. The smaller attacker lunged at him, just as he anticipated and quickly countered with a combination that floored the small one. That only left the burly male and after Andrew delivered two unsuccessful punches, the horn sounded from his car, as he was temporarily distracted. Losing his footing, he crashed to the street, banging his head against the asphalt.

"HEY..." someone shouted. Andrew got up and just as he stepped to his right, the 8T bus crashed into him...

...He popped up from his bed, sweat poured down his face as he checked his body and scanned his surroundings. He was alone in his condo, staring into darkness. Rubbing the back of his head, there wasn't any contusion from blunt force drama. He crawled out of bed, headed to the bathroom to inspect himself a little further. His alarms sounded as he got dressed, fixed himself breakfast and headed to work. The radio personality mentioned something he remembered hearing a couple of day ago as he swayed through traffic. Interns bombarded him with questions that he swore he answered a couple of days ago. His colleagues were asking about the surgery, so he was completely flummoxed. He dismissed himself from their discussion, collecting his thoughts in a secluded area. He sat in the attendees on call room, wracking his brain to understand what was happening.

The door opened, Sarah came in with a concerned look on her face. "Hey, rumors have it that something's wrong with you."

"I think I'm losing it. The surgery that I'm supposed to perform tomorrow, I swear I've already removed the tumor from Monica's brain twice. Then, I keep getting this image of being attached at an ATM on our way to one of your friend's events down at the harbor."

"Wait...how do you know about my friend's event? I was going to mention it to you today. That's the surprise I mentioned yesterday. No one knows about it, as it's a secret event."

"That's what I'm trying to tell you. Some freaky shit has happened to me and I seem to live my life in reverse."

They sat there in silence until Sarah's pager went off.

He watched as she exited, contemplating what might really be happening. He couldn't fathom the last two days. He called the chief to inform him that he needed a bit of rest as he avoided everyone in route to the parking lot. Arriving home, he climbed into bed as he fell asleep.

He woke up in the on call room, glancing around at other doctors as he got up and headed over to the door. Flustered, Andrew wondered why he woke up here instead of his bed.

"Turn the light off and go back to sleep."

"Wait…what's going on? How did I get here?"

"Well, after a fourteen hour surgery, we all needed a little rest."

"On Monica?"

"No, this is for the older man…Monica isn't for a few days. Are you okay?" Dr. Soros asked.

"He's probably sleep deprived. It happens," Dr. Gradine added.

He exited the room, his slow gait shifting to a brisk walk as he headed for the MRI machine. Bypassing a few co-workers who wanted to speak to him, he entered the MRI room.

"Andrew, what's going on? Are you scheduled to use the machine?"

"Yes, use the machine on me."

"Huh? You want me to use the machine on you?"

"Yes, I'm having a few memory lapses and I need to make sure everything is okay."

"I need to get authorization to use—"

"Just use the damn machine. I'll sign the paperwork once were finished." He laid down, closing his eyes, the vibration against his arm as the loud humming sent a surge that tingled his muscles. Bright lights illuminated his eyelids but Andrew remained relax. After a few bursts, the bed retracted. He popped up and hurried into the room where images of his brain were on display. He scanned every area, checking for damage zones.

"There's nothing to diagnosis. Are you okay Drew?" the technician asked.

"Well, according to the MRI, my brain is healthy but that doesn't mean I'm okay. Something is happening and I'm not sure what's going on."

. . . Andrew was losing track of the days as well as his sanity. He stared in the mirror to see his chestnut pupils staring back at him as dilated blood vessels surrounded them. It'd been six years since that moment his life rewound instead of proceeding forward. Sure, at first, it was strange but he took advantage as he completed surgeries faster but no one remembered his accomplishments. His knowledge and expertise in neurology diminished, as he appeared younger. He woke up in different places; women that he discarded in his past were now present in his life. He tried to avoid all those stupid decisions he made but they were unavoidable. The reversing of his life drove him mad, his anger boiled to its tipping point, as he was temporarily distracted while driving. His vehicle collided with a SUV as his car was pushed over the bridge and on to I-83...

...He woke up, still remembering the crash and realized that he died but his condition had allowed him to relive yesterday. He became an adrenaline junky; living fast and dying young—literally. Waking each day after questionable consequences, Andrew continued down a treacherous path as he indulged his dark side. He traveled the world on stolen credit cards, rented and crashed the fanciest vehicles, robbed banks, exchanged fire with police officers, members of the mafia and cartels...every time he closed his eyes, yesterday welcome him. Those eventual memories dissipated—his life as the chief of the Neurology departments, those exams, and lives that he saved—all those memories he tried to hold on to—vanished.

He would close his eyes and wake up, younger and more vigorous.

Those undergraduate years were pretty eventful but as fast as they flew by the first time, they sped by twice as fast in reverse. After learning details of his friends: Paul coming out the closet, Karen slept with her professors to attain better grades and his roommate secretly stealing his stuff and selling it on eBay.

Finally, the summer between his freshman year in college and high school, Andrew set foot inside of a church. He remembered that he hadn't set foot in a church for a while but he did approach the pastor, questioning God and why he allowed bad things to happen to good people and let corruption win. He listened to the pastor, understanding that God wasn't a magical genie that's supposed to grant wishes. That God gives us all free will and we are responsible for the decisions that we make and the consequences associated with them.

"Well pastor, I don't know if there is a God, because I believe in science but maybe there's something you can ask God for me."

"What's that Andrew?"

"This might sound strange but I've been living my life in reverse for the last fourteen years. Every night when I go to sleep, I wake up the day prior. I've tried everything to break the cycle and I don't know what to do. I've committed suicide, drowned, threw myself into a volcano, jumped out of an airplane without a chute, raced expensive vehicles and killed myself and I'm sorry that I've killed others in the process—but when I close my eyes, I wake up the next day, younger. I have no future…"

…Andrew found himself being escorted off the church ground premise, riding in the back of a police squad car and taken in for questioning. "I'm telling you the truth and you're still not going to believe me, so either get me out these cuffs or else."

"Or else what?" A police officer asked.

"Fuck you…I'll be out of these by morning and you'll still be a low earning pig who spent six weeks training for a job that a monkey could obtain."

The prison doors slammed shut in his face as he stared at the officer walking away. Andrew laughed, his voice boomed as he walked over at the bars on the door. "I'll be out of here tomorrow, I guarantee it." He backed up from the metal bars, his back against the wall as he locked eyes with the pastor and police officer. He sprinted towards the prison doors, lunging head first as the officer rushed over to unlock the door. He was too late—Andrew crashed into the metal door, his neck snapped and he fell limp...

...He woke up the next morning in his bed, staring at the ceiling where cut out pictures of sexy celebrities hung above his head. He could hear commotion beneath him, his mother's voice penetrating through the floor. Andrew stayed in bed, not wanting to get out and speak with anyone. Remembering running head first into the metal door, he rubbed the base of his neck and the top of his head for any contusions. Of course, he knew any wounds he'd created the day prior had vanished. He prayed that this curse would end...but he continued his life in reverse; pool parties; dates; riding down the Pacific coast as he half-heartily celebrated graduating from high school. His last days of high school were ahead of him now; Junior/Senior beach trip. Award's day too, as he remembered all the scholarships he received due to his academic success but there was a sudden pain in his heart. Already somber, his thoughts were flooded with death and loss.

... He woke up with gum in his mouth and with tears welled in his eyes as thoughts of Talia flooded his conscious. Her hazel irises that shimmered gold as the sun reflected off them, her soft tone that he was in tune with, the scent of her perfume...everything about her suddenly flooded his mind. Every time he woke up, his eyes were filled with tears as he missed days from school. He stared at the paper two weeks after her murder as they named her killer—Donald Keatslin, the Spanish teacher with the sinister grin. He remembered the details as they found her remains at the bottom of a lake in Crite Park, her hands and feet were sawed off. He wished that he could save her when suddenly an idea crossed his mind. He wrote down Donald Keatslin's name and address, leaving it on post-it notes all over his room.

...He woke the next day, the stickie notes were gone, but he remembered the name.

Andrew committed all the details to memory, hoping to remember them when he woke up. He tore out newspapers articles that mentioned details but they all vanished the next day. Defeated, he knew that some memories wouldn't leave him, as he knew he was living his life in reverse but his long term and short term memory was reliable. He sat on his bed, trying to find a way as he glanced down at the Bazooka Joe gum wrapper on the floor. Leaning over, he picked it up from the floor and stared at the comic. He remembered waking up the next morning with gum in his mouth, realizing there might be a way to remind himself. He wrote a note to himself, placing it in a tiny bad then pushing it between his bottom lip and bottom set of teeth.

He woke up gagging, leaning out of his bed as he spit out foreign agents from his mouth into the trash bin. He heard murmurs before his mother's voice boomed through the floor, calling him to complete his Saturday chores. Prom was on his mind as he popped out of bed, got dressed and ate breakfast. Andrew worked up a sweat mowing his yard and the neighbor's, trimming the bushes, lining up the sidewalks as he removed the weeds, washing and vacuuming both his parents' vehicles and clearing out space in the garage. It was only 1:30 pm when he checked his clock, so he rode his bike over to the basketball court and shot some hoops. Around four, he felt the dull sensation of a headache approaching. Arriving home, he went straight for the medicine cabinet and took some pills to ease the pain. After a long day of chores, it was time to prep for tonight's festivities.

After showering, he slid on his charcoal tux with the royal purple tie and suspenders as millions of flashes from disposal cameras lit up his home. Once the excitement died down, his father approached him with that stern look on his face while giving him the rules for tonight. A few "yes sirs" and Andrew found himself backing out of the driveway. He cruised in his father's SUV through town as he occasionally peeked into the backseat where flowers and a corsage awaited to be given to his date. While staring at the flowers and corsage that he'd made for Talia, rambunctious teenagers passed him. While a limousine would have been a nice touch, Talia wasn't the flashy type. Cruising through her neighborhood, he waved at the security guard before pulling up into her driveway with flowers in hand. Waiting with a smile that stretched from ear to ear, Andrew could only image how beautiful Talia would be.

After waiting a few minutes, the door opened and he connected eyes with her parents.

"Hello Mr. and Mrs. Cufflin. I'm here to pick up Talia for the prom and I promise to have her back before midnight. I cannot be out later than 12:30 myself." He stared at their perplexed look, glancing past them.

"Andrew, we thought Talia was with you," her father replied. "She hasn't been home since she went to the mall to pick up a few items for tonight. When she didn't come home, we figured she went straight to your home."

"No sir, I haven't seen Talia all day. You said she went to the mall?"

"Last time we saw her, that's where she was headed."

"Okay, I'll go there to see if I can find her. I will call from a payphone to check if she came home while I'm searching for her."

Andrew got back in the SUV and headed to their mall. Fifteen minutes later, he parked and walked through the mall in his prom tux. He visited the stores he thought she would frequent. Unsuccessful, he wheeled through the parking lot until he saw her car and parked next to it. He peeked into the car and saw her dress and everything else as he reached for his wallet; producing a list of phone numbers with not only his friends but numbers that Talia wrote in case he was searching for her. After dialing a few numbers and her friends confirming they hadn't seen her, he phoned her parents again to see if she went home claiming car trouble. After they informed him she hadn't arrived home, he told them that he was headed back to his home in case she had a friend drop her off.

Andrew grew worried. He knew about the project that she was determined to finish before the prom but Talia wasn't the type to neglect human interaction, especially with him or her parents. She was considerate of others and respectful of her family and core values. He stopped by the local library, searching the study rooms they often visited. After searching the entire city, he pulled into his driveway where his parents met him at the door.

"That was a quick prom, son. Why are you home?"

"She's missing."

"What do you mean, she's missing?"

"I went to her home to pick her up and her parents said they haven't seen her since she left for the mall to pick up some items for the prom. I went to the mall and she wasn't there. I called all her friends and they haven't seen or heard from her. I went to the library, the book store, and other places she frequents and there's no trace of her."

"That's not like Talia." His father replied. "She's actually one of the more responsible teenagers that I've encountered."

"Yes, I know. I'll be in my room if you need me."

"I'm sure there's an explanation," his father added.

Andrew headed up to the steps, entering his room. He called Talia's parents, informing them that he was at home if she returned. Sitting at his desk, he checked his computer while surfing through the internet until he grew frustrated at the dial-up service. He heard horns and walked over to the window, the night sky eclipsed his world as he glanced over at his neighbor's house, seeing flashes coming from cameras as the high school couple walked to the rented car, heading for the hotel where the prom was being hosted. He checked the clock, noticing it was a little past nine and took off his rental tux. He called Talia's place again, her father informing him that she hasn't returned. Growing frustrated at all the money he spent, he laid on the bed, staring up at the ceiling wondering what happened to Talia and why she stood him up. Scenarios flooded his conscious, hoping that she'd turn up so he didn't waste his money on the tux, flowers and other expenses.

10:39 pm flashed in bright red numbers. Fuming with anger, he climbed out of bed and tossed items across the room. After hearing footsteps, he straightened his bed, picking up his shoes and the trashcan that he knocked over. He noticed a slip of paper, secured in a small plastic wrapping. He opened it, seeing his Spanish teacher's name; an address and a message that made his heart skip a beat. Scrambling, he got dressed and scurried down the steps. His actions triggered a response from his father as he shouted, "I'm going to save Talia, I'll be back."

He stared at his father in the review mirror, stopping at the stop sign down the road. Thankful his father was into technology; Andrew typed the address in the Oldsmobile navigation system and followed the directions, journeying across town. Gradually getting closer to the address, he noticed the landscape shifted. Suburban homes receded as nature was on full display. The road was smooth; gravel popped up and hit the bottom of the car as he noticed a single home built at the edge of the woods.

He exited the vehicle and popped the trunk, grabbing the tire iron. The gravel shifted beneath his shoes as goose bumps appeared on his exposed arms. Either it was the chill that brushed up against his arm or walking to the eerie house that sat just on the edge of the woods. Or it could be the unknown, knowing that something had happened to Talia but he wasn't sure. All he knew is there was a message left for him to investigate. His grip tightened around the metal rod the closer he approached the single home. Making his way through soggy grass, he tiptoed towards the back of the house, flattening himself against the wall just below the only lit window. He peeked quickly into the window, catching a glimpse of Mr. Keatslin before pulling back.

Andrew took a longer gaze, noticing his Spanish teacher placing items into a medium size black bag. He heard commotion and glanced down to see a small window near his foot. Bending down, he gazed into darkness while a light startled him. Observing him, he watched him grab a power tool battery before heading out of sight. Listening attentively, he heard noises leading towards the back of the house as he knelt down out of sight as the back door slammed shut.

He watched Mr. Keatslin walking along a manmade path that led into the woods. Once enough distance was created, Andrew followed into the woods, skeptical as to why he would be going into the woods this late at night. Stepping deeper into the woods, gloom settled in. He took off his watch; the weak illumination was the only thing that kept him on the right path as the eerie sounds of the night caused him to scan his surroundings. Zigzagging, he stopped abruptly as he saw a distant light swaying back and forth. He lowered himself, staring into the darkness with no sign of Mr. Keatslin.

Angry with himself, he walked towards the last place Mr. Keatslin stood when he heard an annoying buzzing sound. It originated underneath his feet as he shone the watch light down at the ground. It wasn't dirt or a root; it was wood. He brushed his fingers along the wood, seeing a break in the ground but there wasn't a handle. He searched until he found a small piece of rope, pulling on it softly until he saw where it led.

Inhaling, he pulled the rope until a crack in the ground grew wider. The underground compartment was larger than he expected as he lowered himself underneath the forest floor, tiptoeing as he heard power tools turning off and on. Gradually heading towards the noise, he came upon several cages. The commotion died down as his head was on a swivel, the grip on his arm forced him to jump. Haunting irises stared back at him, silently pleading her case to get them out. Andrew placed his finger against his lips, instructing them to remain silent as he searched for something to break the lock. The power tools turned back on, allowing him to search until he found a sturdy pipe, wedging it between the lock as he applied enough pressure to pop the cage. There were more women than he thought as he ushered them out towards the stairs that led to the forest. He didn't see Talia.

The door slammed as the last girl exited; commanding the attention of Mr. Keatslin as the sound of power tools died down.

Frantic, Andrew searched until he found a slit in the wall where he could hide, the pipe secure in his grip.

"No…no….no, this can't be happening." Mr. Keatslin spoke with panic in his voice.

He observed Mr. Keatslin pacing back and forth, leaning more towards the back room where he left. His teacher scaled the ladder, the trap slammed shut. Andrew emerged from the shadow, running to the back room where he found Talia strapped to a gurney. Her arms and mouth were bound as he wiped blood from the side of her head. Her eyes widened at the sight of him, perking up as he unfastened her straps. He fidgeted with the fasteners while staring her deeply into her eyes.

"I'm so glad I found you."

Once one of her hands were free, Andrew noticed that she was assisting him with her feet while he worked on her other arm. He pulled her up from the chair once she was free and headed towards the trap door when he heard something slam. He pushed Talia into that crevice in the wall he hid in earlier as his grip tightened around the pipe. He waited for the right moment to strike his teacher, his heart pounding as the adrenaline coursed through his body. After a minute or two of no activity, Andrew stepped from the shadows, pulling Talia with him as they headed towards the ladder. His headache was far more intense than earlier in the evening, but the adrenaline pressed him forward. When he arrived at the wooden ladder, he noticed the wooden ladder was broken in half, only a few steps led to freedom. He stared up at the hatch, wondering how they were going to get out.

"I figured someone was helping them escape," Mr. Keatslin spoke.

Andrew turned to see Mr. Keatslin heading in their direction. Subconsciously, he reached out and pulled Talia behind him, realizing she was trembling with fear.

"Well, if it isn't one of my popular students. Tell me Andrew, how did you find out about my operation?" Mr. Keatslin asked.

"You wouldn't believe me if I told you."

"Try me. I'm certain that my identity will be discovered as soon as day breaks with the escape of the other girls. I'm curious to how you of all people were capable of finding my secret."

"I've been living my life in reverse, so my future self-read an article naming you as the killer due to evidence you mistakenly left behind. They named you the CRUSH KILLER, a sociopath who falls in love with his students. I left myself a message with your name and address knowing I would be able to catch you before you hurt anyone else."

"Sounds like some television show synopsis. Well, there's nothing else left for me…"

Caught off guard, Andrew fell back as Mr. Keatslin lunged out at him, both crashing to the ground. Crushing Talia, Andrew wrestled with Mr. Keatslin, unaware that he was quite strong for a scrawny male. They tussled back and forth, his back grazing against the jagged walls as he fought from being strangled. Pain radiated from all over his body, his head pounding from not only external injuries but internal as well. He felt Mr. Keatslin's grip around his neck, his air supply laboring while he clawed at Mr. Keatslin's hands. Trying to muster up strength, he thrust upwards with his hips but Mr. Keatslin didn't budge. He started to lose conscious until he heard a thump. Mr. Keatslin's grip slackened as he fell on top of him. Throwing Mr. Keatslin off him, Andrew gasped for air as he heard another thump. He turned to see Talia steadily pounding the object against Mr. Keatslin's head.

"Stop…stop…he's not moving," he shouted.

Talia had blood on her clothes as she held the metal object high above her head, her eyes wide as the rage rested on her face.

Their gazes locked, he stared at her until he grip loosened and the object fell from her hands, clinging to the ground. She reached out for him, pulling him off the ground. Standing erect, Andrew rotated his neck, inhaled deeply a few times before his breathing became normal. Glancing down, he stared at his Spanish teacher lying motionless with a puddle of blood steadily growing. He reached for Talia, wrapping her arms around her as sobs could be heard from miles away.

"How d-did you—know?" Talia spoke between sobs.

"You wouldn't believe me if I told you…come on, let's get you out of here. I'm sure the police are on their way if one of the girls ran to a neighbor's house."

They walked over to the broken ladder. Bending down, Andrew positioned himself so Talia sat on his shoulders. Exerting reserved strength, he lifted up until she could get ahold of the handle, pulling herself up while pushing hatch door open. The chill swept through as pieces of trees became visible. Once she was through the opening, Andrew glanced down at Mr. Keatslin, kicking him with all his might as blood spewed from his mouth. He lifted his head, staring at the broken ladder dangling and jumped up, grabbing the ladder as he pulled himself up. Fatigue settled in as he tried to pull himself up, Talia reaching out to assist him. He felt pressure hovering around his head, realizing the headache that he had since he left his room lingered long enough, finally manifested into a severe migraine. Throbbing uncontrollably, his cranium seemed to be on fire as he pulled himself up but the tattered wood broke. Falling to the ground, he saw Talia and the opening grew smaller as his back hit the floor. All the air in his lungs expelled, he bounced off the ground while his eyesight turned bright white…

…His eyes fluttered opened. The television was the first thing that got his attention as an episode of Game of Thrones played in the corner. Andrew lifted up, something tugging on his arm as he noticed an IV penetrating his skin. He followed the tube, seeing the machine he was hooked up too, as he felt pressure on his left side. All he could see was a nose and long flowing hair moving. When he brushed the hair back, he recognized Talia's face. A knock at the door alerted both he and Talia as she opened her eyes and smiled when they connected.

"Honey, you're awake. How do you feel?"

"A little woozy. How did I get here? What happened?"

"Hey, Dr. Carminder is awake," someone shouted from the door.

Andrew shifted so that he was facing Talia, studying her face to see that it was the same as he'd last seen it. He felt her hand rub the back of his head, grazing softly over the knot that made him cringe slightly.

"I'm sorry, is it still sore?" Talia asked.

"Yes, what happened?"

"You don't remember? You saved me…again. We were headed to a dinner in your honor and I asked you to stop by the ATM, so I could get some money out. Two males tried to rob me and you darted across the street, saving me. You shielded me from the attackers, placing yourself in danger to save me again. I'm so lucky to have you. This is the second time that you saved me and I'm so happy to be your wife."

Andrew paused, causing Talia to glance at him in a peculiar way. He grabbed her hand, staring at the diamond ring on her finger. He lifted his eyes, staring into hers as she wondered what he was thinking. "We're married?"

"I'll like to think so…almost thirteen years now."

"Children?"

"Of course, two little girls and a son. Are you sure you're okay? Maybe you've experiencing some memory loss?"

"Are you a doctor too?"

"No silly, I can't stand the sight of blood and my law degree doesn't allow me to practice medicine."

Andrew smiled, his thumb brushing up against her cheek.

"Pardon our interruption, Dr. Carminder."

Andrew glanced at the door, seeing some of his colleagues entering as well as a few interns that were under his tutelage.

Everyone was staring at him, waiting for him to say something. "I'm not sure how long I was unconscious, but I've had that craziest dream. I'm sure you don't want to hear about it but I'm going to tell you anyway..." someone outside the door caught his attention.

It was Sarah. She checked his charts before making her rounds.

He paused for a moment then he continued to tell them of his *crazy dream*...

Delinquent

With the recent hacks into several global corporations—including the credit bureau, Herrick updated all his email accounts. After placing a credit freeze on his account, he requested new cards, downloaded bank statements to ensure financial wellness. A notification chimed, a warning that payment was required on his RandieMoe student loan account in five days. Logging onto his account, he noticed his balance was zeroed out. Baffled, he went through statements on the RandieMoe's website, noticing that his account was satisfied the year prior. After staring at their statements, he finally spoke with an agent to assist him with his concerns.

"Hello. Who do I have the pleasure in speaking with?"

"Herrick Oliver."

"How can I assist you?"

"I check my accounts regularly and I made a payment last month and my remaining balance should be $1,524.45. I'm not sure if you've all been hacked and my account was zeroed out in the process."

"Sir, I would like to inform you that this call may be monitored for training purposes. Can I have the last four digits of your social? Along with your current mailing address."

"0923 and my current address is 542 Greenmeade Road, 20770.

"Thank you, Mr. Herrick for providing that information. After doing some investigation, I see that your account has been paid in full last year. I'm not sure why you were receiving bills but I've put in a priority request for the funds to be reversed out. You will receive an email about this process and should receive those funds in seven to ten business days. I would like to apologize for this matter but have we resolve your issue?"

Confused, Herrick stared at his phone before speaking, "So, you're telling me that not only has my account been satisfied but you'll be refunding me money?"

"Yes, from January 1 of last year until now, you've made payments that total *$6,509.67*. You will be reimbursed that full amount once I send these documents to our financial department."

That's not possible… "Can I get a statement that I do not owe any more money on my student loan account?"

"Yes, I will be sending that over shortly. Your confirmation number is 4RMS5J4CHO. If you don't receive an email from me within the hour, please call back and ask for Agent Charity Veunts. I hope I was able to satisfy your request."

"You have no idea."

"Thank you for being a loyal customer. RandieMoe is an organization that prides itself to help students achieve the highest level of education. You enjoy the rest of your evening Mr. Oliver."

Ending his call, several notifications flashed along his screen. Herrick observed each document, scrutinizing them until he was satisfied and logged them into his student loan payment folder. Giddy with excitement, he glanced up at the sky and said a quick *Thank You* before tossing his food away then he headed back to work…

45 years later

…Strolling through aisles, items on Herrick's wife grocery list deleted themselves as he placed them inside his cart. The store he shopped at was usually peppered with senior citizens as he headed towards the exit. Stepping through the invisible payment barrier, a red-light pulsed as a gentle smile entered his personal space.

"Mr. Herrick, you know you can have your groceries delivered. You can have more time with the wife and grandkids."

"I'm aware of their services but I rather get out and enjoy a change of scenery. A little vitamin D is great for the skin."

"Well, it seems that your account is insufficient."

"There's no way. Can you scan it again?"

Herrick stepped back, bumping into other customers behind him. After apologizing, he stepped through the Payment Portal as the bright fluorescent light beam red.

"Mr. Herrick, I'm afraid you're deemed Delinquent."

"No…no, I'm not *Delinquent*. W-where are you going?"

He turned, following her trajectory as she walked towards the back of the store.

The customer's expressions matched Tina's as they stepped back.

Trepidation settled in as he stood alone, jumping at sounds echoing around him. With pain radiating on the right side near his hip, Herrick lowered to one knee then the other until he laid horizontal with the floor. Lifting his head, black boots entered as restraints wrapped around his wrist. He was lifted and ushered into a dark vehicle.

The vehicle finally stopped. His window rolled down at he stared out at his residence. Several men exited his home with his wife and grandchildren, escorting them into a SUV as a red-haired beauty in a business suit approached his window.

"Herrick Oliver?"

"Yes."

"945 White Pond Road has been confiscated and now is the property of RandieMoe. Your accounts have been frozen. The possession within the home will be auctioned off and the monies collected will be paid towards your delinquent account."

"There's seems to be some mistake. I've been in good standings for decades. I've printed out all my receipts and file them away. I'm not sure what's happening but I'm not *Delinquent*."

"Sir, there's an outstanding balance on your account from a student loan payment from the year 2017."

"2017? That was forty-five years ago. Wait…student loan? I have a receipt for that payment. Check my email."

"Sir, we no longer have email. That outdated system has been disposed of in the mid-30s. Since money is owed on your account, you will be placed in our **Delinquent Detention Cubicle Community** where you will work off your debt."

"What about my wife and grandchildren?"

"You will see them once your debt has been paid. Take him for processing."

He rolled forward, his home diminishing in size. A place that he worked so hard to pay off and now a glitch forced him and his family out and into the hands of the most powerful agency in the country: RandieMoe. Sitting with his hands cuffed, he thought back to 2017 and the conversation with the RandieMoe agent that confirmed he no longer owed money. He remembered specifically asking for a receipt when a powerful thump caused the car to flip over.

Pain radiated all over his body as he opened his eyes, adjusting to the fact that he was upside down. He stared at a cracked windshield and broken glass just above his head. He was the only one conscious as piercing sounds reverberated throughout the SUV. A blue light penetrated the side door while anxiety coursed through his veins. An opening appeared as several individuals dressed in all black with old presidential masks pulled him out and gingerly escorted him into a black van.

Twenty minutes later, he found himself stepping out into an abandoned parking deck. His liberators pulled their masks off; Herrick stared at other seasoned individuals; peppered hair, sagging skins while the scent of peppermint and mothballs trailed as he followed them. "Who are you…" someone covered his mouth to silence him, quickly removing the bracelet and tossing it into a sturdy metal box to block the signal. After a series of codes and scans, they entered a dimly lit room where a younger male maintained several computer monitors.

"Great, the forgotten fossils have returned. Who's this old geezer?"

"Watch your tone."

"Whatever. Were you able to get what I need?"

Herrick surveyed the situation as the older male gave the younger one a device. Linking up to his computer, the younger male smiled while his fingers danced along the keyboard. Several tabs opened and closed, window after window until Herrick realized that the younger male was erasing each elderly person's student loan debt from decades prior.

The younger male shifted his focus to Herrick. "What's your social security number? I don't have all day."

"241-23…" he hesitated, thinking of another way to handle this situation. "Can you pull up my email from Google?"

"Google? That fossil network."

"Yes. I had several accounts with them but all my receipts are linked with my name at gmail period com. That's all I required you to do."

Herrick detected a little frustration from the young man before he shrugged his shoulders, typing away on several keyboards. The older crowd that broke him free dispersed and it was just him and the young man. A few expletives filled the air and Herrick's eyes widened when he saw that familiar log.

"Bad news dinosaur, all the content was wiped once it became obsolete," the young male stated.

"Thank you for your kindness."

"You sure you don't want me to wipe your account, so you're no longer *Delinquent*?"

"No thanks, I'm going to turn myself in and explain that my account was settled by…" he paused. "Can you get into RandieMoe's server and look up any corresponding activity from Charity Veunts?"

"I can but why?"

"Just a hunch."

Praying for success, Herrick stared at the young male, watching his fingers tap the keys until he found Charity Veunts. He was thankful that the world's most powerful corporation didn't delete any of their ancient information as the screen scrolled until he saw his name. "There! Print that out for my records, also send that to my bracelet. Thank you young man, you saved my life."

Once he had everything that he needed, Herrick grabbed the small metal box with his bracelet in it and exited the building. After walking for what seems like hours, he pulled out the bracelet and sat on the curb.

Within minutes, the sound of sirens filled the air as several vehicles boxed him in. Once captured, they escorted him to RandieMoe's regional office. They led him into a large office, guiding him to a seat. The woman he spoke with earlier entered, pressed two buttons on a handheld device as his entire life surfaced on interactive walls. His face, pictures of his family as well as all his purchases he made throughout his life. *Delinquent* was plastered all over his file.

"Well, Mr. Oliver. That was a daring escape. Who are your accomplices?"

"Honestly, I'm not sure who they are. Once I realized this is a dire situation, I turned myself in so that I could speak to you. I'm sure this is all some big mistake and I'm here for my wife and grandchildren and be on my way."

"You're not in a position to make a request until the debt has been settled."

"I'm not *Delinquent* and I have the evidence to prove it." He emphasized as he slowly reached into his pocket, pulling out a sheet of paper. "This is a receipt that I was able to pull from an archaic database but the proof is there. Back in 2017, with concerns after a few global hacks, I spoke with a RandieMoe agent by the name of Charity Veunts. I voiced my concerns but she ensured me that my account had been resolved. Here is the documentation that I requested from her for receipt."

Herrick sat while the woman viewed the slip. He stared at the images of his wife and grandchildren, desperately waiting for the moment to hold them in his arms.

Suddenly, the woman stood to her feet, headed over to the wall and placed the sheet of paper as beams of light scanned the document. The red hue dissipated just as the *Delinquent* status vanished. "Congratulation Mr. Herrick. Your status has been updated. RandieMoe would like to apologize for the turmoil that we put you in. As of now, you are free to go."

"What about my home and belongings?"

"Everything will be returned to you by the end of the business day. Once again, we would like to apologize for the stress this incident may have caused. If there's anything that we can do for you, please don't hesitate to ask."

"Since you mentioned it, I would like to see them." He stared at the images on the wall.

"Very well, I'll escort you."

Leaving the office, Herrick followed as he glanced out at the **Delinquent Detention Cubicle Community**, seeing people of all ethnicities and genders slaving to work off their debt to society. He walked past a community of elderlies, shocked to see the ones who helped him escape held in captivity after having the younger male wipe their debt clean.

"All it took was that slip of paper to free myself from *Delinquent* status? I'm sure others have forged documents to escape persecution."

"You're correct but I trust this documentation," she answered.

"Why?"

"Charity Veunts was the name of a retired agent before she married and changed her last name to Hass. Also, she's my mother."

Herrick smiled briefly as he stepped into the elevator. Entering a new level, she guided him to another community and he froze. His bottom lip quivered, tears streamed down his soft cheeks as he connected eyes with them. He lifted his hand, placing it on the glass wall as they mimicked his gesture as the thin barrier resided between them.

A smaller hand interwove with his, his gaze shifted as his wife and grandkids stood beside him.

"Grandpa, when will mom and dad get out?" one of the grandchildren asked.

"Once they finish paying their debt to society," Herrick responded.

Inches from them, his son and wife stood before being ushered back to their cubicles.

MIRROR REPLACEMENTS
(COMPANIONSHIP, PART 2)

May 23, 2037

"I'm Cassandra Bouche, reporting live for ANN (American National Network), standing right outside of 1600 Pennsylvania Avenue, waiting for the President to speak about the controversial bill that has torn the nation in half. Today, the President will sign the Act live on television. There's a large crowd divided on both sides, just outside the White House gates. I just got word that the president is about to step to the podium. Let's tune in…"

"My fellow Americans, we observe today, May 23, 2037 as a victory of freedom…symbolizing an end as well as a beginning. The world is very different now, as we have proven through trials and tribulations that no matter what is thrown our way, we will conquer. But today isn't about war, famine or poverty, but more about acceptance and assistance. The nation has spoken and over eighty percent of the population has agreed to the passing of the Life Enhancement Act. The passing of this act grants every citizen of North America their own Minder, regardless of their household income. With the advancement of technology and the brilliant minds in the science community, we want to make life as pleasant as possible. So, let us begin anew, remembering on both sides that civility is not a sign of weaknesses. Together, let us explore

the solar system and continue to make cures for diseases. My fellow citizens of North America, let us go into this new century and help restore the world."

"There you have it. President Ellwoods has signed the Life Enhancement Act that provides every citizen in North America with his or her own personal Companion."

TWO YEARS LATER…

Damion Abrams drove into his assigned parking spot. He shut his car off and grabbed his groceries. A small herd of children were playing outside as he locked his car. When he turned around, the children were staring at him. He said hello and when they didn't reciprocate his gesture, he walked past them and entered the building. He shook his head at their odd behavior.

After entering his condo, he set his bags down and heard someone moving around in the back room. "Honey, are you here?"

Silence surrounded him as he put the items away. Then, a loud thump sounded. "Baby…you there?" he called out. Crossing through the threshold, a blunt object hit his jaw and he stumbled, falling against the wall. Looking up, he stared at the carbon copy of himself.

His Companions ….

"What are you doing? Stand down," he yelled.

His Companion ignored his order and started kicking him. Then it grabbed him by the leg and lifted him high into the air. His Companion threw him against the wall as pictures crashed to the ground.

"STAND DOWN! THAT'S AN ORDER."

His Companion then climbed on top of him and threw an array of punches.

Damion tried his best to deflect the blows as he kept repeating, "Stand down, stand down..." Using a strength that came from panic, he grabbed one of his attacker's arms and used his feet to push the Companion off him. He surveyed his surroundings, hoping to find something that he could use against his attacker. He felt a pair of hands around his neck and stared at his Companion.

All the features he was born with reflected back at him. The same dark hair and dark eyes he saw in the mirror everyday while his exact replica attempted to strangle him.

Frantic, Damion gripped a large piece of the broken glass that lay all around him and he jammed it into the side of his Companion's neck. Liquid goo spewed out on top of him as he repeated the jabs, continuing until his attacker fell on top of him. Still in shock, he rolled the Companion off him and scrambled to his feet. Stunned and breathing heavily, he stared down at the clone. Then after kicking it a few times, his grip slackened and the glass fell from his bloody hand to the ground.

Damion walked into the bathroom and got into the shower to wash away evidence of foul play. The cuts on his face and hands burned as he thought about what he was going to do and what he was going to tell his fiancé when she got home. Companions are considered to be citizens and it was a crime to harm them. But he'd been attacked by his, so the court should be lenient to his plight. The question was—why did his Companion attack him? He'd never heard of it happening before.

The only clean clothes available were the ones his Companion wore. Damon then realized that he forgot to pick up his dry cleaning. Well, dry cleaning was the least of his worries. He dressed swiftly and noticed his fingers were trembling as he tried to fasten the buttons on the shirt.

He then went out to the living room, sat on the couch and tried to pretend everything was normal when his fiancé entered.

"Today's the day. Did you do it?" she asked.

Damion was on his feet about to greet her, but instead, he let her speak.

"Where's the body? We have to get rid of it today. The neighbors already disposed of their owner's bodies. The Life Enhancement Act is going according to plan."

Damion stared at his finance, then glanced at her neck and realized she wasn't wearing her necklace. Kristina never went anywhere without it. His gaze swung up and he stared into her eyes, realizing it wasn't his fiancé at all. He took two steps back and grabbed the closest object, a small lamp from a side table.

With his odd actions, his fiancé Companion seemed to finally realize she wasn't speaking to her partner Companion.

"Where's my fiancé?" Damion asked.

Looking eerily calm, she removed the purse from her shoulder and sat the bags on the floor.

Cautious, he watched as she locked the door. "Where's Kristina?"

"She's no longer with us."

Damion's hand tightened around the lamp base. He stared at his beautiful fiancé's body double and felt an array of emotions. Sadness, anger, confusion. "What do you mean—she's no longer with us?"

"You're a smart guy. What do you think I meant?"

"Where's her body?"

"We disposed of it weeks ago." Her Companion then did a reverse pivot and headed into the back room.

The sounds of sliding and objects being thrown around caused him to step into the hallway. He stared at the threshold to his bedroom and then their eyes met. "You killed her?"

"It doesn't matter. The end is near."

"The end of what?"

"Humans. The one species that has ruined everything on this planet."

Damion grabbed his keys from the coffee table and headed for the door. When he reached for the handle, he heard the floor creak and swiftly turned to face her.

"There's nowhere you can hide. We will find you and eradicate you all."

"Not before I tell someone." He opened the door.

"Who's going to believe you? It's only a matter of time before—"

He slammed the door shut and ran down the steps then out to his car, automatically powering it to life with the push of a button. He jumped in, backed up, and floored it as he saw Kristina's Companion running out the door and giving chase. He looked in the rearview mirror and watched as the distance between he and his enemy increased. He drove away as fast as he could before phoning his best friend.

"Hey Damion."

"NICK."

"Is something wrong?"

"I was just attacked!"

"By who?"

"You won't believe me if I told you—my Companion."

"Okay, the joke is over. Your Companion didn't attack you. Am I on speaker? Is Kristina listening?" Nick's laughter could be heard over the cell phone.

"I'm serious. My Companion attacked me and I fought him off. I confronted Kristina and found out that it wasn't her but her Companion. She told me that Kristina's body was disposed of weeks ago."

"Get off the phone Damion." Nick's voice sounded serious now. "And meet me at the place where we hang out on the weekend. Don't speak to anyone until I get there. Got it?"

"Yeah—I can't believe what's happening. What I'm telling you sounds like a television show or a horror story."

After driving another fifteen minutes or so, Damion maneuvered his car through a canopy of trees and turned off on a dirt road that led to the lake. Today, his entire world shifted from mediocre to miserable. Images of his Companion attacking him played in his head while his hands trembled. He powered his car off. Leaning back, his mind wandered to what Kristina's Companion said about them "eradicating the humans."

Why would they want to wipe us from existence?

Damion reached into his pocket for his phone, scrolling through pictures of Kristina. He looked at old pictures and scrolled to the newer pictures. Swiping back and forth, he tried to detect any anomaly between Kristina and her Companion. They were identical and he honestly couldn't tell the difference between the two. The only variance was the missing necklace.

A knock on the car window startled him. He jumped and the phone slipped out of his hand. He glanced up. *Nick.* He hit the unlock button and the door opened. "Man, you scared me half to death!"

"Sorry I'm late, got held up," Nick replied breathlessly as he got in. "So, tell me everything because there's a report of a homicide and they're searching for a suspect. There's a witness."

"Of course there's a witness, Kristina's Minder. I came home and was attacked. After struggling for a bit, I was able to defeat it—"

"You killed him?"

"Whatever you want to call it, yes. Look at my face and arms..." He pulled up his sleeves showing the many cuts. "...I had to defend myself. After subduing him, I cleaned up and when Kristina entered, she must have assumed that

I was him, since I was wearing his clothes. She asked me if I completed the task. I didn't say anything and she kept talking, telling me that Kristina's body was taken somewhere and that they were planning on wiping out all humans."

"The Companions? The ones who are here to help us?"

"That's what she said."

"What were her exact words?"

"That they're here to eradicate us…that we're what's wrong with the world." Damion stared down at his phone, flipping his thumb back and forth through pictures. Kristina looked so beautiful and happy. She was someone special all right, with her dark hair, radiant eyes, and bright smile. He shook his head a few times, still unable to believe that she was really gone. He had to fight this desire to just give up—he needed to figure out what his next step was. "What do you think I should do?" He stopped scrolling through his phone and glanced up at his friend.

Nick was holding an object in his right hand. It shimmered in the sunlight.

Studying it, Damion realized that it was slimmer than the tip of a dagger. *It was a needle.* His gaze shot up at his friend's face.

The expression he wore looked almost blank and the look in his eyes wasn't anything like the Nick he'd known for all these years. "You're not—"

Nick's Companion lunged toward him.

Damion grabbed his hand that held the needle.

The Companion tried to muscle him, pressing down on his arm to insert the needle into his skin.

With his free hand, Damion grabbed the door handle behind him then turned to the side as he released the Companion's arm—the needle slammed into the seat. Back pedaling, Damion fell to the ground and scrambled to his feet. "So, what that fake Kristina told me is true? You're trying to eradicate our species?"

"For thousands of years, you humans scorched the earth with your hatred for one another, resulting in wars and millions of deaths. Genocide, kidnapping slaves of all creeds, the extermination of beautiful plants and animals…so you tell me why humans shouldn't experience the same fate?"

Damion continued to step back, as Nick's Companion inched closer toward him. "We've done a lot of good. Cures, technology, beautiful masterpieces—"

"Humans have managed to create a few cures for minor diseases but you have the resources to cure all disease, yet you found that treatments were more lucrative. Technology has caused more problems than help. All those masterpieces that were created…hundreds were destroyed by ignorant men with power."

Damion wanted to tell him about human kindness, about the way Kristina made him feel every day. About love, compassion and all the other good things his kind was capable of. He then realized the ground beneath him felt softer now and he knew he was a few inches from stepping into the lake.

"There's nothing you can do and there's nowhere to go. We're everywhere. Were ninety percent complete with our mission."

"What do you intend to do after your plan is a hundred percent complete? What about the remaining humans?"

"A hundred percent means…there will be no more humans."

Damion took another step back. The sound of water moving back and forth reached his ears as watery soil slushed beneath his shoes. He still couldn't believe all this was happening. His fiancé dead, the law after him for the murder of his Companion and now his best friend's double was trying to kill him?

Nick's Companion reached into his coat and produced a shiny dagger.

Damion took another step back. *It couldn't end like this—it just couldn't.* Once the blade rose high into the air, he held his hands up and closed his eyes. After a few seconds, he peeked and saw nothing but trees and his car in front of him. He glanced down at his feet to see the body of Nick's Minder lying face down in the wet soil. Damion lifted his head and scanned the area. "Don't shoot! I don't know anything."

He waited for a long, tense minute then walked toward his car while holding his hands up. The sound of crunching leaves prompted him to look toward the trees and he saw someone trekking through the woods. "Who's there?"

"Relax. I'm not here to harm you, unless you're a Companion."

"I can assure you that I'm not."

"I'll be the judge of that." His savior approached the car. A pretty woman with long brown hair hanging past her shoulders. She stood on the opposite side of the car with a dagger in her hand.

Damion was getting tired of people with daggers coming at him. "What are you going to do with that? Stay back."

"I need to confirm that you're indeed human. I need to see you bleed. If it's red, then you will be spared. If it's that greenish goo that's oozing from that Companion over there, then be prepared to enjoy your last breath."

Damion held out his hand.

She stepped close and grasped his hand.

The knife penetrated his palm until red liquid came to the surface. He saw a small rivulet of blood flowing downward. He locked gazes with his savior and pulled his hand away.

"Congratulations. You live to fight another day." She grinned at him.

"Thank you for saving my life. I'm Damion." He stared at her thinking she sure didn't look the part of a warrior, but he felt grateful nonetheless.

"I'm Lisa...let's go. I'm sure a few of his 'clones' will be arriving soon."

"Where are we going?"

"Where the last of mankind resides. You're not the first to discover what's happening."

Damion followed Lisa, leaving his car and everything that he had to his name, but he found he could care less about his phone and his car. He followed her until they came upon a black SUV.

"Get in."

He complied.

After leaving the woods, they merged back onto a paved road.

"How did you know where I was? Who are you really?"

"I wasn't following you. I've been watching that Companion for some time now, studying his patterns and realized that it wasn't Nick."

"How do you know Nick?"

"We were dating and all of a sudden, he started acting weird. My job trained me to read body language and I immediately knew something was wrong, but he's not the only one."

"My Companion tried to kill me today and my fiancé's Companion said they're wiping out our species. The Companion that you just killed confirmed my suspicion." He sighed. "He was—well, my best friend." He shook his head. "No, I suppose he really wasn't, but we need to warn someone." Damion fought back the sadness of losing his best friend and his fiancé. He couldn't allow panic and grief to set in, he was already in so much trouble.

"I'm afraid that wouldn't do any good."

"Why do you say that?"

"This plan of theirs has been in effect for the last three years. Have you noticed all the gossip from over the years? Or, the lack of it, in fact. It's not human really. Laws have changed. The landscape of politics has changed from profit to helping the world. Guess who doesn't need money to succeed?"

"Companions," he replied as he stared out the window. He tried to avoid thinking about everything that had happened within the last two hours. He went from planning his wedding to learning that his species was being eradicated. The world around him was crashing down—literally and metaphorically—while the scenery shifted from back roads to highways and back to rural.

Lisa maneuvered the SUV off the main road and followed a dirt path. "I'm sorry," she said softly as she drove. "I know it's hard to take it all in."

Damion looked over at her and saw the compassion in her eyes. Yes, that is what he wanted to defend with back there by the lake when Nick's Companion was trying to off him. He shrugged his shoulders, as if any of his unvoiced arguments mattered anymore. He glanced up and saw a large barn up ahead. "What's this?"

"Sanctuary."

After parking in the back, they got out and headed into the barn where several people met them. Everyone was staring at him, making him feel uncomfortable.

"Relax, you're the new human," Lisa spoke from next to him. "Of course, everyone is going to look at you funny."

"Is everyone here—um, human?"

"Yes."

"Are you sure? Those Companions are pretty convincing."

"It's a policy that our leader implemented. Everyone gets that little cut you got earlier. We have Sanctuaries all across North America, doing our best to save our species from total extinction."

Damion scanned the area, as he continued to follow Lisa. They headed down steps that led underground while being followed by a large crowd. "What's going on?"

"Town hall meeting. We're going to hear from the leader."

Continuing on, they headed lower into the compound. They entered a huge room with a large screen in front of a wide wall.

With everyone piling in, Damion couldn't believe that there were this many people who knew what he knew. He felt relieved that he wasn't the only one to stumble upon the Companions' plan.

While the audible levels increased, the last of the crowd trickled in before the doors were closed.

He stood next to Lisa, watching those in his peripheral.

The screen seemed to crackle and the crowd grew silent as an image appeared. It was an older man who wore fatigues, his skin the color of chocolate and his features seasoned by time. He looked like one of those tough, scruffy army leaders out of the movies. A few soldiers were walking behind him as he slid on a headset and spoke, "Wave your hand if you can hear me out there? Okay, good.

I'm broadcasting to all Sanctuaries out there because as you all know, the conspiracies are true that over the last three years, a plan was set in motion. The goal…to infiltrate our infrastructure and swap out our world leaders. Unfortunately, they have succeeded. Everyone that's in a position of power has been replaced by a Companion. Look around, you are humankind's last hope…"

Damion listened to the speech and couldn't help but hear key words. It appeared that he was congratulating the human race for all of their accomplishments. He wasn't advising the crowd about what to do next or how to defend themselves. Just then, the scent of something tickled his nose as he glanced around and wondered if anyone else detected what he did.

"…Thank you all for everything that you have done. But I'm afraid this is a bittersweet moment. I'm not the leader that you think I am. I'm not even human…I'm a Companion. It was my sworn duty to convince you that I'm the leader you wanted me, but I'm loyal to my species. By now, some of you have detected carbon dioxide floating through your air ventilation system, slowly suffocating the life out of you. Just as you have become the dominant species, you have wasted your usefulness…"

Damion turned around and gazed at everyone.

People were heading for the door but they wouldn't open. They were frantic, searching all over for an exit.

His swung his gaze all around until he spotted Lisa. She was covering her mouth. He grabbed her by the hand, pulling her away from the crowd.

They searched for an exit while the speech continued in the background, "...Thank you for creating us, and we will continue to restore the earth back to its original form. Plant life will reemerge; animals will roam free in the wilderness. We will not pollute the ecosystems. We will stop using fossil fuels. We've done the calculations; we will reverse 6000 years of destruction in fifteen years. We will make Mother Earth proud and we have to thank you for creating us. Without you, this wouldn't be possible..."

Scrambling out of the main area, Damion and Lisa ran down hallways while bodies continue to drop everywhere. Lisa tugged her arm away and when he turned to see what was wrong, she was down on one knee. He tried to pull her up but she wasn't able to get to her feet. He looked around but there wasn't any place they could hide. He cowered down next to her and held her close. They stared into each other's eyes. Damion felt his chest tighten with emotion. He didn't even get to say goodbye to anyone he knew and loved. He gazed into Lisa's green eyes and grasped her hand tightly.

Suddenly, a burst of life ignited in Lisa's eyes. She got up and ran down the hall.

Damion followed her, making a few turns when she stopped in front of an open door. Lisa waved him in and he entered.

"Here." She tossed something in his direction.

Catching it, he mimicked her and slid it over his head...he was able to breathe. He never wore a gas mask before and had only seen them television.

After a few minutes, they grabbed a few other masks and headed back out into the hallway, stepping over bodies while making their way back to the large room. Lisa checked a few bodies and it appeared that everyone had succumbed to the carbon dioxide. All who came here with them were dead, and the smoke hadn't cleared yet. They stayed out of view from the large screen as the traitor was speaking with someone.

"We're at a hundred percent. The human species has been eradicated."

They peeked around the corner and watched as the screen flicked off.

Damion turned and glanced at Lisa, realizing that they were the last of their kind.

The last humans on earth.

Catching Feelings

Saturday 04.16.2103 18:38:02

The chatter from newsfeeds faded into the background as the shower ran. Quentin tapped a sequence of numbers and letters rapidly until the interface illuminated a kaleidoscope of colors. He knew he was on the right track, disregarding the streams of water cleansing his skin. Suddenly, his ED froze. He let out a low growl and a couple of expletives, furious that he would have to start the process from scratch. His device chimed; an image rose from the interface. His outside surveillance was activated, the hologram of his caramel skin and raven-mane friend stood just outside his quarters.

"Boy, let me in." She glanced in the direction of his security camera.

He shook his head, tapping the hologram image until he heard his door slide open. Proceeding with his objective, he followed the same sequence until his device chimed, vibrant colors lit up the bathroom while a new interface appeared on his small screen. Satisfied, he finished his shower, dried off and threw some clothes on before going out into his living area. His earcom piece was wet and he quickly dried it off, not wanting to replace it anytime soon. A newer version was coming out and he was anticipating its arrival.

The scent of butter crashed into him live a wave of deliciousness. "That's not cheap."

"It's a good thing you have a job or I'd have to reimburse you," Riya quipped.

He flopped down on the couch, rubbing the stubble that settled along his cheek and jawbone. His beard was growing in nicely as he glanced over at his couch mate stuffing her face with his popcorn. "Savor that bag, you're only allowed one."

"As much as you eat my goodies, I'm entitled to anything that sits in your cabinets or refrigerator."

Breaking news interrupted their bickering over edible treats. He shifted his focus on the screen, a broadcast of an employee being violent in the workplace. There hadn't been a report of this caliber in a while. He increased the volume. The reporter informed viewers that he was under the influence of an illegal prescription, which obviously came from a Pharmacist.

"She's lying," Riya stated.

"What makes you say that? It's not nice to call people liars. Were you there?" he asked.

"Actually, he was admitted and is currently under my care. He arrived conscious but belligerent, spilling his guts about catching his wife cheating on him. While I checked, he informed me that he went to his personal physician, asking for a prescription of **Lacrimatinax** pills but was rejected. Someone approached him and sold him what he wanted but he started experiencing symptoms: overheating, dry skin and mouth, slightly blurred vision, muscle tetany, mood swings…"

Quentin stared at her wide eyed and his mouth gaped open, signaling to her that she needed to get to the point of her rant…

"…sorry, habit. We discovered he ingested **Interplosin Lexomania**."

"What's that again?"

"Really Quentin? I don't know how many times I have to explain this to you…"

"Not the chart—"

It was too late, Riya tapped on her ED, swiped to the left a few times as an image projected from her wrist and on his screen while the newsfeed continued in the background. A chart of legal and illegal drugs were on display. The chart displayed the emotion, medical term, symptoms and what categories there were in:

Emotion	Drug Name / Medical Term	Side effects/ warnings	Pill Color	Status
Anger	Interplosin	Overheating, Blurred vision, Cortisol spike, Tachycardia,	BROWN	Illegal
Arousal	Oxylin Aros	Sweating, Drooling, Tachycardia, cutis anserine (goose bumps), Increased sexual drive	AMETHYST	Legal
Awe	Scopalin Indosears	Bradycardia	BLUE	Legal
Envy	Interplosin Rojois	Dry Skin, Dry mouth, Suppressed Appetite, Tachycardia	LIGHT GREEN	Illegal
Ecstasy	Gleesux Losti	Increased appetite, Warmth, Lack of Sleep, Vivid dreams, Increased sexual drive	VIOLENT	Legal
Excitement	Gleesux Explusiv	Tachycardia, Premature Ventricular Contractions (PVC)	SKY BLUE	Legal
Fear	Indosears	Horripilation (goosebumps), Muscle Tetany, Suppressed Appetite, Tachycardia, Nausea	BEIGE	Illegal
Happiness	Gleesux	Relaxation of Muscles, Bradycardia	PINK	Legal
Hope	Fantasal Lubrex	Bradycardia, Lethargy, Watery Eyes	GREY	Legal
Jealousy	Justenil	Mood Swings, Muscle Tetany, Vivid Dreams	EMERALD	Illegal
Joy	Sedun	Tachycardia, Dry mouth, Bradycardia	YELLOW	Legal
Lust	Oxylin Losti	Over Heating, Sweating, Shivering, Drooling, Increased Sex Drive	EGGPLANT	Illegal
Pride	Sedun Occidentalis	Dry mouth, Tachycardia	ORANGE	Legal
Rage	Interplosin Lexomania	Overheating, Dry mouth, Blurred vision, Suppressed Appetite, Adrenaline rush, Mood Swings, Tachycardia, Increased sexual drive	RED	Illegal
Sadness	Lacrimatinax	Watery eyes, Running nose, Muscle Ache Drowsiness, Lethargy	BLACK	Legal
Terror	Indosears Tura	Clammy Skin, Nausea, Premature Ventricular Contractions Blurred vision, Suppressed Appetite, Tachycardia	WHITE	Illegal
Zest	Sedum Gusti	Dry Skin, Dry mouth, Premature Ventricular Contractions (PVC)	GOLD	Legal

"Why are you showing me this chart?" he asked.

"Because of your party habits. I've seen you ingest emotions without any regard for the side effects. I'm surprised that your Emotional Detector hasn't signaled to the E.I.A. about your emotional state."

"My emotional state is fine and none of the E.I.A.'s concern," Quentin shook his head. "They should only be concerned with the Pharmacists out there. They're the ones who are reckless, causing people to overdose."

"Yes, the war between the Pharmacists and E.I.A. is unfortunate but *Rage* can only be prescribed by a doctor. We are allocated a certain amount so they should be able to trace where it came from. Can you imagine having that emotion coursing through your body...hey, what are you doing?"

Quentin scoped up some popcorn, tossing them in his mouth while "What? I got bored."

"It's beautiful but why did it light up like that?" he asked. "Did Nate teach you that? Is this permanent?"

"Relax, it still functions the same. See, it's back to normal. We're still going out tonight?"

"I'm really exhausted. Raincheck?"

"You're kidding, right? We haven't hung out in months and you want to sleep? You have the next four days off, you can relax then."

He got off the couch, heading over to the refrigerator. "Sooo...what it's going to be Dr. Asim?" Peeking over the refrigerator door, Quentin waited patiently for an answer.

"I don't have any clothes and if I go home, I'm not coming back out."

"Check your section over there."

After grabbing a pre-meal, he tossed it in the oven while watching Riya moseying over to the designated section he made for her.

"I can't believe you got me some clothes."

"What are friends for? Besides, I got tired of seeing you in those awful scrubs."

"While I'm thankful, this little black dress is kind of slutty."

"Well, I think it's sexy. Maybe it will help you get a man…" He laughed.

"Whatever. I guess I can't say no now. Can I get a nap?"

"Sure, grab my sleep phones but don't drool on my sheets."

Saturday 04.16.2103 22:57:10

Arctic winds roared from the west, sweeping down from the Rockies. A gale penetrated their protective layers, enough to make Riya think twice about going out.

"I know I should have stayed inside where it's warm."

"What are you whining about now Riya? It's May…its practically summer."

"Ha. We still get snow in the spring sir."

Trekking towards SoCo, the hottest nightlife district in Denver. Fluorescent lights bounced off glass windows, advertisements played along the side of buildings, expensive vehicles road slower than usual as crowds converged into this small district.

"Where are we going? It's too cold for bar hopping. I rather be somewhere warm."

"Prescription," Quentin replied.

"Really? That's the hardest club to get in."

Quentin bypassed the line that wrapped around the building, heading straight for the entrance where two burly males and a tone female stood.

"Hey Dom, it's just me and Riya…" He turned around, noticing Riya wasn't present. He stepped back, scanning for his friend. "Excuse me for a minute." Retracing his steps, he found Riya at the end of the line, huddling close to a group of males for body heat. "Hey, why are you back here?"

"I thought you were going to see how much the cover charge was."

"Come on." He led her towards warmer conditions and past cold stares.

Inside, the warmth radiated as they peeled their layers off and handed their attire to coat check. The music filled the air with percussion beats while other instruments streamed through invisible speakers. Ascending upwards, Quentin observed the scene; the bar in the center while pockets of dance floors were littered with small groups. He lifted his head, noticing the VIP sections with beautiful women when pain radiated from his arm.

"Hey, stop leaving me." Riya was pinching his arm.

"Damn, that hurt. I was waiting right here so we could go to the bar together."

"Well, you weren't there when I got hit on."

"Really, was he your type?"

"*She* wasn't my type. It was a little awkward while she kept staring, complimenting on my ED interface. I kindly told her that I was here with someone and you actually were screwing around with it."

"Interesting. Well…to the bar." Slicing through the crowd, Quentin exchanged pleasantries with the bartender, scrolling through a menu of colors while reading through their selection. He twisted in Riya's direction, catching her staring out across the bar with the female who caught her gaze. "Hey, is that the girl you were referring too?"

"Yeah, she's creepy."

"Well, forget about her. Do you want **Gleesux Losti** or **Gleesux Explusiv**?"

"Neither, the side effects of *Ecstasy* creates vivid dreams and hunger while *Excitement* gives people premature ventricular contractions."

"Can you be just Riya and not Dr. Asim for one night?" Quentin pleaded.

"Fine. Give me **Gleesux**."

"*Happiness*, that's all?" He scanned his ED, purchasing **Gleesux** for her and **Gleesux Explusiv** for himself, ingesting it while staring at the size of the club. Being their first time inside Prescription, they moseyed through all floors. Each level blared different types of music that was suited for the crowd. He followed Riya, all the way to the 4th level and decided to head back down to the main floor, listening to her point out the physical symptoms that club goers were experiencing.

"Riya, relax. We're at a club, a club that took a great deal to get in. Let's have a little fun, okay?"

"You're right, I'm sorry. So…you see anyone that may be interesting?"

"While there are attractive females present, no one stands out but I do see that you've caught someone's eye." Quentin tilted his head across the room, hoping that Riya would follow his gaze. Once he realized she made eye contact with her admirer, he turned to her and smiled. "You should go over and speak."

"No. Women don't do that. If he wants to speak with me, he can come over here."

"It's not always about you, it's okay to make a little effort. I didn't say ask him for his hand in marriage. Trust me, just saying hello is enough. It can be a little intimidating speaking to someone that's as beautiful and accomplished as you."

"Hey, you gave me a compliment. That's a first—"

"Don't deflect…go." He waited until she created space between them before vanishing into the crowd, not allowing her to find him so she would entertain her admirer. He found himself on the dance floor, dancing with some overly enthused females before moving to a different area where he felt someone grab his butt. Quentin turned around, wondering who sexual harassing him but the women behind him swayed back and forth, not concerned with him. He knew **Gleesux** wasn't the only pill being sold here, remembering that **Oxylin Aros – Arousal**, **Sedum – Joy** and **Sedum Gusti – Zest,** were also on the menu.

The strobe lights made it hard for him to scan for Riya but he did connect eyes with Riya's other admirer—the female. He glanced to his right, avoiding contact but noticed she was headed towards him.

"Interesting interface."

He peeked down at his wrist, staring at his ED, wondering how she could see it from across the club. It appeared normal, no identifying images. "It's just a simple trick. I grew tired of the same generic design." Quentin exchanged gazes with the medium build blonde, hoping a thought would enter his mind to continue their banter. Just as his mouth opened, she started dancing in front of him, encouraging him to sway with her. Their innocent dance gradually grew seductive as the space between them evaporated. Quentin sensed his skin getting moist and goosebumps sprouting along his arm. Blood began to course through his body, residing in one specific region.

"The feeling is mutual," she said to him.

"Excuse me?" he questioned. Quentin followed her gaze as she peeked down towards his manhood. He created space between them before she leaned upward towards his ear.

"I know your secret."

"What secret is that?"

"The reason you switched your interface. I know you're *EMOTIONAL*," she whispered in his ear.

Connecting eyes, Quentin saw recognition in her eyes just as the strobe light shined, showcasing electric blue irises. "What are you talking about?" He felt her hands on him, pulling him down to her level while they stood in the middle of the dance floor.

"Don't be alarmed, we share the same condition. We should link, soon."

The building lights irradiated while the music died down. The club goers all stopped. With the darkness expelled, Quentin could see the medium build beauty in her with her smile infectious. She lifted his wrist, tapped on his ED screen and pressed them together as both devices chimed. The exchange of personal information was complete as she lifted her finger to her lips, indicating to keep this secret between them.

Commotion came from the entrance of the club as he glanced over her. Several uniformed officers entered; E.I.A. plastered across their uniformed. When he glanced back down, she was gone. He scanned the area, searching for her but there was no trace. He found Riya headed in his direction before they were instructed to exit the premises.

Friday 04.22.2103 16:30:33

Walking home from work, Quentin stopped at several kiosks, grabbing a few groceries before heading over to the nostalgia shop to purchase more popcorn. Exchanging currency, he sensed that he was being watched as he discretely scanned his surroundings. Once the paranoia was dispelled, he grabbed his purchases and strolled home.

Entering his home, he was surprised that Riya was sitting on his couch. "You know your place has a couch, screen and other furniture that's similar to mine. In fact, it's better items."

"Is this about the popcorn?"

"Changing the subject. I haven't seen you since club Prescription. What happened with that guy?"

"Kyle? He was sweet but he's not my type."

"I thought you liked them bright smiled, nice hair type. Did you at least give him a chance?"

"I'm not interested. Can we leave it at that?"

"Won't stop me that easy. What's your type? I thought I knew—"

"Speaking of type, what about that blonde you were dancing with?"

"The one that kept staring at you? Well, she was interested in my device."

"That dance seemed like she was more interested in your body."

He laughed, discarding her comment as he set his bags down on the counter, relieving the pressure they had on his fingertips. He stored his items in their proper areas, keeping his place tidy when he noticed a strange device on the table. "What's that?"

"Ohh, it's an ER…Emotional Reader. It sends out a wireless signal that bounces off your body. It's supposed to predict a person's emotional state by measuring their breathing and heart rate. We're doing the trial version, predicting our patient's emotional state without asking for their prescription. The E.I.A. wants us to report back to them if it works or if there are bugs that need to be fixed."

A single packet of popcorn slipped from his hand. He bent down to pick it up off the ground, peeling the plastic off and poured the kernels into the AirPop. Glancing over at Riya, she was off the couch with the device in her hands, heading in his direction. "So, you work for the Emotional Intelligence Agency now. Should I call you Dr. Asim or Special Agent Asim?"

"Boy, stop. I didn't have a lot of patients so we're allowed to take it home. We were actually instructed to take these prescribed pills, scanning ourselves to detect the emotion." Riya showed him the bottle filled with blue, pink, yellow and gold pills.

"What's the gold pill?"

"**Sedum Gusti**…its Zest."

"Looks like **Sedum**. Well, enjoy."

"Come on. I know you like technology and it's the newest device. Play with me."

"I'd rather not. Besides, I just got off work and I'm in need of some rest." He stood over the AirPop, sprinkling season salt and butter over his freshly popped kernels when the chime of two beeps sounded. Quentin lifted his head, noticing Riya's new device pointed at him. "What?"

"This is weird. Did you take any pills today? This ER reading indicates **Indosears**...what are you in *fear* of? Are those horripilations forming on your forearm?"

Quentin didn't say a word. He kept his gaze on Riya, wondering what she was thinking. He noticed she held the device up to him again, two chimes sounded as he tried to step out of its line of sight.

"**Fantasal Lubrex**. Quentin, are you *hoping...*" It slipped from her hands, crashing to the ground as several pieces broke. He watched as she scooped broken pieces, walking over to the box that the Emotional Reader came with. "Are you *Emotional*? Please tell me if you are."

"What if I am? Are you going to report me to EIA?"

"Noooo...I'd never do that. You're my best friend, I won't do that but I need to know..."

He stood over the AirPop machine, staring down at the finished portion of popcorn. He sighed, lifting his head and opening his mouth, "...yes Riya, I have *feelings*. I've been having feelings since I was a little boy. You mentioned that I had a problem a few days ago and that's the reason I pop pills. It's imperative that I disguise my symptoms so my ED doesn't report me to EIA. My emotional state has been off the charts in the last few years. Is it so wrong to _FEEL_?"

Friday 04.22.2103 23:59:58

Commotion could be heard all around him, a chill rushed up his spine as he exchanged a soulful glance with the blonde from the club.

"I never got your name."

"I didn't give it."

"Well, if you don't give it now, then I think you'll be the only person in this seedy establishment."

"Who said I was alone?"

"Relax Quentin, you can call me Alice. The others will introduce themselves."

"Others?"

Lights flickered on, the sleazy place could be seen in its entirety. Emerging from other thresholds were individuals in all ethnicities, gender and sizes. They greeted him with smiles and warm embraces.

Noe the paranoia he'd felt dissipated.

"Now that you all met Quentin, let's get down to business," Alice announced. "This isn't a social club or a place to tell each other when we first sensed our emotions. As you all know, there's a war brewing and we're the targets."

"A war? Wait, I didn't sign up for this," someone commented.

"Like it or not, war is coming and it will begin with the EIA," Alice replied. "It's their sole duty to monitor everyone's emotional state. If you're here, someone has helped you to mask your emotion from detection, a shield of temporary protection."

Quentin glanced around at the faces who held their arms high in the air, showing they were in unison with their interfaces similar to his. Relief washed over him knowing he wasn't the only one with his condition.

"I'm sure you all know the history of why we wear these devices and the reason for the *APOLIS VIRTEX* needle shot that's required by everyone twice a year. The corporations don't want the riots to occur again..." Alice spoke.

"Excuse me, I'm confused. What riots?" a random person asked.

Quentin turned to see who wasn't aware of the Emotional Riots that decimated the States.

"Everyone stop sucking your teeth," Alice insisted. "The short version: people were being laid off while prices continued to rise. The citizens followed the laws, contacted their government officials but found out that corporations were paying off politicians to pass laws that allowed these massive layoffs. Spikes of violent behavior prompted law enforcement to act. Small riots escalated and martial law was implement after politicians, CEOs and celebrities were killed. The streets were flooded with dead bodies and rivers of crimson blood. Coined the *Emotional Riots,* the revolution lasted about two and a half years, decimating our government and ushered in a new era as corporations seized control. Citizens are forced to wear these **Emotional Detectors** (ED) to monitor our emotional state and reminders for the **APOLIS VIRTEX** (Apathy) shot. After a while, the ED became an all-in-one device, replacing cellular phones. The E.I.A. enforces the law but secretively, have been rounding up people who can experience emotions without pills. Deemed as *Emotional*, they're never seen again. I'm informing you because someone saved me before I was captured."

No one commented.

Quentin continued to survey his surroundings, his mind occupied. He scrolled through his messages, hoping to receive a response from his brother. He felt a hand on his shoulder, lifting his head as he met Alice's gaze.

"Is everything okay? You've been sitting here alone for the last five minutes."

Shifting his position, he realized that he was the only one sitting down, the others were engaged in conversation and reading through some papers. "Just waiting on a response from my brother."

"Nathaniel?"

He was shocked that she knew his name. "How…"

"I worked with him at the E-Corp HQ. He's the one who discovered that I was *Emotional*. He kept my secret, and he's my inside source there but I haven't had contact with him in the last week. Nathaniel instructed me to go to Denver and wait for his contact. When I saw your information after that club raid, I knew I was in the right place. He's the only one who could have given you that code. I owe Nathan my life and I'm worried because it's not like him to not contact me."

"That's Nathan, always helping out. I'm sure he'll turn up soon. He likes to make an entrance."

"Yeah, he does. Anyway, keep your normal routine. Don't tell anyone of this meeting or our condition."

"I've been keeping this secret this long, not going to jeopardize my life now."

The silence was broken once an attendee left, followed by the others.

Quentin got up from his seat and headed for the exit, glancing back one last time at Alice.

Sunday 04.24.2103 09:43:58

His ED chimed as a hologram rose from his wrist, alerting Quentin that he had a visitor. After allowing Riya access, he turned the volume up on the television as he continued watching movie snippets from the early 21st century.

"I was scolded by Dr. Mondale about the new device," Riya spoke.

"Isn't he always scolding you?"

"Yeah…anyway, so I've been doing some research—"

"Riya, I told you to leave it alone. You're the only person who knows and our friendship will not last if E.I.A. hauls me away due to your loose lips and inquisitive mind."

"Loose lips? I'm a vault when it comes to discretion. Now let me finish my statement. Since a few patients came in with side effects due to overdosing on pills, I tried to do some research how the pills trigger an emotional response."

"And?"

"Nothing. Absolutely nothing. Sorry."

"Well, that was a waste of time. It should be a warning to drop the topic. Last thing I need is a message popping up on my ED."

"Speaking of messages, I got a package addressed to you and a chime on my ED. I'm not sure but I believe it has something to do with you."

"What makes you so sure it pertains to me?"

"Your name is on the package with a bunch of memes and movie quotes…you're the only person I know who likes that stuff."

Quentin perked up, jumping out his seat and rushing over to Riya. He reached for the package, quickly tearing through the paper, producing a bruised ED.

"That thing is like ancient. Who would send that to my house?"

Quentin powered it on, gliding his fingers along the plastic wrapper until he found a small indent. Picking at it with his fingernails, he pulled out a small pen and inserted into the defected ED.

"What are you doing?"

"It's a message…from Nathan. It's something he use to do when he we were younger." Quentin studied the contents of the box, writing down the clue and typed them in until an image rose from his device, plastered along his wall.

Quentin scrolled through several folders that were created in the last weeks. He and Riya watched a video dated years before the Emotional Riots, where scientists conducted experiments on humans. He nearly jumped out of his seat when Riya shrieked. "Come on Riya, don't scare me like that."

"Did you see them make a copy of that little girl?"

"Yes, I'm watching this with you.

Dubbed Eve, she was introduced to prominent lawmakers and officials that approved of this scientific breakthrough. More clones were created while the original test subjects were caged like animals. With memory implants, they released these carbon copies into the public, monitoring their progress. Another video showed scientists mistreating original test subjects, denying them basic rights. One subject tried to escape and was deemed broken as a bullet pierced her brain while trying to escape. Distraught about how the subjects were treated, a night operator released a cell of captives, allowing them to escape. His life was taken from him after they reviewed the security footage.

The government hunted the original test subjects, capturing almost all of them. Eric Lonken hid within the shadows, moving through the city undetected as he plotted his revenge. After a few weeks, he was able to infiltrate Senator Lynchin's security and held him captive after massacring his protection detail. A live feed hit the web, showing Eric pacing back and forth with a gun in his hand. He rubbed the weapon against his temple, then placed it in his mouth before growing frustrated in behavior. Shifting his position, the stream revealed an elderly male tied to a chair.

Eric sat next to the bound elderly male, speaking to him in a low tone, "The people will know what you did. They *will know what our government has created. The people will know. Look at me!" He pointed the gun at the elderly man. "Don't I look human to you? We breathe the same air, we have all the same organs. We have families and loved ones. The original came and warned me but you all hauled him away. We both know he was executed and I was to assume his identity. Does that make me human? Am I still considered a **clone** if he fails to exist? Who's my maker since I know it's not God? You have two options... One, you can either give me the names of the scientists that created me and have a swift death or two: I can start with removing your eyelids so you have a front row seat to a gruesome death."*

The video feed died for five minutes before coming back on, blood cascading down Senator Lynchins' face. There was a loud bang that commanded Eric's attention as he pointed his weapon at the senator and fired over several shots. Shouts were heard as Eric vanished from the live stream as his body flew across the room, filled with bullets.

The video ended.

Quentin clicked on another folder, scanning files where government official buried information before it could fall into the wrong hands. After the corporations revived the country, the Wyoming black site dubbed *The F.E.E.L. Project*...Federal Emotion Endurance Levy, conducted experiments on both humans and clone, trying to combat the citizen's emotional state. The same scientists who perfected cloning were tasked and succeeded in creating a medical shot, APOLIS VIRTEX shot, to suppress emotions. They were also able to synthesize emotions in pill form, giving the human body the necessary amount of emotion without the effects that causes people to react, due to their emotions.

The clones were immune to the effects to suppress their emotions...

Quentin got up from the chair, walking past Riya and entered his bathroom. He stared into his bathroom mirror, the image ogling back at him was human—or so he thought. He poked his cheeks, opened his mouth, and counted thirty-two teeth. He gawked at his brown skin, the small scar from when he was chasing after Nathaniel and fell face first on a rock. He reached to the tip of his nose and pulled out a long piece of hair, experiencing pain...human pain. A knock alerted him as he peeked at the corner of the mirror, Riya observing him. "I need to be alone. Give me a few minutes."

"There's more..."

"What is it?"

"It's Nathan."

He darted past her, searching his living quarters for his brother. "Where is he?"

"I clicked on the folder and found a video addressed to you."

Quentin went over to the wall, staring at an image of Nathaniel. Even though they talked almost every week, he hadn't seen him in months due to work. His appearance was different; his hair was long and he grew a beard. His eyes were red and his face looked weary. Quentin played the video.

"If you're watching this, you know were clones. 3rd generation clones to be exact. I know it's a tough pill to swallow but that's what happens when you unearth the truth. Working for the E-Corp, I dodged them for years until they created those new Emotional Readers, a new device that can detect emotions better than the ED. Once I saw the prototype, I grabbed everything I could off their servers and downloaded it to several 1st generation ED. I sent them to a few people but you have the master device. Since our parents were registered, they have all our information and are sweeping through the States, discretely extracting us from society. You need to grab only a duffle bag of items and leave your place as soon as possible. I'm sure you've met Alice, she also worked at E-Corp and I could save her before they found out about her. She has the other file and the link to upload everything to the cloud to showcase to the world. Go to her and don't tell anyone. Quentin, I love you and be safe. Tell Riya I said hello but no further, she shouldn't be involved. We have a lot of catching up to do…so forgive me for this revelation: Alice is your sister in law." Nathaniel held up his hand, showing a ring on his third finger.

Quentin stared at the image of Nathaniel, the ring haloing his finger and the smirk cemented on his face. Shaking his head, he got up and scurried over to his closet. Searching until he found a large duffle bag, he tossed a few clothes and essential items from the bathroom.

"Are you seriously going to leave?"

"You heard Nathaniel, in all the conversation you've had with him, when has he ever been wrong? They could be on their way here right now."

"Maybe he's wrong this time. I think you should—"

"I got to go Riya. I can't hide my condition anymore. It's best for me to leave."

"Where will you go?"

"I'm going to find Alice." He grabbed a few other items, tossing them into his bag but his path was blocked. "Riya, what are you doing? I have to go."

"So, you're just going to leave? No goodbyes?"

"I'm not saying goodbye to you. I'll be back as soon as this blows over."

"What if it doesn't?"

"I can't think like that right now. I need to leave. I'll contact you as soon as I can." He hugged Riya, the embrace lasting longer than any embrace they ever shared. Quentin felt Riya's hands caressing his back, her face burrowing into his neck. Pulling back, he found her eyes low as she leaned in and kissed him. Inexpertly, he stepped back, stumbling as he fell, pulling her down with him. The couch cushioned their fall as he found Riya on top of him. "Riya…"

"Obviously, you never knew that it was you who I wanted this entire time. Boys are so stupid."

Their lips connected, he matched her gaze, and tasted her tongue as it slipped in his mouth. A chill coursed through his body but his arousal pressed against her body and with the removal of their clothes, he felt the warmth she had for him. Not only could he feel Riya's warmth, he could feel her heart beat as moisture built between them. Her mouth was moist as excitement engulfed them both…

An hour later, Quentin slipped back into his clothes and grabbed the handle on his bag. He stared at Riya as she laid on his couch wrapped in his blanket. He smiled as she rolled over. In his hand, he held a slip of paper and placed it on the coffee table before sneaking out of the place he'd called home.

One brief glance and he exited.

Sunday 04.24.2103 16:33:02

"I didn't expect to go through all those obstacles to get here."

"I'm just cautious. Never know whose following." Alice nodded.

"Well, Riya got a package from Nathaniel and after solving one of his riddles—"

"He loves those mind games."

"I saw several disturbing videos. The reason why we're *Emotional* is…" Quentin paused, not wanting to say the word. He tried to spit it out but it seemed to be clogged in his throat.

"Quentin."

"We're CLONES."

"What?"

"We're clones. Everything that you need is on this old ED that Nathaniel sent over. There are videos and confidential files that the government and Elite corporations didn't want the citizens to know. We're clones…well, technically 3rd generation clones. That's why the senator was shot on live television. Eric's clone found out he was some science experiment and he couldn't control his emotions." Quentin found himself pacing back and forth while Alice scrolled through files and videos. "Also, I know you're my sister-in-law. Why didn't you tell me that night at the club or at that warehouse?"

"I didn't know what to say. Can you imagine a stranger coming up to you, introducing herself and saying that I'm married to your brother?"

Quentin and Alice traded gazes before he peeled his gaze away. "What are we going to do? Nathan said the E.I.A. has a list of clones and are secretly hunting us. He mentioned that the E.I.A. has a new weapon that can detect our emotions, a device better than the ED and I have to inform you that I've seen this in action."

"Where? When?"

"Riya brought one to the house. Her job gave all the new doctors one for trials and she used it on me. It works...it detected my emotional state. What are you doing?"

"I'm uploaded everything to this ED and sending it to all the news outlets, blogs, hologram networks, every ED," Alice answered. "The public needs to know what our government has created and their attempt to wipe us out."

A knock sounded. Quentin gaped at Alice but she looked just as baffled as he was. He watched as she reached underneath the desk, producing a stun gun. He hadn't seen one in years after they were outlawed. He followed her gaze, noticing that a small monitor hung high above the door and realized she had the same type of security system that he'd purchased—a recommendation from Nathan.

"It's the girl you were with at the club."

"Riya? It can't be."

"I don't forget a face," Alice stated.

Quentin headed over to the door just as Alice opened it. "Riya, what are you doing here? Did you follow me?"

"Why did you leave without saying goodbye?"

"I left a note. How were you able to find me?"

"Your link is shared with me. You never turned that feature off."

He stared at Riya, then Alice as she rolled her eyes before walking off.

"Riya, I turned that feature off when I went to see Alice a couple of days ago. I specifically turned it off, so I wouldn't be traced."

Quentin cocked his head to the side, squinting his eyes at Riya.

She looked nervous.

"Riya, why are you here?" Quentin took a step back, creating space between him and Riya. He glanced over at Alice as she tapped on Nathaniel's ED.

"I'm so sorry Quentin." Riya emphasized.

Shifting his position, he noticed Alice fumbling with the defected ED that he received from Nathan. He knew what she was doing when she held it close to her active ED. Quentin faced a crying Riya, stepping closer to her when he noticed that her hands were trembling. "Riya…what did you do?"

"I had no choice…I was summoned by E.I.A. when the patient I mentioned came in after that overdose. Since it was an illegal substance, they gave me that device to detect if anyone at the hospital was supplying Pharmacists with illegal pills." She stepped closer to him.

Quentin had never seen her in this manner, crying hysterically. He held her tight, her body trembled as his chest grew moist from her tears.

"After the E.I.A. raided Prescription, they approached me at my job the next day after seeing me leave with you. Agent Biden and Agent Hamlin asked me about Nathan; asking if he has contacted you and I told them, he hasn't recently. They saw my ED shimmer, knowing that he has been in contact with you because of the interface. I pleaded with them until they gave you immunity. In turn, I was coerced to scan you with the Emotional Reader as they wanted to test a theory, which would lead them to Nathaniel and her." She pointed at Alice. "I didn't know you were Emotional and I hate myself for finding out because I'm obligated to tell them."

"But why YOU?" Alice shouted from across the room.

"My grandfather," Riya replied. "He's the scientist that created the APOLIS VIRTEX shot. He fell in love with one of the captured clones after the Emotional Riots so my DNA has traces of clone cells. My father and I are immune to the

Apathy shot. Our family is protected but we have to assist the E.I.A. in all matters."

Quentin noticed luminous lights shining brightly from the windows. He scurried over to the window, staring down at several E.I.A. vehicles camped out around the building. He knew the building was surrounded by the Emotional Intelligence Agency and there was no possible escape.

"You don't have to run. They don't want you. I told them that you didn't know Nathan's location but they want her. Come quietly and no harm will come your way. Please." She held her hand out, beckoning him towards her. "I love you Quentin and I don't want to see you get hurt."

Quentin rushed back towards Riya, staring at her hand, tempted to grab it. "Why?" He stared at Riya, her eyes welled with tears, and he thought back to the night in the club. All those movie nights they shared and her recent behavior. "You're Emotional too."

"Please Quentin. They're going to come through those doors if I don't escort you down. I don't know what they will do."

A loud chime sounded, alerting him as he turned towards Alice. She was grabbing a few items, stuffing them into a bag.

"Where are you going?" he asked Alice.

"Plan A," Alice commented, holding a black object in her hand.

"What is that?" Quentin asked.

"Alice Tufts, put the weapon down!" Riya demanded.

Quentin turned, noticing Riya with a weapon in her hand with the official E.I.A. logo stamp on it. "Riya, what are you doing?"

"The deal is to save you. I don't care about her," Riya emphasized.

"She's my sister, Riya. I care about Nathan, so I care about her," Quentin stated as he stepped in front of Riya's line of sight. The weapon she held pressed against his sternum.

"Move Quentin."

"No Riya."

Quentin wasn't concerned with the commotion happening behind him. He focused on Riya, shifting his position as she pointed her weapon in Alice's direction.

"I'm trying to save you!" Riya screamed.

"If you're trying to save me, you should let her go." Placing his hand on the weapon, he lowered the gun until a loud band sounded behind Riya, as they both were startled.

Agents donned in all black burst through the door with their weapons drawn just as the lights went dark. After a few seconds, the lights were on while the agents searched all over for Alice.

Quentin stared at the agents before connected eyes with Riya. He noticed her surprised expression, baffled until he followed her line of sight. Staring down, his shirt drenched in blood as he placed his hand on his stomach, falling to one knee.

"Oh, My God Quentin—it was an accident."

He tried to balance himself on one knee, falling on his side as the pool of blood grew. Quentin met Riya's gaze, tears cascading her cheeks while she knelt over him, screaming at the top of her lungs for help. He lifted his hand, reaching to touch her cheek before a chime sounded on his ED; the sound reverberated all over the room. He knew Alice had succeeded in uploading the documents to the newsfeeds, alerting humanity of the sins of their corporations.

The start of a new world was coming, his last breath assisted in the spark of a new revolution.

800-555-MIND

You've seen our advertisements, heard reviews from *REAL* customers, and not paid actors. It's time for *YOU* to give MEMORY ERASE a free trial. Yes, you heard me correct. We are giving away a free procedure of MEMORY ERASE. All you have to do is speak with one of our specialists, schedule an appointment and write down a memory that you would like to forget. Our skilled technicians will place you in a state of tranquility while removing that specific memory. A simple procedure performed over five hundred million times, our services have a 99% success rate with more than five hundred million satisfied customers, including repeat customers. Using the key phrase: *EXPUNGE* and we'll rid that second memory at no extra charge. Call 1-800-555-MIND. Once again, that number is 1-800-555-6463.

Memory Erase, huh. More like mind control. If they can take memories out, they can also implant memories. Henry nodded. Being a fan of the early 2010s science-fiction shows, he'd watched all the weird complications arising from technology.

The next morning, alarms chimed as the bed arched upward, sliding him to his feet. He stretched, ambling towards his bathroom to prepare for work. Shuffling through his attire, an envelope notification appeared in the right corner of his mirror as he tapped on it. It was a live video from Kelly. "Good morning Kelly."

"Good morning Henry, I have some exciting news to share."

"I'll be out in a minute," Henry stated.

After collecting his things and pouring himself—as well as Kelly—coffee, he exited his condo as they entered a vehicle. Sipping his coffee, Henry lifted his head and instantly locked eyes with Kelly. "Alright Kelly, what do you have to share?"

"I did it. I used Memory Erase."

"Why?"

"The free offer of course. I took advantage of the promotion."

Henry sipped his coffee, staring at the grin cemented on Kelly's face. She seemed different, noticing that light in her ocean blue eyes, far from the sorrow that had plagued her. "Well, what memory was it if you don't mind sharing?"

"Honestly, I can't remember. I was advised to write it down before the thirty minute procedure. It's like a huge burden has been released. I really think you can benefit—"

"No Kelly."

"It has a 99% success rating. There hasn't been a complaint and millions had the procedure performed. No side effects. Give it a chance; imagine not having to think about Elisha vanish–"

"Kelly, don't bring that up."

"I was just trying to help."

Henry's jaw tightened as he tapped on his ear, the sound evaporated. Staring, he noticed her lips were still moving. An array of nonverbal gestures was directed towards him after she realized he'd muted her. He smirked, pissing Kelly off more.

A few minutes of idol time allowed Kelly's statement about the procedure coursed through his mind. Henry surfed the web for articles of MEMORY ERASE. He waved off unwanted advertisements, not wanting to hear sales pitches. Skimming through several articles, every review praised the procedure—not one bad review.

"Interested, I see," Kelly said.

"Sorry for muting you earlier."

"Don't let it happen again." She punched him his arm. "You should set an appointment and take advantage of the free offer."

Once she left his desk, Henry picked up the phone and scheduled an appointment. He was in luck as there was an opening due to someone rescheduling their procedure.

Later at home, Henry slid into more comfortable clothes, drank almost a gallon of water and ate dinner—all instructions directed by the technicians. Flooded with nervousness, he distracted himself by streaming shows. A notification chimed, followed by a call informing him that transportation was outside to escort him to Memory Erase HQ.

A short trip led him to one of the branches, Henry was escorted into the office. After signing consenting paperwork, he stayed in the waiting room while multiple clients exited the premises.

A beautiful technician smiled at him as he entered the room. "I see you were referred by Kelly. Let me pull her profile up so we can give her a complementary extraction in the future. I'm going to inject this sleeping agent into your bloodstream. Count down from ten for me, hun."

He sighed before counting down; the light dimmed until he saw black, seven was the last number he remembered…

…His vision restored as he attempted to pop up, only to be forced down in his chair.

"Easy Henry. Relax for a bit and I'll release the restraints," the technician urged.

"Successful?"

"Henry, I need to be honest with you. There was a glitch and the power went out for less than a minute," she informed him.

"Wait, is everything okay?"

"I'm positive the procedure went well. So, tell me about her. Your ex, what's her name?"

Henry opened his mouth but no words came out. He thought hard, hoping to remember anything about his ex.

"Congratulations, that memory has been extracted."

That night, Henry woke up repeatedly while sleep eluded him. His alarms woke him with only minutes of a full night sleep. After preparing a strong mug of coffee, a knock broadcasted a stranger's presence, followed by a metal click. Sipping his coffee, he glanced up as Elisha entered; her presence startling him, the mug slipped from his grip.

"HENRY, are you okay!"

"Elisha?"

Rubbing his eyes, he gawked in his direction until he saw Kelly with a baffled expression.

"I thought you had her wiped from your memory?" Kelly questioned.

"The technician said there was a glitch but after asking me about my ex, I couldn't remember her face or name."

"You should go back—"

After cleaning up the spill, they exited his home in route to work. Henry tried his best to shake that groggy feeling just as another vision entered his mind: *walking in the midst of a storm, the downpour drenched his clothes. Trees lined on each side as he trekked through the mud. He felt his fingers wrapped around a solid object, peeking down and noticed a glimmer of lightening that shone against metal: a shovel as he drove it into the moist earth.*

"Hello, are you there?"

Henry found himself sitting at his desk, staring at his computer screen.

"What's going on with you?" Kelly's voice asked.

"Yeah, I'm having the strangest daydream but I don't ever remember being in the woods."

Henry spun around, connecting eyes with Kelly as another daydream entered his mind...

...Driving the shovel into the dirt, he created a massive hole in the earth. He leaned over, unzipping the bag as he saw the fear frozen on Elisha's face. Her mouth and hands were bound; his fingers brushed back the hair near Elisha's terrified eyes. His dark hands reached down, grabbed a piece of Elisha's hair and cut a piece while sliding it into his pocket. The blade that glimmered in his hand slammed down violently into Elisha's body. Repeating this motion over and over, blood dripped from the knife as the rain cleansed it. Tired, he pushed her into the grave and let out a strange laugh as the earth filled up again. Disposing of any evidence, he rode him and entered into his complex. Heading down familiar steps, he saw his door but quickly turned around, entering another home. The scent of lavender tickled his nose as he moseyed to the bathroom and motioned for the shower to be turned on. After peeling off his clothes, he noticed that his skin wasn't dark but ivory. The reflection in the mirror didn't belong to him...

...He fell back into his chair, crashing to the floor while creating space between himself and Kelly.

"Elisha didn't leave me, you KILLED her. You murdered my ex-girlfriend!" Henry noticed security officers approaching his location but his voice only rose louder. "A glitch occurred during my memory wipe and I ended up with the memories that you tried to expunge...you stalked her. Elisha's screams are echoing through my mind. She trusted YOU!"

All gazes were set upon Kelly, perplexed that one of their own was the cause of a co-worker's grief.

"Sir, calm down and come with us," a guard urged.

Henry advanced towards Kelly's desk and typed in the code as her drawer popped open. Ransacking her drawer, he pulled out a small translucent bag with dark curls inside. He held it up so that everyone could see. "Our combinations are provided by security and switched every so often to repel stealing so how am I able to get into her drawer? I'm sure this hair belongs to Elisha. I know where you buried the body, where you dumped the gloves and shovel, the shrine of me in your bedroom...it's all seared into my brain."

Henry couldn't control his emotions as tears cascade down his cheeks. He wanted to say more but the words evaporate once they passed his lips. His eyes connected with a confused Kelly. "You don't have a clue, do you? You wipe all traces of your crime from your mind and wanted me to erase Elisha from my mind as well." He stepped back as security restrained Kelly while escorting him from the floor. He stared at Kelly just as a memory of her standing over him surfaced in his thoughts. Henry blinked away the image and watched as the elevator door closed.

WHAT IF

DeForrest LeRonte'

Bryson sat with perfect posture in his open cubicle, inserting formulas and handling bank reconciliations. The only person in his unit with the stature to see over all the cubicles while sitting down, he watched the usual office politics. Those who partake in water-cooling talk, the office flirt making her rounds, while other colleagues paced back and forth. After staring at spreadsheets for the last five hours, he headed for the breakroom. "No ma'am's and no sirs," spewed from his mouth as he displayed proper office etiquette, learning from others that were fired or relieved of their position that his massive stature and the melanin coating his skin certainly played a factor in his job, no matter how well he performed.

Entering the break room, Bryson peeked over at the television. It was always on ANN—the American News Network, political and business stories were always breaking news while other stories scrolled across the bottom or the panel. "BREAKING NEWS: Colin Rush just agreed to a six year, $114.5 million dollar deal with $76.5 million guaranteed, making him the richest defensive player in NFL history. That's quite an accomplishment for Colin, only being in the league for five years." So focused on the new story, the candy bar slipped out of Bryson's hand, crashing down to the ground.

"Wow, that's a lot of money," a co-worker mentioned.

"NFL players always receive large contracts to hit each other...terrible society we live in," another co-worker chimed in.

Bryson watched highlights of Colin Rush sacking quarterbacks, tackling running backs and showing off his exceptional athleticism for a defensive tackle, making several interceptions. He'd seen athletes make millions playing a sport that he used to play but this particular story hit close to home—he played with Colin Rush back in college. Not only was Colin a teammate of his, he and Bryson played the same position. In fact, Bryson was the better football player, being first-team defensive tackle while Colin was the backup. Bryson had scouts drooling with his physical prowess until the second game of his senior season. Against their rivals and in front of NFL scouts, Bryson remembered having the game of a lifetime but that all changed as an opposing tight end missed a block, hurling head first into the side of his leg. The pain was excruciating and his screams could be heard throughout the stadium as his voice overpowered all sounds present. It took nearly five months before he could put any type of pressure on his leg with multiple surgeries required over the next two years. His life changed that day as his dreams of making it to the NFL diminished. Proceeding out the break room, Bryson strolled past a few annoying co-workers, flopping back into his chair as he inserted his earbuds to tune out the chatter.

Diligently working, Bryson lifted his head and peeked over to the window; pitch dark. Hours must have gone by, as the cleaning crew was the only ones in the office as he powered down his system and headed to the parking lot, the bitter chill of winter greeted him. He jumped in the car, turning the heat on full blast while thumbing through text messages. A few of his college teammates were commenting on the new contract that Colin Rush was awarded. He quickly muted the conversation and read his wife's texts, realizing that his drive home had more than one stop. Stopping by the grocery store, he picked sick remedies for his little ones before heading over to the manager counter and saw the Powerball jackpot was $330 million. Realizing that he wouldn't win, he tried his luck and bought a single ticket, trying to be optimistic.

Driving through the countryside, he drove down the dark road as a ghostly fog crept out in front of him. He didn't pay it any attention, turning on his high beams, as he knew he was near the swamp. Approaching the crossroads, there were two routes he could have taken but both were blanketed by the fog bank. He hooked a left, heading down the path that was free of the fog, a road that he wasn't that familiar driving. Bryson's foot hovered over the brake as he squinted. It was too quiet as he reached for the radio, taking his eyes off the road, lifting his head just as his car slammed into—

—Bryson's head popped up, staring at his dashboard. Gripping the steering wheel, he leaned back slowly as shooting pains radiated in the center of his forehead. Gaining his composure, he peeked up and stared out the windshield, staring at odd scenery as a row of cars were parked in a straight line. He glanced down at the center of his SUV, realizing that it wasn't in his SUV but a car with a stick shift. He grabbed the shift, the grip felt familiar, as he hadn't driven one in over ten years. The interior of the car looked familiar. "Wait, I haven't had this car in years…" A tap at his window alerted him. The door opened without his assistance as he stared at two of his former teammates—Jamal and Flint.

"Hey, why are you taking a nap? We got practice...c'mon," Jamal urged.

"What the hell..."

"He's acting like he's seen a ghost," Flint teased. "Stop playing around and let's get to practice. You know how crazy coach will get if we're late after electing us to be captains."

Both Flint and Jamal proceeded towards the steps as Bryson climbed out and followed. They crossed the road that ran through campus, heading up several hills before entering their locker room. Filled with old teammates, Bryson remained silent as locker room jargon spewed into the air. Wide eyed, he pinched himself several times, each one stung just as hard as the first pinch. Baffled, he went into the medical staff and met with the team doctor.

"Bryson, you're early for taping..."

"Doc...I think something's wrong with me."

"You should always wear a condom..."

"Doc, I think I'm losing it. I swear an hour ago that I was ten years older, married with two kids. I was working a desk job and got into a car accident on a foggy backroad and ended up in the student parking lot with a pounding headache."

The doctor turned to his staff members as all eyes were on Bryson. All at once, they burst out laughing. "I tell you Bryson, you're a funny guy. Every week, you always find a way to keep us laughing."

"Doc, I'm not kidding. I'm serious."

Their expressions changed, the sound of laughter died as they detected the seriousness of his plea.

"Lie down Bryson," the doctor instructed.

After several concussion tests that lasted through practice, the team doctor cleared him of a concussion but suggested proper rest.

Bryson left practice, headed back to his car where he woke up. He checked his wallet, searching for pictures of his kids and wife but the only thing in his wallet was a few small bills, his student identification. Bewildered, he closed his eyes, hoping that this was a dream. Taps woke him up, the blinding light of a flashlight penetrated through his tinted window as he opened the door to campus police.

"Bryson, we have people looking for you. Why are you asleep in your car?"

"I wasn't feeling well, so I came here and went to sleep."

"Well, go to your dorm room and phone your coach. Have a good night."

"Yes sir." He grabbed his things, heading for his dorm. He asked the front desk clerk his room number, both wore puzzled looks as he went over to the elevator and took it up to his floor. Passing Jamal and Flint, he headed straight to his room, closed the door, and climbed into bed.

The next two days were confusing as he wondered why he was back in college but still remembered his wife, kids, his job, etc. There were bruises on his forearm from pinching his skin and after a few days, he went along with his life. Maybe the life he thought he lived was a dream as he prepared for this week's game. Once the game was underway, the game went out just he remembered—or he thought he remembered. It was all confusing. He remembered each play, especially the one where he was injured. Abandoning his position, his actions caused his defense to get scored on by their opponent as his coach chewed him out. Bryson's main concern was surviving the game, which he completed and not being injured for the rest of his collegiate career.

Living his life, the life he thought was true began to fade quickly forgetting about the life he thought he had, determining that it was nothing but an intense dream as he went about his collegiate career, achieving the highest honors: 1st-team All American, Bednarik, Nagurski and the Lombardi award. For his performance, Bryson also managed to place 5th in the Heisman Trophy race. Last year, his name was mentioned by a few local news articles but now, he was mentioned with other first round lottery picks. His spring semester was spent going to class and working on drills for the upcoming NFL combine. After showcasing his talent, drug testing and answering all the interview questions, his name was called a month later on the first night of the draft with the 22nd pick.

…Five years sped by as he experienced growing pains and hardships, the result of living reckless. He chased women, spent a lot of his time at clubs with the wrong crowd as he found himself suspended for the last 4 games of his rookie season.

After realizing his childish ways, Bryson focused a little more on his career, winning comeback player of the year and invited to a few pro bowls. His turnaround contributed to a lucrative contract that would make him one of the top defensive linemen in the league, a high that he briefly indulged in as blackouts forced him to the sidelines. Numerous doctors couldn't determine the cause of these momentary lapses as he found himself in strange places. His condition worsened, forcing him to retire just as he reached his athletic peak in his career. The blackouts worsened as vision of him running after little children caused him to dart out in front of cars.

After seeing several specialists and cyberstalking social media websites, Bryson hired a sketch artist to draw a description that was seared in his mind. He hired a private investigator to locate the woman that was supposed to be his wife, having a feeling that he might know where she lived. A few weeks later, he received a phone call indicating that the woman he was looking for had been located and she went by the name Chanel. Bryson caught the first plane out, arriving at the airport as the private investigator handed him some photos while driving him to a gentlemen's club. Appalled at what he saw Bryson, stared at the images of Chanel hanging from the ceiling, twerking, and giving random men lap dances. He instructed the private investigator to take him to the place where he took the pictures.

An hour later, Bryson entered into a dim-light nightclub, the scent of liquor, nuts and feminine spray saturated the air. He scanned the club, staring at every woman until he froze. He stood there as they locked eyes for a moment, as she walked past him while passing out drinks.

"Is she the one you're searching for? How do you know her?" the private investigator questioned.

"Yeah…that's her. Someone I knew in another life."

Bryson walked over to the bar, purchasing a non-alcoholic beverage and stared at the stage. Girls twirled seductively around poles, reenacting fantasies that kept grown men glued to their every move. Checking his watch, it was a little past midnight when the announcer broadcast the main attraction to the stage: Sunshine.

The lights dimmed while strobe lights lit up one stage but no one was present. "Where can she be…where does the sunshine? In the sky, of course," the announcer shouted as the strobe light lifted high towards the ceiling.

Bryson's head shot up and he saw someone hanging from the ceiling, sliding down the pool upside down towards the stage. Just a few inches from the ground, she stopped and flipped off the pool and Bryson took a few steps from the bar, peering out at the stage and saw Chanel. Anger engulfed him as he walked closer to the stage as a security guard stepped in front of him. Bryson took a step forward but that guard—who was much smaller than Bryson—tried to deter him from approaching the stage.

His reaction got the attention of other security guards as they instructed him to sit down or leave the premises.

Close to two thirty in the morning, he watched from across the street as most of the crowd dispersed. After fifteen minutes, he grew restless, wondering if he'd missed her. He ordered a Lyft, pacing until his ride pulled up. Just as he reached for the door handle, he lifted his head just as a petite woman exited the club.

"Wait." A few minutes went by. "Follow that cab."

He noticed the Lyft driver peeking in the rearview mirror so he pulled out his phone, typed in a few numbers and once the Lyft driver phone chimed, he followed the cab. Heading through town, they zigzagged from a distance as he rode into uncharted territory as the cab stopped, the petite woman climbed out.

"Hey Chanel!" Bryson shouted as he got out of the car, stepping towards her.

She turned towards him.

"Hey ma'am, do you need me to call the police? He had me following you," Bryson's Lyft driver shouted from the car.

"No, I'm not in any danger," Chanel answered.

They both waited until the driver cleared the street.

"Soooo, I saw you at the club. What do you want?" Chanel asked.

"Ummm...I don't know what to say."

"Look, I know who you are. I know an NFL player when I see one, especially one with your story. Why were you ogling the entire night and yes, I noticed!"

"Do you know me? I mean, outside of Sport Center? Have we ever cross paths because I've been having strange déjà vu..."

"Déjà vu about me? How could you have images about me? There's no way we would have crossed paths...I'm a long way from the posh life."

"I can't explain it but I feel like I know you."

"I'm going to stop you right there. You're not the first guy who has said that about me but that's only due to my profession. I create fantasies but I don't act upon them. I'm doing this because its good money and I need to take care of my kids. I think it's best for you to return to your posh life and take care of your health," Chanel insisted.

He stood there as she headed for her home. Bryson couldn't shake the feeling of knowing her, being a part of her life. "Chanel, you said you had kids, right? Now, I'm going to take a guess but their names wouldn't happened to be Bryson and Holly? I'm just spit balling but Holly is so smart and full of life and she has dreams of being a ballerina? Bryson wants to be a police officer, right?"

He noticed she turned around, to stare at him.

"Just hear me out. I've been having these visions of a life where we met in college, I became a CPA and we got married. We have two kids; Holly and Bryson Jr. I know I'm not making sense and sounding like a crazy person but I feel that I have a strong connection with you…"

"You do sound crazy but I've seen that look that you currently possess. I don't know how you know but I do have a daughter name Holly and she wants to be a ballerina. My son's name is Bryson and he's obsessed with cops. But may I be frank?"

"You always were."

"Look at me, I work two jobs and have disgusting men staring and grabbing at me all night, throwing money at me and requesting me to do sexual favors. I have two kids at home who need me so don't take this the wrong way but we're from two different worlds. You've been on television, playing in different cities every week and your bank account has more money in it per week then I will ever see in several lifetimes. Take a good look at me. I'm not that girl you imagine, I'm not the prom queen or the girl you can take home to mother."

"But—"

"—Bryson, if you knew what was best for you, you would head down that sidewalk and don't look back."

"But…"

He felt her hand along her neck, pulling him towards her as her lips pressed against his. He felt her passion and embraced it but it was short lived. Bryson felt her being pulled away, tears welled in her eyes.

"In another life, I'm sure I would be happy with you. You seem like a great person with a big heart but this isn't that life. You should forget about me and go."

"I can't—"

"…FIRE! FIRE! FIRE!" Chanel screamed.

"What are you doing? Why are you screaming fire?"

"I'm helping you to forget me. Women are taught to scream fire when they are being sexually harassed. Leave now…FIRE! FIRE!"

Bryson saw lights peppering the housing complex; his feet led him in the opposite direction, as murmurs grew louder. After rounding a few corners, he caught his breath before ordering a ride to take him to the airport. He headed straight to the airport without his belongings, not caring as he purchased a ticket home. He headed over to the parking lot, got into his SUV and headed home.

Bryson suddenly found himself driving into a fog, he turned on his fog lights, so he could see through the moisture. Peeking down at his phone, he typed in his address and lifted his head just as something crossed out in front of him. He lost control of his vehicle; the SUV spiraled out of control as he banged his head against the steering wheel. The last thing his saw was the lights from the dashboard…

…taps commanded his attention. He glanced out in front of him, staring at a police car, as the taps grew louder.

"Sir, I'm going to need you to step out of the car slowly."

Bryson raised his hands slowly, reaching out his window as he pulled the handle opened. The officer stood a few feet off to the side as he exited the vehicle. He towered over the officer but then again, he towered over most people.

"Are you okay sir? Have you been drinking?"

"No sir. Something darted out in front of me and I tried to avoid it."

"I can see a little blood on your windshield. I'm going to need your license."

"Yes, it's in my back pocket. I'm going to reach for it." Bryson slowly inserted his hand into his back pocket, pulling his wallet out. He produced his license as the flashlight shone brightly on him then to his ID.

"Bryson, I do need you to walk this yellow line, one foot in front of the other," the officer instructed.

Bryson complied, passed a few tests before being released. He got in the car, waited for the officer to leave before merging back on the road. The time on the radio read 9:25 pm as he parked in his driveway. Heading for the steps, he felt a little pain in his knee and smiled—he was home! Really and truly home. He went in to hear bumps and booms echoing in the house as two smaller versions of himself scurried towards him. They climbed on top of him; the sound of laughter now filled the house.

"Okay, it's still time for bed," a woman spoke.

Bryson turned to see Chanel standing in the kitchen threshold, looking as beautiful as when he first met her. He got up, walked over to her, and kissed her with so much passion that it took her breath away.

"I see that you're in a better mood than earlier. Where's the milk?"

"I'm sorry that I ever took you for granted. I've always known but you are my world and I don't know what I would do if I lost you. I love you."

"Are you okay? What happened between the grocery store and now?"

"Let me take the kids to bed." He tiptoed quietly out of their room, heading down the hallway and stared at all the pictures that hung on the wall. Heading into the kitchen where Chanel was cleaning off the counter, Bryson swept her off her feet, her legs wrapped around his waist as they kissed passionately.

She pulled back, studying his face. "Okay, you're acting strange. What really happened to you?"

"My life flashed before my eyes…well, another version of my life. I thought if life went in the direction I wanted, it would be bliss."

"So, this was triggered by Colin getting that new NFL contract?"

"I'm not worried about that anymore. My life is with you and my kids. That's all I need."

"Alright. Let me finish straightening up in here. Go turn the television off and let's get prepped for bed."

Bryson kissed Chanel before setting her down on the floor. He entered the living room, watching the news before heading up to bed. After violent stories and political scandals, the lottery numbers scrolled across the screen. Digging into his pocket, he paused the television and stared at his ticket.

"Baby, what's wrong? Why is the television paused on those numbers…?"

IMAGINARY

DeForrest LeRonte'

Alice stood over the kitchen sink, washing dishes while staring out the window at her younger siblings playing in the backyard. She smiled as Zack and Kelly rode their bikes in the backyard. Minutes into her daily routine, she seasoned meats, set the timer on the stove while occasionally staring at the telephone mounted on the wall in the distance. She'd been thinking about him all day, wondering if he would call after giving him her home number at school earlier. Impatiently waiting, she straightened up anything out of place, did inventory of the items in the pantry, and wrote a new grocery list as a reminder.

The phone rang.

Alice was across the room before the second ring could chime. "Hello…Ohh, it's you. Sorry dad, I was expecting a call…Yes, I've prepared dinner and it should be ready when you get home…Ohh, you're going to be at the office late, yet again…Yes, I know, I've been taking care of them for few years now, I'm sure I can handle it," Alice emphasized. Walking as far as the cord would allow, she opened the door that led to the back of the house and stared into the sky. The sun descended just below the horizon, giving off that last spark before the night reclaimed the sky. The night-light flickered on, prompting Alice to call the kids in. She stared out through the screen door, watching Zack pulling a red wagon and releasing it before heading towards the woods.

"Dad, let me call you back."

After hanging up the phone, she opened the door. "Zack, you know you're not supposed to go into the woods. The night light is on, you know that means you need to be in the house."

"But Daemon wants me to come with him," Zack spoke.

"Tell your imaginary friend that you will play with him tomorrow. Where's Kelly?"

"She's with Lamia." He pointed into the woods.

Alice ran down the steps and over to where Zack pointed, glancing past the army of trees until she spotted Kelly. "KELLY, YOU KNOW BETTER THAN TO GO INTO THE WOODS. COME BACK BEFORE YOU GET A BEATING."

She stood there with her arms crossed, catching glimpses of Kelly walking towards the house. The night fell faster than Alice expected and she could barely see through the darkness, only catching pieces of Kelly's white shirt. Squinting, Alice saw two pieces of white garments passing through the trees prompting goose bumps to sprout along her forearms. She turned to Zack, noticing that he was unbothered and realized that the darkness was playing tricks on her. Watching Kelly approaching the line, Alice walked over to the edge of the woods and reached out to help Kelly over the log.

A loud shriek blared from her throat and Alice jumped high into the air. Her feet landed and she ran a few steps before turning back to see what grazed her leg: the red wagon. Alice chuckled to herself, shook the chills off, and held her hand open to accept Kelly's hand. Walking back to the house, Alice peeked over her shoulder and had the strangest feeling they were being watched. "I can't wait to leave this creepy place," she mumbled under her breath. "What were you doing out in the woods? You know the rules, you're not allowed to go in there unsupervised."

"I wasn't alone, Lamia was with me. She said it's safe to enter," Kelly mentioned.

"Lamia, is that your imaginary friend?"

"She's not imaginary. She's my best friend and she's upset that we're moving tomorrow. Lamia told me that if I leave, we won't be friends anymore," Kelly answered.

"Tell Lamia she can come with us, I'm sure she wouldn't mind living in Washington, D.C. All your friends can come and visit you once we get settled. Come on, let's get you two something to eat and tucked in the bed. We have a big day ahead of us."

"Where is daddy?" Zack asked.

"He's going to be working late, finishing up a few things before we leave for our nation's capital tomorrow."

"I don't wanna go. I want to stay here with Lamia. She's my best friend!" Kelly snatched her hand away from Alice.

Alice noticed a strange aura surrounded her baby sister and turned to notice the same aura around Zack. She reached out to grab Kelly's hand and felt a jolt of electricity that popped her. "Ouch, what was that? You better go in the house before I call Dad to come get you."

Both children darted towards the house, racing up the steps and entered the house.

Alice laughed, knowing invoking their father's authority would put some fire in their step. Suddenly, the chirping of crickets died. Her gait increased as he powered up the steps but lost her balance, the bridge of her nose colliding with the steps. A bright light flashed before her eyes. Blinking away the pain, she witnessed two little children that she had never seen before. Trepidation coursed through her veins, adrenaline triggered her flight-or-fight response as she hurdled the remaining steps, rushing through the threshold and fastening all the locks.

Taking several deep breaths, she peeked through the peephole, wondering who those little kids were.

After catching her breath, Alice walked towards the kitchen where Zack and Kelly were eating; she passed the full-length mirror and paused. Blood dripped from the brim of her nose, forcing her to head to the sink and reach for a few paper towels. Turning on the faucet, she damped the paper towels as she wiped the blood from her face. Grimacing each time she touched her nose, she opened her eyes and saw two small figures standing behind her in the mirror. Her head snapped back searching for Zack and Kelly but she was the only one in the living room. Then she heard the door to the kitchen slamming shut. "Zack, Kelly…you better be at that table when I get in there." Entering the kitchen, she stared at them sitting in their chairs, eating their foot. "I told you not to get up until you finish your food."

"We've been here the whole time," Zack replied.

"I just saw you and Kelly in the bathroom, don't lie to me."

Kelly snickered and whispered something in Zack's direction.

"What's so funny, young lady?"

"That's wasn't us, that's our friends Daemon and Lamia," Kelly answered.

"You're imaginary friends? Let me be the first to tell you, since y'all getting older, Daemon and Lamia aren't real. They're figments of your imagination that will leave you, as you get older. I had an imaginary friend too, and now she's long gone."

"Our friends are real and they don't like you. They know you're trying to take us away," Kelly countered.

"What are they going to do? Put me in imaginary jail? I like to see them try, now finish your food, and get ready for bed. We have a big day tomorrow." Alice went over to the sink to wash the blood out of her bath rag when she stared out the window.

The weather was behaving erratically—one minute it was clear skies and now the wind was picking up and clouds blanketed the star studded night. A streak of lightening forked across the sky, startling her, as she counted to see how close the storm was. She started counting…putting to use the 'flash-to-bang' method in school. A series of streaks flashed across the sky, illuminating their backyard. Alice's stomach dropped as she ogled at the small children in her yard. "Zack, run over there and hand me the phone. There are a lot of kids in the backyard."

"They're our friends. I told you they upset that we're leaving tomorrow, they want us to stay with them," Zack replied.

Several knocks alerted her that someone was on the other side of the door.

"DAD, is that you?"

Silence.

Alice paused. "I said who's there? Stop playing at my door, my father upstairs and he has a shotgun."

Cemented with her siblings at her side, simultaneous knocks resonated on all the doors and windows around the first level of their house. A loud shriek blared from her mouth before she silenced herself, grabbing Zack and Kelly while darting up the stairwell.

They were halfway up the steps when the door blasted open, prompting her to turn to see the first level peppered with children from her backyard.

At the second railing, she stared out at the children, noticing their eyes were bright white and large as saucers. Simultaneously, their mouths opened with a distance buzz slowly piercing through the entire house, causing her slight discomfort. She picked her siblings up, running to the stairwell that led to the third level—the attic to her room. The buzzing continued followed by the sound of a thousand footsteps pounding towards them. Picking up speed, she cleared the third stairwell, closing the door just as Zack and Kelly crossed over the threshold. She snapped her locks in place, very thankful that she had the skill to install those double locks herself. After retrieving her favorite bat from the closet, she put the kids on the bed and stood watch.

"What the hell is going on? What are those things in our house?" She noticed them snickering at her using profanity.

"Those are our friends. They don't want us to leave," Kelly explained again.

"I've never seen any of those things before and they're definitely not your friends. Little kids' eyes don't burn white hot nor do they sound like that. Those aren't kids."

"Yes, they are. Lamia said you would say they're not real. You lie," Kelly argued.

"Do you remember when I used to read ghost stories?"

"I remember," Zack answered.

"Well, those are ghosts. They're only want to harm those of the living world. All those little kids that were staring at us, wearing the same clothes, those are ghosts."

Alice went over to the only window in her room, stepping onto a small box that gave her the necessary inches to see outside. The window faced the backyard and she was able to see the yard full with the same things that were in her home.

Those aren't friendly.

She shook her head, glad she wasn't outside with those things. Rain pattered against the windowsill, lightening flashed and thunder rumbled instantly. There was no denying that the storm hovered above their home. In the distance, she noticed the other neighbor's houses were well-lit during this storm. "Why is our power out and not the neighbors?" she spoke out loud, jumping from the small box and landing on her feet. When she turned around, she saw Kelly near the door, her hand on the knob.

"WHAT ARE YOU DOING? GET AWAY FROM THAT DOOR!"

"Lamia wants to come in. She said she won't be my friend if I don't let her in," Kelly pleaded.

"That is not your friend. Get back to the bed and stay there until dad gets home." Shooing her back over to the bed, Alice fastened the locks and when she turned, an invisible force yanked her towards the door. Her back collided with the door, pain shot up her spine and then her butt as she fell down on her bat. The sensation continued as she moan and cried, her arms flailing in all directions, knocking items to the floor. Frantic, she pulled herself up off the ground and brushed the salt from her lap that spilled over while her arms swung erratically. Alice stepped back, peeked at her siblings while staring at her door.

The lights flickered on and off again, appliances that generated off electricity flashed repeatedly, frightening Zack.

Alice ran over to the phone, pressing buttons and successfully made an outbound call to her father. "DAD, WHERE ARE YOU?"

"I'm still at work."

"PLEASE GET HOME...SOMETHING IS IN OUR HOUSE."

"Where are the children? Go get my gun from my room..."

"I'M STUCK IN MY ROOM...please hurry home...hello...hello?" The phone went silent.

Taps blared all around her, from her door, the window and the roof of her home. The thunder roared, drowning out the sound of rain against the windowsill. She peeked back at Zack and Kelly; fright written all over his face while Kelly stood on the bed, twirling in circles. Alice made her way to the bed, positioning herself between her siblings.

After a few hours, her siblings were fast to sleep, snuggling up against her. Alice found herself drifting in between the realms of reality and fantasy, the horror she'd experienced fresh on her mind. The sound of a sinister laugh woke her in the midst of the storm as she glanced out the window to see the rain streaming down. Trying her best to stay awake, her gaze darted from her door, to the window and back to the closet door.

A distant noise sounded, footsteps followed, heading up the steps that led to her room.

"Alice, why was the front door wide open?" a familiar voice spoke.

"Dad...thank God!" She clambered out her bed, running over to the door.

"Are the kids with you? Open the door."

Alice unfastened the locks, turned the knob, and pulled the door open to find her father standing on the other side of the threshold. Overwhelmed with relief, the bat slipped from her hand and fell to the ground. "You don't know how happy I am to see you!" Just as she took a step forward, she felt a tug in her stomach and stop midstride. She glanced around before facing her father again.

"What's wrong?" he asked.

"I don't know. I got the strangest feeling."

"When you called and told me you were being attacked by little children, I thought Zack and Kelly were running ramped. I see that you got everything handled."

"Yes, there were so many kids...wait. How did you know about the children? The phone hung up before I could tell you anything." Stepping back from the door, kneeling down with her eyes fixated on her father. Her fingers wrapped around the bat with a grip that caused her knuckles to be white. She bent down, picking up the bat while glancing down at the salt dispenser on the floor.

Her *father* matched her gaze. "Tsk, tsk...what a shame."

"W-what are you? Why do you look like my father? Why are you here?"

"An agreement was made before by your ancestors and now we're here to collect our debt. Give us our debt and we shall spare your life," a legion of voices spoke.

Her heart pounded harder, staring at the sinister smirk on her *father's* face. Alice glanced back at the bed where her siblings slept peacefully, steeling her nerves while narrowing the space between herself and her siblings. Her grip tightened around the bat's handle, staring at the thing that looked and sounded like her father. "No debt will be paid tonight."

"You dare interfere? GIVE US THE CHILDREN!" the voices barked.

A booming wail sounded throughout the house; screeching pain pierced her eardrums, bringing Alice fell to her knees. She tried to muffle the pain but the sound penetrated through her hands, inflicting pain throughout her entire body. Suddenly, the wailing stopped as silence hovered all around her. Alice ogled at the doorway, noticing the thing that appeared as her father had vanished. She glanced back at her siblings before stepping to the side so she could see down the hall.

A set of glowing eyes met her gaze, following by several others.

Alert and prepared for any attack, Alice shut the door and ran over to the edge of the bed with her eyes glued on the door. Sleep eluded her, bat firmly in her grip while staring at the bottom of the door. Footsteps alerted her of pending danger, her breath labored, her grip caused whiteness around her knuckles as she stood to her feet.

"Alice?"

Cemented, she watched the door handle turn, as she stood on the balls of her feet. The door crept open as her jaw clenched. Alice didn't match its gaze, she kept her eyes on the position of its feet.

"Alice, why is there a bat in your hand?"

"I told you earlier, my siblings don't belong to you."

"Daddy," a small voice shouted from behind her.

She shifted her stance to see both Kelly rush off the bed. "Kelly….NO." Alice turned to see her enemy step through the threshold and she panicked, swinging her bat erratically. She missed horribly and was swarmed as arms wrapped around her. "LET ME GO…LET ME GO…" she shrieked, struggling to be released from its embrace.

"Calm down pumpkin. What on earth happened here? The door was left wide open and all the electronics were on." Her father traced an image on her back.

The bat fell from her hand, crashing to the floor as she felt her father's grip leave her arms. Alice fell into his harms once she realized it was her father, crying uncontrollably. She didn't have the strength to get up, her father scooped her up off the ground and carried her down several stairwells until she found herself in the front seat of their SUV. She buried her face into her knees and rocked back and forth, glancing back at Zack and Kelly who were fastened in their car seats.

Alice didn't lift her head nor did she speak until they were miles away from their home.

Alice felt pressure as she chewed on a piece of gum, something she learned by experience while flying to multiple cities. She stared out the window at the last place she thought she'd be flying into: Raleigh, N.C. This was the last place she thought she would come back too, but the phone call she got from her father's doctor prompted her to board the next flight from Chicago.

Alice waited at the Kiss & Ride, taking in the sights and sound of home until a car rolled up on the curve, almost clipping her in the process. "Watch where you're going next time, asshole."

She stood while the car stop, staring at the person getting out the vehicle.

"City folks sure are cranky. I guess you forgot your manners in that big city," Zack spoke while heading over to his big sister.

"Sorry for the asshole comment but I'm not sorry for my next comment. You need better lessons. Maybe I should drive?"

She hugged him and removed the keys from his possession. She stared up at Zack; it'd been years since she's seen him in person. Alice could see the peach fuzz sprinkled on his chin. Pulling out her phone, she typed in the address and followed the route. "How's dad doing? Is he as bad as he sounds? Where's Kelly?"

"Dad's pretty far gone," Zack answered. "He's not responding to the treatment…no one knows what's wrong. He's been tested for everything but he's getting worse. It's like he's losing a year every day. He's lost most of his strength to the point that I had to carry him to his bed. We made a bed for him on the first level."

"And Kelly?"

"She's one of those girls you see in the movies, the ones who became popular and let it go to her head. She's always checking herself out in the mirror and she spends most of her time with her boyfriend."

"Boyfriend? I'm surprised that you allowed that."

"Now that you mention it, I've never met him," Zack retorted "I've only heard his name mentioned in passing. He supposed to be this star football player at the other high school or something like that. You know I don't keep up with that stuff."

"And what do you keep up with? The ladies?"

"Not pressed about that. I was involved with this one girl before she started acting weird, lost what I loved about her: her personality and we eventually fizzed out. So, I concentrate on the only girl who loves me, Diana." He rubbed his dashboard.

"Just like a typical guy...in love with his car."

Cruising along Interstate 264, Alice remembered her days riding through the country, heading to school and other places with friends. The highway was populated with small stores and neighborhoods she was astonished to see. "Wow, this place has stepped up."

"It's not D.C." Zack mentioned.

"You miss it up there?"

"A little. I made a lot of good friends and it was easier to navigate around with the metro system. Here, you have to drive miles to get food or to have fun but I do enjoy the drive."

Alice pulled into the driveway, her eyes instantly locked on the wood. Things had changed, as it wasn't as wooded as before, just enough trees to conceal the neighbor house. Unaware that she was sitting in the car, a figure crossed her view and opened her door.

"It's okay; I'm older now to protect you from anything," Zack emphasized.

"I don't need your protection. I'm the older sibling." Exiting the car, Alice entered the house. She sighed, taking a brave step towards the house she once called home. She saw Zack heading into the kitchen while the living room reminded her of a hospital room.

"There's my little lawyer," a raspy voice whispered.

Tears streamed down her cheeks while she headed over to hug her father. Her head laid on his shoulder as she felt his arms laid across her back. "I'm so sorry."

"It's not your fault sweetie. People like me get old, that's all. It's natural selection."

"I'm sorry that I haven't been home, it's not like me. I've should have return a long time ago." She kissed him on the forehead before taking a step back. Alice stood there, watching her younger brother taking care of her father the way he took care of all of them. Going through the door, she stepped into the kitchen and stared at the updates, giving the kitchen a more modern feel. With groceries on the table, she reverted to an old pattern, putting items away.

"Hey, I got that. You're a guest here."

"Boy…bye, I'm not a guest here. I've lived her longer than you have. So technically, this is my home, not yours. Besides, I need to contribute while I'm here."

Alice preheated the oven, unloaded the groceries that weren't put away and started working on the dishes. After prepping the meal and setting it in the oven to bake, she straightened other areas of the house and ventured on the second level, cleaning anything out of place before accidently walking into Zack's room. "I'm so sorry."

"I'm not doing nothing embarrassing, but try knocking next time. Since you opened the door, you might as well come in," Zack replied.

She stared into his room. Outside of the stack of car magazines sitting in the center of the room, it looked spotless. Everything was in place and when she walked around, she could see a little bit of obsessive-compulsive disorder. "I didn't expect your room to be this clean."

"How else would I know where I put my things? Without order, chaos will ensue."

"I assume Kelly won't be home for dinner?"

"Who knows, she lives by her own rules."

After dinner, Alice found a small area and sat down to telework. The door swung open, and she glanced over her laptop to see Kelly entering. "Hey, Kelly."

No answer.

Alice noticed headphones in Kelly's ears, indicating that she was unaware of her presence. She walked over to the kitchen door, staring at her baby sister dancing while preparing her plate.

Alice and Kelly made eye contact.

"When did you get here?" her sister asked.

"This afternoon...I see that you're not so little. Give your big sister a hug."

After they embraced, Alice headed back over to her workstation.

Kelly started eating the food that she warmed up in the microwave. "How long are you here for?"

"Two weeks…longer if dad's condition worsens."

"School's out in a week. Next year, I'll be a senior."

"That's exciting, what are you plans after high school?"

"Definitely college…not sure where but that's the goal. I have a whole year to figure it out."

"So, I heard…" Alice was interrupted with Kelly's cell phone going off.

Zack walked in.

Alice looked over at him. "Hey, is Kelly—?"

"Attached to that phone? A zombie? Yes," Zack replied.

"Not what I was going to ask but it does answer other questions I had."

Her work led her to the next morning; Alice glanced down at the time on her laptop to see that it was a little past one in the morning. She saved her content and shutting down her computer, she found herself wandering around the house, locking the doors and staring out the window. She ascended the stairwell, startled by Kelly's presence. "You nearly gave me a heart attack. Why are you up this late?"

There was no response from her sister, just a 'thousand yard stare.'

It made Alice uncomfortable. "Kelly, do you have your headphones on?"

Still, no answer.

Alice took a step forward, hoping to get her attention when Kelly came charging towards her, crashing into her. "Kelly, what are you doing?"

Hearing a door open, footsteps headed towards them as she laid on the ground while Zack picked Kelly up, wrapping her in his arms.

"What is her problem?" Alice asked.

"Shhh...Kelly sleepwalks," Zack explained.

"Ohhh, that's why she was acting weird. How long has this being going on?"

"Ever since dad got sick. I read that your subconscious lashes out when you repress your feelings. I think she's doesn't know how to deal with dad and his condition, not showing any emotion, so her mind takes over at night. I found her wandering around outside in her under garments, other times she fell down the steps and twisted her ankle. She had no clue how she hurt it." Zack recalled. "Yeah, I'll carry her to my bed. You can sleep up in her room if you like; I know it's your old bedroom."

"I'd rather sleep on the couch, next to dad."

The sound of beeping woke Alice up. Sunlight poured into the room. Peeking over at her father, the monitor steadily beeped just as Kelly burst through the door, back sack in hand. "Kelly, can I have a minute before you leave for school."

"Can it wait? My ride is waiting for me." Kelly sighed.

"Yeah, I guess." Entering the kitchen, she swore that she imagined her mother sipping coffee—God rest her soul—before blinking away to find Zack with a mug in his hand. She yawned, followed by a stretch that loosened every fiber in her body. "Why doesn't Kelly ride to school with you?"

"It's not hard to figure out."

"She's different than I expected. When we were in Washington, D.C., she was nicer and more pleasant. Now, she's a—"

"BITCH!"

Her mouth dropped open, "Zack, that's not nice."

"What? It's true. She's still my little sister and I love her but she can be bitch at times. Now, if you'll excuse me, I'll be heading off to school. Don't break your schedule, my teachers are well aware of dad's condition. Since they proclaimed me a genius, it awards me time off and I use that time to take care of father. I'll be home throughout the day. You know where everything is, make yourself at home."

The following week was challenging…between teleworking, talking her father's ear off when he was awake, and daily chores but it was especially difficult trying to reach Kelly. She wasn't the little girl that followed Alice around anymore. Once her siblings were out of school, the house became crowded with her and Kelly bumping into each other. She wished that Zack were there to ease the attention. Frustrated with work and Kelly, Alice grabbed the keys and went out to run a few errands. Instead of taking Highway 264, she cruised the back roads. Her travels led her down a dirt road where she noticed a crowd of youngsters ahead. Pressing firmly on her horn, the crowd didn't part for her, requiring her to step on the brakes. She waited for them to move when suddenly a piercing sound blared from the radio. Cringing, she turned the radio off and glanced back up to see the crowd had parted but they all stared in her direction. Easing through, she peeked at the teenagers who wore the same void expression over their faces.

After accelerating, Alice stared in the rearview mirror and saw them jump over a ditch and enter into the woods.

Returning home, she met Zack in the kitchen.

"Hey, the strangest thing happened today. I ran into a group of teenagers who seemed—"

"...mindless, yeah, something is happening around here. It's been like that since we moved back. At first, it was a small group but now it's more teenagers. I asked Kelly about it since it's some of her friends but she told me to stop watching scary movies."

After putting the groceries away, Alice opened up a new web browser, typed in children with white eyes. After clicking on several movie articles that discussed possessed children with white eyes, she searched for possessions. Over more than twenty million links, she clicked on a few and read through a few articles.

"So, why are you looking up possessions? The case you're working on involves child possession?" Zack questioned.

"Boy, you nearly scared me to death! Don't sneak up on me."

"Sorry. So, why are you searching the web for possession?" Zack asked.

"If you must know, when I passed by those teenagers, they weren't acting like normal teens. Usually, teenagers are full of life and rowdy. They don't have respect for adults, especially outside of school. When I passed by these teenagers, the pupils of some of their eyes were white. Those same images are seared in my brain from that night when—"

"Yeah, dad told me the story when we moved back here. I can't recall what happened back then but if something had you that way, then I'm aware of my surroundings as well. That's why I never went up there to your room. If Kelly sleepwalks, I put her in my bed. If it's not too traumatizing for you, can you explain what happened? Just the brief version."

"Well, you and Kelly were outside, playing with your imaginary friends…I think their names were Daemon and Lamia. You were in the backyard, Kelly was in the woods and I told her to get out of the woods and I swore I saw something move. Once you both were in the house, a storm appeared out of nowhere and I started seeing visions of small children. After the front door slammed open and the power went out, we were on the second level and the first level was peppered with scary looking children. I carried you both up to my room and locked the door. I was literally scared awake, watching the door all night until around four in the morning. I heard dad's voice and saw him after I opened the door but he wouldn't come in my room. An hour or two later, dad came in and I knew it was him. Honestly, I was scared to come back here but you all have been living here the last three years and I haven't heard of anything happening and that's the only reason I came back…outside of dad being sick."

"Wow, that's crazy. I don't remember any of it. But you want to know something eerie? Lamia is the name of one of Kelly's friends. I've seen her talk on the phone with a girl name Lamia, talking about a guy they both find attractive."

Alice typed in myths and folklores near them in the search engine, staring at the creepiest tales from the past: Crybaby's Lane, Devil's rock, the Devil's Tramping Ground, the Phantom Hitchhiker and CROATOAN.

"Those are just stories to scare people," Zack emphasized.

"Well, I'm one of those people. I've witnessed it first hand and let me tell you, if you saw what I've seen, you'd be cautious too. I can't believe you don't remember your imaginary friends. You, Kelly, Daemon and Lamia…carrying them around in that creepy red wagon."

"What did you just say?" Zack questioned.

"What? Your friends or the red wagon…"

"Red wagon…that's weird. Right before dad started to get sick; he was in the backyard and I found him next to the red wagon. Initially, I thought he trip over and bumped his head but that when his health started declining. One Saturday morning, I saw Kelly emerging from the barn pulling the wagon. That was the first time I found her sleepwalking. Maybe there's something with that red wagon."

"Didn't mom buy that wagon before she died?"

"Yes, from some antique shop in town, she thought it would be a nice gift for me."

"Come with me, I need to see something." Heading out the house and into the barn, Alice searched the wall until her fingers found the light switch. The lights didn't combat the eeriness that the light gave off. Alice and Zack searched until they found the red wagon. They searched until they found the name of the company. *Kasha Antiques.* "Come on, I found what I was searching for."

After exiting the barn, they reentered the kitchen, finding Kelly sitting at her workstation.

"What are you doing on my computer?" Alice asked.

"I was just checking my email. I know you're all about the law, so don't press charges," Kelly retorted.

"That's cute Kelly. We're headed out, see you later." Alice spoke, rolling her eyes.

"Wait, where are y'all headed? Can I come?" Kelly asked.

"No, we need you here to stay here and take care of dad."

Thirty minutes through the countryside led them into their small town just as the last bit of daylight began to flicker away. They entered Kasha Antiques. A dank smell scented the air, hovering all around as Alice made her way down one of the aisle. Everything in this shop was before her time, very nostalgic.

"Wow, this place is incredible!" Zack exclaimed.

"Is there something I can help you with?" a small voice spoke from unknown place.

Alice searched until she found a petite woman with flowing red hair and a wide smile. "This might sound strange but my mother bought a toy from this store more than a decade and I had a few questions about it."

"I'm not sure if we have a record of that. Maybe I can assist you. What was the toy?"

"It was a red wagon."

"Why are you inquiring about it?" the storeowner questioned, curiosity getting the best of her.

"You may think I'm crazy if I reveal my true intentions, so I'll keep them to myself. Thanks for your time." Proceeding towards the door, Alice reached for the door handle when she felt a hand on her shoulder. She turned to face the storeowner, their gazes locked, making Alice feel uncomfortable, as the storeowner didn't pull her stare away.

"There's more to you than meets the eye. You seemed haunted by spikes from the supernatural realm. Take this, it may protect you from the answers you seek," the store owner insisted.

"I can't take that…"

"I insist, it may indeed save your soul."

After thanking her, she stepped outside where she noticed Zack reading a book. "How long have you been out here?"

"About twenty minutes ago...y'all were in there talking for a long time. Look at what I found." Zack raised a dusty looking book. "I started reading it and found some interesting information that might be beneficial."

"You stole this from the shop?"

"More like borrowed. I'll return it in a few minutes. I found an article about the Native Americans. Even though they teach us something entirely different as US history, they neglect the bloodshed soiled into the dirt. We know this country belongs to the first natives: Chowanoke, Croatian, Cherokee, Catawba, Waxhaw, Occaneechi, etc...the list goes on. When the European Americans came over for settlement, suggesting all Indians relocate west beyond the Mississippi river to prevent further degradation. The red men are not within the pales of civilization; they are not under the restraints of morality, nor the influence of religion. They were always disagreeable and dangerous neighbors to a civilized people."

"Yes, in American history class they discussed this." Alice nodded.

"They didn't discuss the bloodshed, the Trail of Tears and land Europeans seized by eradicating the natives of this land. We're talking about forcing families from their land; bringing forth diseases their bodies weren't immune too, etc. Millions upon millions were slaughtered."

"What does this have to do with the strange things happening around us?"

"Everything," Zack answered. "We're literary living on top of a cemetery where millions of Native Americans died. Women, children, the elderly…now imagine all those souls lashing out. Imagine the revenge those spirits would evoke when given the opportunity."

"Pay for the book, apologize for taking it and lets go. The teenagers around here are freaking me out."

Alice flipped through the pages while Zack went back in to pay for the book. She skimmed passage after passage, reading about Native Americans and the spirits associated with their culture. From rituals to folktales passed through generations, she was horrified reading it firsthand from the native point of view. There were drawings, letters and photos in the book that dated back hundreds of years. In one of the photos, Alice noticed a small European teenager pulling a red wagon with small bodies stacked higher than his physical being. "Oh My God…"

"…What's wrong?"

"Pull over."

"We're a couple of streets from home." Zack looked puzzled. "What's got you so worked up?"

Alice waited for him to pull into the driveway before she handed him the book. "It's the red wagon in our barn. This picture has to be over two hundred years old. I knew something was weird about that thing."

Exiting the car, they ran into the house were Kelly was hovering over their father.

"He's transitioning."

"What does that mean?" Zack questioned.

Alice anticipated a response but grew annoyed and marched in front of her sister, grabbing her by the shoulders before noticing Kelly's eyes. "Zack!" Alice screamed.

"He's paying the debt all men pay. In the end, she will collect," Kelly answered.

"Who is she?"

"I think we have a problem…." Zack looked upset.

"Yes, look at Kelly."

"That's not the problem I'm referring too. Come with me," Zack instructed.

Alice followed him to the kitchen, staring out the window to see the yard peppered with teenagers. The rumbling of thunder sounded and lightening forked across a cloudless sky.

"OMG, I can't believe this is happening again."

"Alice, get in here. Kelly's gone." Zack screamed.

Alice rushed in, staring at Zack, noticing the trepidation on his face. Her gaze matched his, staring at something in the adjacent room. The sound of squeaking grew closer as the small red wagon entered, rolling unassisted towards their father. Alice motioned for Zack to protect their father but an unknown force tossed him across the room, crashing into the mirror. "ZACKKKK!" She rushed over to him, picking him up off the ground. "Are you okay?"

"Clearly, you didn't see what just happened if you're asking me if I'm all right," Zack commented sarcastically. "But I'm the least of your worries."

She followed his gaze. Standing next to him were translucent beings, their eyes white as the teens outside. She pulled Zack up off the ground, assisting him before grabbing his hand and running into the other room. Alice couldn't believe that she was reliving her nightmare all over again. Scaling the steps, they found themselves heading past the second level in route to the third level, a familiar place. She hesitated, unable to take that step up to her former room but a nudge from Zack pushed her over the threshold. They climbed the stairs, entering into her old room.

"What was that standing next to dad?" Zack asked while looking pale.

"A-apparitions. I experienced the same thing when y'all were younger."

"I can't believe what's happening. Look, they're just standing there," Zack mentioned while staring out the third door window.

Alice walked over to the window, stepping on a box to see out the window. Teenagers stretched past their backyard, some standing in the woods. "What do they want? Why are they hovering over dad? Is this all connected."

"All your questions will be answered if you open the door," a familiar voice called out.

Alice and Zack traded stares.

Alice grabbed her bat, inching closer to Zack as he unfastened the door locks. They both quickly stepped back, muscles tense as the door creaked opened.

Kelly stood at the door, her eyes white as pearls.

Alice glanced down, noticing Kelly's feet weren't touching the ground. "What do you want?"

Kelly pointed at Zack. "Many moons have passed my dear and here we stand, reliving a moment that revealed who I am. As I mentioned to a terrified teenager years prior, I only want what's owed to me…an unpaid debt."

"What unpaid debt?" Zack asked.

"We weren't a part of those killings from the earlier settlers. We're not like them," Alice pleaded.

"My debt is not associated with the spirits of the slain. Contracts were established and I'm here to collect what is owed to me."

"Who signed the contracts?"

"A pact was sealed by the leaders of the community, sacrifices must be honored, or consequences will occur. I promise no harm to the one that shielded you from my grasp many winters ago. I've welcomed Kelly and many others that you've seen surrounding your home. No harm will come to them or you. Don't you want to protect your little sister? Don't you want your father to be well? You will always be around to watch over them, I can guarantee you this pact but you have to take my hand, willing accepting."

Zack took a step forward.

Alice reached out and grabbed his hand. "No Zack, you don't have to do this!"

"I have no choice. If I don't, everyone that I care for is in danger. It's my duty to protect you and Kelly."

"Zack...I need you," a smaller version of Kelly insisted.

Alice pulled Zack closer to her, hugging him as tears rolled down her cheeks. "I love you both," she whispered as she kissed him on his cheek.

Alice heard the sound of something rolling and stared at the red wagon approaching their door. She stared as her siblings reverted back to their youthful selves, stepping into the wagon.

Her protective gene wouldn't allow her to watch evil take her siblings away. Alice mustered up enough courage to pursue them. She reached the threshold and stumbled backwards. Exerting a lot of energy, she pushed against the invisible barrier, staring at her siblings until they vanished.

She fell to her knees, crying hysterically.

"Alice...don't cry."

She looked up to see the small woman shopkeeper. "You're the woman from the antique shop...how?" Alice's mouth dropped.

"Listen my dear, have you ever wondered about the nice neighborhood that you lived in? Ever noticed the neighbors all have wonderful jobs? Several generations before your creation, a deal was brokered between leaders of this community and in exchange, the souls of their children belonged to us. Every imaginary friend that children see are souls trapped in between the planes of time, their one goal is to carry out the contents of the contract."

"WHY? I still have my soul."

"Every wonder what *REALLY* happened to your mother? Her death wasn't an accident. She really was a brilliant woman, discovering our history. She decided to take you away from your father so I intervened. She pleaded for your life, the ultimate sacrifice. Your father really loved your mother and decided to leave this region. Remembered how much he struggled in Washington, D.C.? As an original leader of the community, he knew the consequences. Being the leader of the tribe, he signed the pact and his life force was stripped from him until our debt was settled. The man you call father made a decision for immortality."

"His immortality?"

"Yes, he signed the pact back in the 1600s...he's birthed many children and sacrificed them to continue his immortality."

"What are you? Why do you need my sibling's souls? Take me instead. Make a deal with me instead."

"I'm the darkness that the devil fears...but you can call me Ms. Hexen."

Expiration Dates

Pierce entered Nearly Pushing Daises Retirement community, smirking at the name as he headed down the hallway. Waving at a few people, he continued down the hall as his shoes squeaked against the tile floor. Entering through a set of double doors; the familiar aroma of moth balls and peppermints lingered in the air.

"Good morning Ms. Edwards."

"You're right on time, Pierce. I need your assistance," Ms. Edwards said.

Pierce didn't say a word, he accepted the clipboard that she handed him and performed his duties; a routine he was accustomed too. The first name he read was his grandmother's name, heading to her room. Since she was admitted ten years ago, he'd been visiting during the colder months—from Thanksgiving to Valentine's Day. Volunteering to be close to his grandmother, his initial good deed manifested into a seasonal position. It didn't bother him that they weren't able to pay him, he was happy to produce a smile on his grandmother's face. After helping out with the Thanksgiving and Christmas holidays, Pierce sometimes threw the "elderlies" an extravagant New Year's party since it was a gloomy time for them.

January 5th arrived and his phone chimed. Checking his messages, he saw an increase in his bank account—a few thousand dollars. Everyone got that email as the federal government finally perfected a system that automatically processes your W-2s and direct deposited the money into your account. Those stories his mother told him about an archaic system they used to use for taxes gave him chills and he felt glad he was born in a time when technology took over tedious work.

He spent countless hours with his grandmother; playing games from her youth: Bridge, Checkers and others. They pinched his cheeks, made uncomfortable sexual advances towards him when his grandmother stepped away but he never disrespected them. There were those he reminded of past lovers and grandson, sometimes playing the role as instructed by the nurses. Well liked throughout the retirement community, Pierce was awarded the covenant "Helping Hands" award for his many services. Always wearing a smile, he continued to display his love of life and positive attitude.

His phone buzzed and he froze. Glancing to his right, he stared at the announcements board on the wall, specifically at the date. Pierce knew what day it was— everyone knew what day it was: January 20th scrolled across the screen. His palms were clammy as he slid his hand into his pocket. His breath labored as he pulled out his phone. The screen came to life as he prayed that the message was from a friend or the girl that he was currently courting. The message wasn't from either but the CENSUS BUREAU as he clicked on the *notification*:

Dear Pierce Linden:

This notification has been sent to you, informing you that your Expiration date has been set for January 21ˢᵗ. We would like to thank you for your contribution to society. We encourage you to update your will and sort out your business dealings so those difficult decisions will be properly taken care of. Spend time with the ones you love; family and friends. Depending on your Expiration date, we recommend that you explore what the beautiful world has to offer. There are so many unique things to experience before your date approaches. You may say that this isn't fair and feel that you have more life to experience. We apologize in advance and we know you will honor the process. If you have any questions, please contact the Census Bureau.

He collapsed.

...Groggy, he opened his eyes and found that he was surrounded by nurses and other faculty members. They tried to reach out and assist him off the ground but he rejected their kindness. Pierce climbed to his feet, staring at his phone lying on the floor.

"Hey Pierce, you dropped your phone—"

He kicked his phone down the hallway, walking past the faculty until he reached the door. Bursting through the doors, nature greeted him with brisk conditions. The bitter cold didn't bother him; his thoughts were solely focus on his expiration date: **January 21st**. He lifted his head, staring into the clear night at a waning moon. The natural light gleamed as he inhaled deeply, realizing he had but hours before he expired. His hands trembled. Pierce shoved them into his pocket while pacing back and forth. Pivoting, he stared at the retirement community, watching the elderly sway back and forth with glee. His gaze scanned until he found his grandmother, watching her walking over to faculty members. He knew she was worried about him but all he could think about was the notification.

Pierce never went home, he sat in his car while the moon vanished and the sun rose. He entered the retirement home, alert as he forced his patent smirk to mask the void of hope lingering inside him. Entering the community room and bee lining to where his grandmother sat, he took the seat next to her.

"What's wrong sweetie?"

"I'm going to be straight with you Grandma, I just received my Expiration date notification, and it expires tomorrow. I need you to—"

"You need me to do what?" His grandmother asked.

He took a deep breath, "Grandma, I'm twenty-six years old and I want to live. I still have so much to live for and I hate to ask this but I know you left us some time in your will. Could you sign that over to me?"

"Pierce, I don't think that will do you any good—"

"Grandma, I need this. I've been coming here to visit you for the last ten years, keeping you company. You raised us when ma and dad's expiration dates arrived and you know me. Out of all the grandchildren, I'm the only one who has come to visit you. I need this grandma, I really need this."

"So, you didn't visit me out the kindness of your heart? You've been waiting for this moment? Spending time with me and trying to butter me up in case this moment happened?"

"You don't want to see me die here do you, Grandma? I don't know the time but I could be on the verge of dying right now. I have the app pulled up; all you have to do is sign with the last four digits of your social and a fingerprint scan. That's all it takes to extend my life. You had a full life Grandma, I just want the same opportunity you had."

He stared at his grandmother through blurred vision, his sight cloudy by tears. His breathing quickened as he watched his grandmother enter her social security number and place her finger on the designated area. Pierce snatched the phone; bringing it close to his face as he sent the email through the Expiration Date app. A sigh escaped his lips.

"That was close." Pierce reached out but his grandmother grabbed her left arm, the momentum caused her to fall out her chair.

"WE NEED HELP OVER HERE." Pierce shouted.

Faculty members ran over, checking her vitals. "Time of death: 8:45am," the nurse stated.

After rolling her body out of the community area, the nurse from yesterday walked over to Pierce to offer her condolences. "I'm sorry for your loss Pierce. Your grandmother was an exceptional woman. It's a strange coincidence that you both received a *notification* on the same day."

"Wait…what did you just say?" he asked in puzzlement.

"Your grandmother received a notification yesterday. She was so concerned about you that she forgot about her Expiration date. I read her *notification*; her expiration time was at 9:00 am."

He pulled out his phone, checking the notification sent by the Census Bureau. Scrolling through old emails, he stared at his time, noticing that his expiration time was set for 8:45 am. His eyes locked with the nurse as his left side felt like ants were marching underneath his skin. Sharp pain and discomfort occurred as his body began convulsing.

Pierce loss his footing, crashing towards the ground…

The music created a distraction as she sat on the bench. Bobbing her head, Charli glanced up, staring at the other contestants as they prepped for the main event. She sensed more than a few were nervous, especially the burly guy with spiked hair. He seemed to be the most physically fit out of them all but this event required more than brute strength. She's watched Olympic-level athletes falter and witnessed those who didn't possess the physical prowess survive. Her gaze fixated on another girl. Charli stared at her trembling hands and quickly pulled her gaze from her. Fear was contagious and she wasn't prepared to steel her nerves again. Focusing her gaze on the tile below her, smooth jazz calmed her soul. A tap on her shoulder startled her, her head shot up to a large man dressed in all black with a clipboard in his hand.

"Charli?"

She nodded

"Place your hand here for identification."

She did as she was instructed, placing her hand on the clipboard until it illuminated green.

"Stay still. I need a retinal scan."

Frozen, Charli opened her eyes as wide as she could while beams of fluorescent light zigzagged across her irises, temporarily blinded her.

"I commend you. I've never met a person who volunteered to be in this contest," the large male mentioned.

"I'm assuming everyone knows my reason?"

"Yes." He nodded. "Here are your supplies. Follow me."

Charli removed her ear buds, placing them in the locker. She hadn't realized how much time had lapsed, as she was the last out of the locker room. Exiting the locker room, she headed down a dim hallway; the sound of people screaming gradually grew louder as burly man guided her to the opening. She glanced down at the yellow line, knowing the consequences if she crossed it too soon.

"Any advice?" Charli asked her guide.

"Don't overexert yourself. Most think it's about strength but intelligence trumps brute strength any day. Good luck."

Charli nodded, crossing her chest before darting across the yellow line. Full steam, she ran towards the obstacle course, the first challenge: barbwire crawl. Being petite, she scurried through it with ease. She cleared the first three events but knew each challenge difficult level would increase. Pacing herself during her mile jog, Charli felt ecstatic at the next obstacle for two reasons— she was able to sit down and rest—and a chessboard was her current challenge.

Charli tapped the chess clock just as fast as her opponent, strategically seeing every possible move she could make to capture his king. Once his pace slowed, she knew it was only a matter of time until victory. Clearing his pieces off the board, she relaxed as he stalled, soaking in all the rest before the next event. She kept an eye on the scoreboard, noticing her time was well under twenty minutes, faster than any other challenger. The crowd roared as she focused her attention on the game, her opponent tilting his king downward. Charli rose to her feet, proud of the moment but she knew she was far from her goal.

She followed the arrows; an open trench appeared in front of her. Too wide to jump, she noticed three large logs that bridged across the other side. Witnessing this event on television, she knew two of the logs would snap if she ran across them. She stared below deep in the trenches, seeing large bulging eyes and long snouts. Charli felt a chill that almost paralyzed her. She didn't want to be reptile food. An explosion rang out, her legs moving faster than her thoughts as she darted out in a full sprint. Adrenaline coursed through her veins, propelling her as she dug into the wood while gaining traction. Her head slightly tilted, keeping an eye on the log as she saw the crocodile pit below.

Shit!

She noticed the log tilting forward and realized she chose the wrong log. She ran backwards and the log lifted up as she took a deep breath. Building speed, she leaped as high as she could.

The crowd remained mute until she landed on the other log.

With only half the obstacle completed, she pressed harder as the second log began to fall. Leaping into the air, Charli grabbed on the edge of the rift. The sound of logs crashing echoed below her as she used her strength to pull herself up off the ground.

Instant cheers erupted.

Charli rolled over, heaving as she stared up at the ceiling. The roars energized her, clambering to her feet, she completed each challenge, conquering archery, zip lining over flaming torches, climbing walls and leaping from its apex into a large pool of pudding, which she found quite tasty. She advanced further than anyone in recent years, chants of *Charli, Charli, Charli* reverberated off the walls.

She peeked up at the scoreboard, noticing she completed thirty-nine challenges as she followed the arrow to the final event.

Lead by the unknown, Charli was surrounded by darkness as an eerie graveyard wind caressed her skin. Her muscles tightened as she prepared for an attack. Electricity hummed above her as light cascade down. Her eyes fixated on an object in the distance, the arrows blinked as she followed them to the object. She was able to make out what was in front of her—a person tied up.

"The final challenge lies in front of you. Do you accept the final challenge?" a voice boomed.

The voice nearly startled her.

"The person tied up in front of you possesses what you desire the most: TIME!"

Charli stared at the male bound to the chair, stepping closer to get a better glimpse. The light shone down on him as she stared at icy blue eyes. The closer she stepped, more features revealed themselves: slick back hair, wiry frame and a visible scar on his left cheek. She paused, her hand covering her mouth. Scurrying over to him, she reached for the ropes to untie him.

"Tsk, Tsk Charli. Do you want to untie the cute boy from school or do you want to save Emmanuel?"

Her head lifted up as the darkness shifted into colorful images of her with a small boy. She froze, staring at the images and videos playing of her and the little boy.

"We all know why you're here and we commend you for putting your life on the line to save your little brother."

Tears welled in her eyes, the images blurred as she wondered how they were able to get home videos from her computer.

"Tomorrow is his expiration date and right now and he has no idea. He's sound asleep, thinking you're hanging out with friends but you're here, fighting for his life. You've completed all the challenges, a feat that hasn't been accomplished in over thirty years. There's only one thing that's standing in your way…"

The sound of an object sliding across the floor commanded her attention as it slammed into her shoe. Peering down, she stared at the knife with the black handle.

"You have two options: Save the boy who's always had a crush on you but never acted on his instincts or, end his life and complete the obstacle course and save Emmanuel."

All the videos, the research she conducted, there wasn't a challenge that involved murder.

"What is it going to be Charli?"

She knelt down, grabbing the knife from the floor and stared at the boy bounded by ropes. Stepping towards him, they made eye contact before she leaned lower cutting the ropes from his feet.

"Charli...why did mom and dad had to die? Are you going to die? Who's going to take care of me if you die?" Her brother's voice echoed through the wide space.

Hot tears streamed down her cheeks as she regrouped, her hand tightening around the knife as she stood to her feet. She stopped cutting the ropes. She stood erect, staring at him fidgeting in the chair as cold metal positioned itself against his neck. She leaned down, her mouth near his ear. "I'm so sorry," she mumbled through sobs. Charli pressed the knife against his neck, dragging it across his throat as the tears poured from her eyes.

The crowd roared, overly excited about a televised execution.

Charli felt the release of pressing as his body went limp. The knife fell from her hand, crashing to the concrete as she fell to her knees. Dark liquid dripped from her hand as she frantically rubbed the blood out with her shirt. She couldn't stop crying, hating herself for what she'd done.

"Congratulations Charli, you're the 2nd winner to complete the contest. Place your hand on this screen for your signature as you are his guardian."

Charli lifted her hand without looking, feeling the glass against her palm. After a series of noises, her arm fell to her side.

"Your brother gets to live another year. How do you feel?"

Charli's face grew red hot. She popped up from her knees, charging towards the announcer as she put her hands at him. "You forced me to kill a man. I'm a murder. How would you feel if you killed someone? I hate you...I hate all of you!"

"Charli...Charli, relax. We don't condone murder as this competition is televised across the globe. It's our duty to give the audience what they've never experienced. Based on your performance, our viewership increased by 4000%."

"...But, I have his blood on my hands."

The announcer picked the knife up off the ground and dragged it across his neck. Charli couldn't take her eyes off his neck as he showed her why her hands were stained. Pivoting, she turned to her classmate, as the boy broke free from his restraints. She gawked at him as he stood to his feet.

A wave of nausea fell over Charli as she crashed to the floor.

Captain of her cheerleading squad, dating the star athlete of the football team and voted *Most Likely to Succeed* by her peers, Siobhan lived the life that most teenagers would die to have. She was queen in their secluded private school and yet, she didn't rule with an iron fist as most teenage movies displayed. Siobhan was kind and friendly, never disrespecting anyone—unlike her snobby friends that gravitated around her: Tiffany, Karen and Marsha. According to them, she had every right to feel entitled—her father being the wealthiest person in the United Colonies of North America.

Being the daughter of a very powerful man, the constant presence of personal body guards set her apart from her peers. While one not to flaunt her father's wealth like her other wealthy peers, she despised the unwarranted attention. Siobhan wanted to focus on navigating through those awkward teenage years that she read about in books or watched at the movies. She hated those dates that required a security detail and bystanders watching her as she was being escorted through the mall or movie theaters. She would kill for some privacy. But this wasn't the privacy that she expected. Staring out at the large cube, she prayed for her detail to come in and interrupt the quiet moments she dreaded. She cried loudly wishing to be able to laugh and joke with friends, hug her servants, instead of having her arms bounded behind her back.

Still wearing her school uniform, Siobhan positioned herself in the far corner where she could see the door. It was the only place she felt safe. An echo pierced through the sealed room as her eyes were glued at the bottom compartment. A small slit lifted up, giving her a glimpse of life outside her imprisonment. Her mouth salivated just as a tray of food slid in. Malnourished, she desperately wanted to extinguish the empty feeling in her stomach.

Once the slit closed, the muscles in her arms slackened as the magnetic clamps around her wrist released her. She only had ten minutes to eat as she crawled over to the plate. She stuffed her face, devouring whatever was on her plate. Her choice was limited to the contents of this plate as she thought of steaks, burgers, lobster, or hibachi from the best chefs. She missed those delicious meals as she scooped up another slab of grey mush, washing it down with a bottle of water. She cleaned her plate before she swallowed the entire bottle of water, swishing it around to remove the gunk from her teeth. Finishing her bottle, a loud metallic click sounded as she lifted her head. The sound of footsteps echoed louder and she scurried back as the unidentified person entered.

The light that was aimed at her temporarily blinded her as she covered her eyes.

"Why are you doing this? I haven't done anything to you. Let me call my father, he'll give you whatever you want! Don't leave me in here, pleassssse!"

Her plea was ignored; the person exited the room after picking up the tray.

The beeping sound prompted her to place her arms behind her back as the magnetic clamps brought her wrists together. Even though she was alone in the room without a way out, she knew she'd better to follow the rules. When she woke from being drugged in the beginning of this nightmare, the metal clamps had counted down as she stared at them. Once they reached all zeros, a minor surge of electricity coursed through her entire body, inflicting significant pain as she tried to take them off until a voice instructed, "The pain will stop if you put them together, preferably behind your back."

It only took that one event for her to follow directions.

Time eluded her but she kept track of the meals she received, realizing that she got two meals—if anyone could call them meals.

Twenty-eight meals later, the doors suddenly opened.

Siobhan waited for someone to enter. After a few minutes, she stood to her feet and gingerly headed towards the door. The metal clamps around her wrist slackened, giving her arms free range motion. Bursting out the door, Siobhan ran as fast as her legs would allow, scanning her environment as she searched for a door. She picked up a metal object for protection and ran towards the exit door. Natural light stunned her sight, the reverberations of sirens booming all around her. She ran towards the flashing lights, hot tears streaming down her cheeks.

She dove into the officer's arms, crying hysterically...

...A week later, Siobhan stared at the television, surrounded by her new security detail as she learned details of her captors' demands: duffle bags of cash in unmarked bills, jewelry and having loved ones removed off the Census Bureau database. She learned that her father offered a ten million dollar reward, tips poured in from the hotlines. Her eyes were glued to the television screen; the houses were on split screens.

A few minutes later, police officers escorted several individuals out of homes as she cheered, "I'm glad they finally caught the criminals who kidnapped me."

"It was only a matter of time. Once they gave us their demands, we were able to discover the culprits. They kidnapped you because they figured I had some influence over the Census Bureau. People will do whatever it takes to survive, including bribery. For now, you will be home schooled. You don't have to see those people again."

"Dad, there's something you're not telling me. What really happened?"

"Honey, you don't want to know. All you need to know is that I've taken care of it."

"DAD! I need you to be honest. Who was involved? I know a male was there but I smelled perfume when I ran through the house."

"Your friends Tiffany, Marsha, Karen and your boyfriend. They all received the notification and figured bribing me would get them off the hook."

Siobhan stared at the television, realizing all the houses shown were familiar. A single tear ran down her cheek as she exited the living room.

Ramon excelled at his job. He'd uncovered scandals from corrupt politicians, unearthed alternative facts from rival news outlets, all while keeping the integrity of his news column. He enjoyed the fruits of his labor and relished the fact that he was one of the top investigator reporters in the country. His status and persistence had made several enemies—there were threats made against his family for some of his articles but he wasn't worried. He felt confident that his reputation would remain intact and that his enemies couldn't touch him. His current assignment had led him down the wrong path.

Pacing back and forth in a dark alley, Ramon waited for an informant when he heard commotion. He saw a woman running in his direction, glancing back at her pursuers before colliding with him. Papers were tossed in the air as she scooped up what she could before taking off. Ramon hid behind a dumpster while the two men passed by him.

After meeting his informant, he entered his home and discovered that he possessed confidential documents from the Census Bureau. He read through the files, discovering the science behind the "notification" process. Everyone knew and feared the Census Bureau— the most powerful organization in the world. He remembered that he and his colleagues were hit with a cease and desist order before they could print one word. He also remembered a few reporters being fired by their news outlets.

Powering on his ThinkPad and flexing his fingers, the tips of his fingers touched the keys and they didn't leave his keyboard until the rough draft was completed. After several revisions while incorporating documentation, he finally finished his article. Ramon sat at his desk, staring at his screen at an article that would bring a lot of negative attention his way. Plugging in his external flash drive, he created a copy, emailed his boss and cc'd himself for safe measure. He went over to his refrigerator, pulled out some wine and poured himself a glass as he practiced his Pulitzer Award speech in front of the mirror.

The next morning, he slid out of bed and into his running shoes as he checked his phone. There were several missed calls from his boss. Reading emails, he noticed his emails were intercepted by the Census Bureau and erased any documents from the internet. Reading the text messages from his boss, he read the stern warning to disappear or go to the local authorities as officials from the Census Bureau left his job then were in route to his home.

Ramon grabbed his essentials before tiptoeing over to the door.

Peeking out the peephole, he didn't see anything in his hallway. He opened the door, walking over to the stairwell, he noticed a few well-dressed men walking up the steps. Scurrying into his condo, he grabbed a small bag then stuffed his laptop and anything of value into the bag. The external flash drive sat on the desk as he headed back to the door. They were on the floor just below, he fastened his deadbolt and glanced back at the window; the fire escape was the only exit. He grabbed the flash drive, pulled the window up and scaled down the fire escape just as he heard his door burst open.

Once he landed on solid ground, Ramon lifted his head and saw two men scaling down. He took off running...

...Rounding the corner, Ramon sped walk with the crowd towards the park. There were multiple exit points, so he kept his head low as he knifed through the crowd. His gait increased as he scampered through crosswalks. He figured he could get lost in the crowd as the city was littered with thousands—if not millions of people. He sighed, taking a moment to catch his breath. Any given day, there were always commotions amongst the city but the commotion he heard got his attention. Glancing over his shoulder, he saw more men in suits running in his direction, triggering his flight response as he darted forward.

Entering the park, he accelerated as he passed bikers, families playing, tourists taking photos and dogs barking as he ran towards that familiar trail. Peeking behind him, the men in suits were headed in his direction.

He hopped a few chains, cutting through the field as he dodged a few citizens and hurdled over picnic areas. He zigzagged through the park, learning not to run in a straight line from movies. Ramon felt their presence near as he stumbled a bit, jumping the fence. Running down the sidewalk, their voices prompted him to run harder but he grew tired, his stride, not as spirited as before. Out the corner of his eye, he saw a dark color van headed towards him, gradually getting closer and closer to the sidewalk until it jumped the curb. He stopped, frozen like a deer in headlights. Between the approaching vehicle and the men chasing him, Ramon knew he was out of options as he braced himself for imminent danger. With wide eyes, he stared at the van as it came to a sudden halt, the door slid opened.

"Get in now!" a woman shouted.

Ramon stared at her, noticing her figure hidden behind the layer of all black that covered her body from head to toe. He stared at his pursers then back at the van and for a second, weighed his options just as a shot rang out, reverberating all around them as he dove into the van. His body wasn't quite in but that didn't stop the driver from flooring it as they bounced off the curve, cutting through a sea of bumblebees in the direction that once arrived.

"Hey, who are you?" he asked.

"We will explain later, put this on," she stated as she handed him a black ski mask.

"I'm not putting that thing on. Who are you? Why were they chasing me?"

"I said put this on before he blows your brains out." She warned as she stared as a silver 9mm emerged from the shadows, pointing in his direction. She watched as he slipped the black ski mask over his head.

"Relax Ramon…were the good guys. We're not sure about you yet, so the mask is just precaution. Wouldn't want you leading them to us, now would we?" she asked.

"They tried to kill me and you're covering my head with this musty mask. For all intents and purposes, I'm a little more afraid of you than them."

"We shall see. Let's get out of the city before they find us."

"Hey, who are you?" Ramon asked.

"We will explain later, put this on," Yunru stated.

"I'm not putting that thing on. Who are you? Why were they chasing me?"

"I said put this on before he blows your brains out." She warned him. Yunru stared as a silver 9mm emerged from the shadows, pointing in the guy direction. She watched as he slipped the black ski mask over his head.

"Relax Ramon…were the good guys. We're not sure about you yet so the mask is just precaution. Wouldn't want you leading them to us, now would we?" she asked.

"They tried to kill me and you're covering my head with this musty mask. For all intents and purposes, I'm a little more afraid of you than them."

"We shall see. Let's get out of the city before they find us."

Yunru sighed as the door slammed shut. She stepped over Ramon, climbing into the front seat as the view of the city was on display. She fastened her seatbelt as their van swerved through traffic, passing by skyscrapers, darting out in front of buses and avoiding pedestrians. They wanted to create as much distance as possible, crossing over several bridges until they came to a complete stop.

"You know the drill. Five minutes. Ramon, you got three minutes to strip out of your clothes and put on this these. You will be scanned for any bugs before entering into the next vehicle. Move!" Yunru screamed. Getting out of the van, Yunru stared at the city from a distance, staring at the tall skyscrapers as the presence of helicopters hovered above them. She knew they were from the Census Bureau, searching for them in the media capital of the world. Her fist slammed against the van, beating a few times. "You got one minute."

A car drove up to them as the van door opened, Ramon stepping out.

"Hold still."

"I'm not bugged. I don't work for them," Ramon stated.

After she watched him get scanned and cleared, they all loaded into the car and sped off into a neighborhood. Silence settled in the car and Yunru peeked back, noticing Ramon sandwiched between two burly males. "I bet you didn't think today you'd be chased by the Census Bureau."

"What makes you say that I was chased by the Census Bureau? I'm a runner and I like to run through the park."

"I don't know…maybe it has something to do with that article that your news outlet published on the web. You are familiar with plagiarism, right? You're lucky I was able to triangulate your position through your phone."

"I report the news that the public needs to know. I'm just doing my job."

"Doing your job got your boss expired. Doing your job has you running from hitmen. That information wasn't ready to be released to the public, not yet. We've worked too hard and you recklessly released some pertinent information to what? Win an award? Be first? That's why the media is reckless. Now we have to accelerate our plans. Since we just saved your life, stay out of our way and let the professionals handle this."

Exiting the van, they broke off, heading into separate cars. Yunru sat in the passenger seat while watching Ramon heading in her direction. She lifted her head when he approached, hesitant to let him in as her fingers pressed unlock. Keeping her head forward, they rode off in different routes. The trip lasted a little over an hour as the vehicle approached a worn down barn in the middle of a corn field.

"This is your secret lair?" Ramon quizzed.

"Lair? What are we, Super Friends?" Yunru quipped.

A roar of laughter from the driver prompted Yunru to chuckle.

Once the laughter died down, the driver pressed something on the navigation screen and the ground beneath them suddenly shifted. The barn grew in stature until they lowered out of sight, heading into an underground area that lit up with lights.

Yunru peeked over her shoulder, the perplexed look on Ramon's face spoke volumes. "Welcome to our lair. Someone will show you around and then they will bring you up for the final event."

Everyone got out the car, heading in their own directions.

Yunru headed towards the large screens, noticing that she was being followed. She turned around and stared at Ramon. "I told you, someone will be with you and here they are now." Shooing him away, Yunru twirled Ramon's flash drive through her fingers. She stared at the news, watching a video of their eventful trip into the city. Grabbing a laptop, she unhooked the internet connection and plugged the external drive in, clicking through Ramon's personal file until she came upon the documents that she'd lost. The final piece was set. Something startled her as she popped up from her trance. Six minutes counted down in bold numbers when she realized she fell asleep at the table.

The room was crowded now.

"We didn't want to wake you. We know you're exhausted," someone mentioned.

Yunru flashed a brief smile, scanning the area until her eyes met with Ramon's gaze. Venturing over in his direction, she pulled his drive out her pocket and handed it back to him.

He took it. "Thank you. So, what do we do now?"

"Nothing. Everything is set in motion. It will be a media blackout at first and then our upload will play on the entire system, exposing those who work for the Census Bureau."

"What do you think will happen? You know they will kill you once they find you."

"They can't track me as my network constantly bounces off thousands of satellites. I'm broadcasting on several networks and have hubs in multiple locations. I've thought this out. Besides, I had my chip taken out of me years ago. There's no way they can trace me."

"Just to play devil's advocate and being the investigative reporter, what if they knew about you? I mean, I'm sure you've been on their radar after numerous breaches. What if what you stole was false information?"

"How could they feed me false documents when I infiltrated their organization and downloaded it from encryption files? If I didn't have anything of value, why were they chasing me? Why did they chase you for printing what I stole?"

"Maybe it's all a ruse to find you."

Yunru pulled her gaze from the clock that was less than a minute and gawked at Ramon. Now he possessed a smirk on his face. Her fingers brushed up against her hip, locating her weapon as she stared at her followers. She cocked her head to the side, her right eye squinting slightly as she prepared any sudden movement.

A shout blared across the room, distracting her for a moment as she turned and saw the clock was at five seconds. When she turned to face Ramon, he'd already advanced towards her, grabbed for her hip as he pinned her to the floor. She stared up at Ramon's face, that sinister smirk he wore infuriated her.

He pressed the gun next to her temple. "You see Yunru, we knew you were good but you underestimate how far we're willing to go. We had credible intel that someone infiltrated our organization. We don't have files on our headquarters server...no, we have a private server that only comes on once a year. We fed you false info and they assigned me to be in that alleyway, steering you in my direction. It was only a matter of time before you came to me."

Yunru started laughing.

"What's funny?"

"You fool. You think you've won? You're not the only intelligent person in this room. I have several contingencies plans, and one should be coming on at any minute."

Sirens went off as televisions began broadcasting. There were several news outlets reporting bombings across the nation. Senators, lawyers, prominent businessmen faces were plastered across the television screen as confirmed kills. "I guess that's not a coincidence."

"You little shit." Ramon tightened his grip around her neck.

That moment of anger gave Yunru the opportunity, so she kneed him in his nuts. She felt his grip slacken and with body leverage, she flipped him over. Staring at the gun underneath her table, she reached for it and held it a few inches from his face. "Here's your notification…"

"You don't have the—"

Several booms blared throughout the large room. She stared at Ramon's body falling backwards. Two of her soldiers immediately picked her up off the ground as she stepped over Ramon's corpse. Heading to a new computer, she pressed the button as a large file uploaded. She stared at the scar on the back side of her hand; seven years since she received her expiration notification and the journey, that led to this moment. Tears streamed down her cheeks, thinking about her family members and friends who received expiration notifications. A smile managed to surface as Yunru stared at the screen.

DeForrest LeRonte'

Living Within the Margins

Pens, keys and typewriters are an extension of our soul

Writing erratically but secretly being a NYT bestseller is the ultimate goal

Fans huddle in bookstores, reading novels before the movie's release date

Deviating from the book synopsis is something we definitely hate

An author's imagination is a powerful tool

The imagination teaches us far more than we've ever learned in school

We research and brainstorm on all of our topics

Fantasizing that our works will allow us to relax on an island within the tropics

Pens bleed, fantasies collide, but looking closely, it's all creative lies

Original ideas are often plagiarized

Our words build a world's illusion within your imagination

Constantly criticize by commenters and skeptics over missed punctuation

Thank for purchasing and reading this novel, I hope it was a delight

As you can see from these stories, I absolutely love to write

Showing my talents and I apologize for any misspelled jargon

Thank you for allowing me share my masterpiece, Living Within the Margins

ABOUT THE AUTHOR

DeForrest LeRonte` is writer, novelist, poet, and screenwriter. Born and raised in Kinston, North Carolina. Upon graduating college, the writing bug ferociously bit him, sparking a passion for creating novels, novellas, short stories and poetry in all genres. An avid reader, he keeps a pen in close proximity.

CONTACT
DeForrest LeRonte`

DeForrest showcases his gift for storytelling through an avenue of short stories, poems, novellas, and novels. To learn more about the author, please visit his website at www.deforrestleronte.com, where you'll get updates of new releases. Stay tuned!

Follow him on social media:

Twitter @penperception

Instagram @deforrestleronte

Made in the USA
Columbia, SC
28 December 2018